D1254873

MAN FIND

KRISTA SANDOR

CANDY CASTLE BOOKS

Mountain Daisy: *Do you think you know it when you find what makes you truly happy?*
Mountain Mac: *Like when you've found everything you never knew you needed?*
Mountain Daisy: *Yes.*
Mountain Mac: *Yeah, I think you know.*
Mountain **Daisy:** *How?*
Mountain Mac: *It just clicks.*
Mountain Daisy: *I get pretty deep after eleven.* 😊
Mountain Mac: *Or sleepy. It's late for you, Daisy.*
Mountain Daisy: *Want to chat tomorrow?*
Mountain Mac: *Always.*
Mountain Daisy: *Sweetest dreams, Mountain Mac.*
Mountain Mac: *Sweetest dreams, Mountain Daisy.*
End chat...

1

CADENCE

"You're sure you packed your toothbrush, Bodhi?"

Cadence Lowry shifted the pickup truck into park and glanced behind her at the gap-toothed, smiling boy with sparkling green eyes.

His father's eyes.

"Yes, Mom! I checked back at the house when you asked me and *again* five minutes ago when you asked me the same question," the six-year-old replied, pulling the toothbrush from his backpack and waving it for her to see.

A tightness pulled in her chest. "This is the first time you've gone to a sleepover birthday party. I just want to make sure you have everything you need. Did you remember to pack Mr. Cuddles?"

Bodhi unzipped his pack and pulled out a Teddy bear limb. "Yep, I packed him all by myself!"

"When did you get so big?"

"Last week when I turned six," her son answered, matter-of-factly.

She swallowed past the lump in her throat. "Well, don't grow up too quickly."

A mischievous glint sparked in his eyes. "I can't help it, Mom. Maybe if you didn't make me eat so many vegetables, then I'd stop growing."

Cadence stifled a grin. "Sorry, B. You still have to eat your vegetables."

Bodhi's brows knit together, and she could see the wheels turning inside his head.

His eyes went wide. "What if we got rid of oatmeal and bananas for breakfast and had cinnamon rolls and doughnuts instead? I bet that would keep me tiny forever."

She unbuckled her seatbelt and patted his leg. "Sorry, little man. Oatmeal with bananas and a tablespoon of peanut butter mixed in is like—"

"I know! I know!" her son groaned. "Gas in the tank. Eat right to keep right."

Cadence stilled, remembering how, when she was Bodhi's age, she'd beg her grandmother to buy the sugary cereals her classmates had talked about.

Cinnamon Toast Crunch, French Toast Crunch, Cap'n Crunch! Crunch, crunch, crunch! Growing up, she'd never tasted any of *The Crunches*.

With an easy grin and a gentle pat to the back of her head, Grandma Helen had weathered her whining and never gave in to her pleas. And day in and day out, every morning, until she went off to college, just like her grandmother, Cadence had a bowl of oatmeal with a cut up banana and a dab of peanut butter. It was her grandma's specialty, which was always waiting for her on their small table by the kitchen window in the cozy bungalow they'd shared two hundred miles west of Denver across the state in Grand Junction, Colorado.

You don't want that sugary cereal, dear. You need gas in the tank to get you through the day. Eat right to keep right.

She could almost smell the Folgers Instant Coffee and hear

the spoon clinking inside the mug as Grandma Helen stirred in a splash of skim milk as they sat together, just the two of them.

How she missed her grandmother.

"Can we get ice cream tomorrow after I get back from the sleepover party?" Bodhi asked, pulling her from her thoughts.

Cadence glanced out the window at a sprawling home with balloons tied to two large pillars near the main entrance. "I think you're going to have your fill of ice cream at Porter's birthday party."

"Can I eat as much ice cream as I want?" her son asked, wide-eyed.

She schooled her features. "Just don't eat too much. You don't want to get sick."

Bodhi nodded sagely. "Yeah, it was really gross when Logan Klein threw up all over the lunchroom at school. Remember, Mom? Carson Davis dared him to drink six chocolate milks in a row." Bodhi shuddered. "Milk even came out of his nose!"

Cadence nodded. Of course, she remembered. She taught second grade at Bodhi's school, Whitmore Country Day, and Logan was her student, up until a week ago when the school year ended, and summer break began.

Despite being officially off the clock, she went into teacher mode. "Logan went home sick and didn't get to have double recess with the rest of the school that day," she added, hoping her son would make the connection.

Bodhi's brow crinkled. "Maybe I'll just have two scoops of ice cream and stop after that."

Cadence breathed a sigh of relief. Message received.

She smiled at her son. "That sounds like a good plan. Are you ready for me to walk you up to the door?"

Bodhi glanced up at the majestic home and his little shoulders sagged a fraction.

"What's up, B?" she asked, but she knew the answer.

Aside from Whitmore being the school Bodhi attended and where she taught, it was also Denver's most prestigious private elementary school. While the majority of the students came from the wealthy upper crust of Denver society, a quarter of the children, including her son, were there on scholarship, thanks to the Bergen Foundation, a mountain sports company headquartered in Denver, that generously donated to the school every year.

She loved teaching at Whitmore. She loved knowing her son was just down the hall. But Bodhi had started noticing little differences between his simple life and the lavish lives of many of his peers.

They lived in one-half of a small 1930s paired home near the park, not a sprawling mansion that backed up to a golf course.

They didn't take fancy trips that spanned the globe.

They didn't own a plane or drive a luxury car.

And it wasn't just the financial differences that set him apart from his classmates.

At any school event that included parents, while the majority of his peers came accompanied by two parents and often many extended family members, Bodhi only had her.

The boy glanced at the wrapped present on the seat next to him. "Do you think Porter will like what we got him?"

Cadence gave her son her best *go team go* smile. "I know he's going to like it. It's a Lego fire truck, and you know how much Porter loves fire trucks."

That was a bit of an understatement.

Bodhi's friend Porter Boyd's proclivity for all things fire and rescue went beyond obsessed. Porter had just finished first grade in her friend and colleague Abby Quinn's class. He had a reputation for pulling the fire alarm any time the teacher wasn't looking to get the first responders to show up at Whitmore. Porter was a year older than Bodhi, but the two became fast friends on the playground, and despite a little nose-picking and alarm pulling, Porter Boyd was a pretty great kid.

"Yeah, you're right, Mom," Bodhi said, toothy grin back in place. "Porter's going to go crazy for the fire truck."

It wouldn't always be this easy. On a teacher's salary, they'd never be able to afford a flashy car or give lavish gifts. But she'd take this small victory.

She glanced at the Post-it note stuck to the truck's dash with the party information scribbled in her handwriting then checked her watch. "Come on! Let's let Porter know you're here and ready to help him celebrate his birthday."

Bodhi grabbed his backpack and the present, and they got out of their old Ford F150 pickup truck. They headed up the path and walked past a fountain and a row of manicured hedges before reaching the front door.

She went to ring the doorbell when Bodhi gasped.

"What is it, honey?"

The boy cringed. "Oh, Mom! I forgot to tell you."

"What?"

It could be anything when it came to little boys. Play-Doh smooshed into the couch cushions. A glass of milk he'd tucked under his bed two months ago. A family of spiders currently residing in an old shoebox.

"Does this have anything to do with insects or science projects gone awry, Bodhi Lowry?"

He shook his head. "No! I wanted to tell you that you've got paint on your cheek."

Cadence leaned in and caught her skewed reflection in one of the door's stained-glass windows.

"Holy pickles and relish!" she said under her breath.

A form moved from behind the door, and Cadence quickly licked her fingertip then rubbed at the streak of paint.

Agreeable Gray.

That was the actual name of the paint slashed across her cheek. And as lovely as the color looked on the walls of the duplex-like connected homes she owned, known as a paired home, where she and Bodhi lived in one of the two-bedroom units as the other sat vacant. There was nothing agreeable about showing up with it smeared all over her face.

Any of her second-grade little girls would have immediately alerted her to this.

Boys...not so much.

"Bodhi, why didn't you mention this earlier?"

He cocked his head to the side. "I thought maybe you did it on purpose. You kind of look like a football player with that stuff they put under their eyes or maybe a zombie."

A zombie!

She squinted and tried to catch her reflection, but it was tricky to make anything out in the ornate colored glass.

Maybe her son was right! Teaching full time plus raising a child plus watching handyman videos late into the night to learn how to complete basic home renovation projects could make anyone look like a zombie—paint or no paint.

Cadence turned to her son, giving up on the panes of fancy glass. "Did I get it off?" she asked when the door swung open.

Cadence dropped her hand and pasted on a grin. It was a slippery slope being both a Whitmore teacher and a Whitmore parent. Luckily, Sandy Boyd, Porter's mom, never tried to get any school gossip out of her like some of the other parents.

"Bodhi! Ms. Lowry! It's great to see you!"

"Please, call me Cadence. School's out."

"Oh, we know! Porter is counting down the days until the Bergen Adventure Summer Camp begins. Will you be teaching there again this summer?"

Cadence nodded. "Yep, Bodhi and I will be there!"

Renovating the paired homes wasn't cheap and to supplement her income, she'd started working summers at the Bergen Adventure Summer Camp. The best part was that, like teaching, she could have Bodhi with her, and the instructors got to enroll their children in the day camp for free.

A grinning Porter wearing a plastic fireman's helmet joined them at the door. "Hi, Ms. Lowry! Hey, Bodhi! I got a new bike for my birthday." The boy pointed behind him into the vestibule of the house where a shiny blue bike was parked.

Bodhi craned his head. "You don't need training wheels?"

Porter beamed. "Nope! My dad taught me how to ride a bike without them."

At the mention of the word dad, Bodhi's smile dimmed. Cadence patted her son's back; her throat growing tight with emotion.

Sandy Boyd took a step back and gestured into the house. "Why don't you both come in. Are you able to stay for a few minutes, Cadence?"

Cadence checked her watch. "Actually, I'm running a bit late. I'm supposed to meet Abby Quinn in fifteen minutes."

Porter's eyes went wide. "Miss Quinn? My first-grade teacher?"

Cadence chuckled. "That's right."

"Tell her hello from us," Sandy said with a warm grin. "Her wedding to Brennen Bergen isn't too far off, is it?"

"Only a couple months away at the end of July," Cadence answered.

"What a romantic story those two have! And to think, it all started with him volunteering in her classroom at Whitmore," Sandy mused.

Sandy wasn't wrong. It was a romantic story. Once Denver's biggest playboy, Brennen Bergen, one of the three Bergen grandsons and an heir to the billion-dollar mountain sports empire, had fallen hard for her dear friend while volunteering in her classroom.

Their love story had gone viral when Brennen proposed to her at the school gala in front of the news cameras covering the event.

But anything the Bergens did was deemed newsworthy in this city.

The Bergen family—the same family that funded the Whitmore scholarships—was considered Colorado royalty. Based in Denver, their billion-dollar mountain sports empire, comprised of retail stores and resorts, spanned the globe. Bergen Adventure Summer Camps were an offshoot of their Mountain Education Department that not only supported winter activities for children at their ski resorts, but also summer camps scattered throughout the Denver Metro area.

"Come on, Bodhi! Let's go join the rest of the kids in the backyard," Porter called, setting off through the house.

Bodhi started after Porter then looked over his shoulder and ran back as the part of her heart that beat only for her son fluttered in her chest.

He took her hand and gave it three little squeezes. A squeeze for each word—their secret way of saying I love you.

She held his green gaze and gently squeezed his hand four times in response.

I love you, too.

Bodhi released her hand and glanced over at Porter's new bike. "Mom, when I get home tomorrow, can we take the training wheels off my bike?"

He'd been hesitant to try to ride without them. And truth be told, it was hard enough for her to get on a bicycle, let alone, try to teach her son to ride one.

"Sure," she answered, doing her best to keep her voice steady. "Now, enjoy the party and listen to Mr. and Mrs. Boyd."

"I will, Mom. I promise," he answered.

Sandy patted Bodhi's arm as he ran past her into the house.

"We'd be happy to bring Bodhi home after the sleepover tomorrow. Does three o'clock sound all right?"

"That would be great! Thank you!" Cadence answered.

While she loved having Bodhi with her when she worked on the house, it was often a one step forward and two steps back process. She'd paint a wall. He'd accidentally step in the paint tray and track paint all over the hardwood floor. A few extra hours to work on her own would help get her closer to being able to rent out the unit—something her bank account desperately needed.

She wasn't supposed to be renovating a 1930s Denver paired home by herself on only a teacher's salary. But life had thrown her one heck of a curveball, and Cadence Lowry wasn't one to give up or give in. Armed with a stack of Post-it notes and a to-do list, she was a force to be reckoned with.

She had to be strong for her son. There was no Prince Charming waiting in the wings to swoop in and save her.

Not anymore.

Porter's mother bid her goodbye, and Cadence headed back to the truck as the sound of children's laughter floated from the backyard. She smiled when she heard Bodhi's sweet belly laugh join the chorus of voices.

He was the only man—albeit, a little man—in her life, and that's the way it had to be.

She got inside the truck, glanced back at the Boyd's home, and touched the simple gold band she wore on a chain around her neck. "He's getting so big, isn't he?"

Her phone pinged, and the breath caught in her throat. But when she looked at her phone, it was just a text from her friend, Abby.

Abby: *I found a daisy doorknob at the antique shop. I swiped it up* *before a very cranky lady got to it. Are you on your way? She's really giving me the stink eye!*

Cadence stared at the screen and released a sad little sigh. Of course, she was happy to hear from her friend—and the doorknob was a lucky find. She'd dedicated herself to following the plan of renovating the Denver paired home with as many original pieces as possible, which included finding two more sets of two-and-a-quarter inch eight-point glass doorknobs with daisy centers. These lovely knobs were the last historic items she needed to find, and she'd been searching Denver antique shops and online for the elusive knobs for the last year and a half.

But doorknobs weren't what had been weighing heavy on her heart.

She was hoping the message had been from someone else.

Someone she knew only as Mountain Mac.

She put the key in the ignition and headed toward Denver's Antique Row. Thanks to the light Saturday traffic and the city parking gods throwing her a bone, she found a spot right outside the shop.

She entered the store and froze at the commotion unfolding in front of her.

Standing a few feet away next to a shabby chic bassinet, her friend, Abby Quinn, clutched a pair of glass knobs to her chest while a small woman with beady eyes reached for the goods.

Cadence shook her head. Yep, this really happened. She'd seen actual fights break out at flea markets and vintage shops. People looking to score the next million-dollar one of a kind item scoured these places like vultures, and it could get real—faster than you could say *Antiques Roadshow*.

"One, two, three! Eyes on me!" Cadence called out, but the beady-eyed woman didn't stop and continued pawing at her friend.

"I already tried that!" Abby answered, angling her body away from the handsy woman.

Cadence looked around. There was no shopkeeper in sight, but she did see a light switch.

Time to take it up a level.

She flipped the switch, and the shop went dark. "Heads down! Thumbs up!" she called, evoking the teacher trick that could silence a rowdy herd of children in two-seconds flat.

She could only hope it would work on an obsessed antique doorknob fanatic.

The woman stilled and squinted her eyes in the dim light. "What did you say?"

Cadence stepped forward. "I said, heads down. Thumbs up."

"Why in the world would you turn off the lights and say that?"

Cadence took another step forward. "Because, ma'am, it looks like you need a little time out. We don't grab things from others. We use our words."

"But I could sell those doorknobs on eBay for double what they're asking for here," the woman whined.

Cadence clucked her tongue. "It looks to me like my friend Abby had those doorknobs first."

The woman stomped her foot. "But I want them."

Abby maneuvered around the woman, then turned and held her beady gaze. "It's hard when we don't get the things we want. But I know that next time you see someone holding something you'd like to play with, you'll ask first."

The woman nodded. "Okay! Can I have the doorknobs?"

Cadence shared a look with Abby and bit back a grin. "No way! Finders keepers, losers weepers, lady!"

"Well, I never..." the woman huffed and pushed past her, leaving the store.

The shop door slammed behind the rude woman, and Abby laughed. "You are one naughty schoolteacher, Cadence Lowry."

"That woman needed some serious redirection. And we work our asses off during the school year. Come the first of June, I use my Jedi Knight teacher powers for good...and for evil."

Abby handed her the glass knobs. "Nice touch using the light switch. Now, please tell me I didn't almost lose a limb for the wrong glass doorknobs."

The lights came on, and an older gentleman in a newsboy cap ambled over. "Ah! I see you've found my latest find."

Cadence glanced down at the knobs as the light sparkled off the cut glass encasing the delicate daisy-center design, and she could hear Aaron's voice.

This is it, babe! This is the house. The daisies are a sign. We can make this work. We can live in one side and rent the other. This is where we're going to raise Bodhi. This is where we're going to grow old together.

"Miss?" he said gently.

She shrugged off the memory. "Yes, I've been searching for these. I'm renovating a 1930s paired home in Denver's Baxter Park neighborhood."

The man raised an eyebrow. "A paired home! Those are quite rare in Baxter Park. Are you renovating one or both of the connected units?"

"We're...I mean, I'm renovating both."

He frowned. "By yourself?"

Cadence lifted her chin. "Yes, by myself. Why would you even ask that? Is it because I'm a woman?"

He put up his hands. "I meant no offense. It's simply quite an undertaking to renovate one historic home, let alone two."

She let out a heavy breath. "I'm sorry. I didn't mean to jump all over you. You're not wrong. It can be challenging at times."

Challenging wasn't even the half of it. It was a lot taking on a renovation. It was a heck of a lot—especially for someone with zero building knowledge.

The man gave her a kind grin. "You've got spirit. I imagine there's not much you can't do when you put your mind to it. The daisy knobs suit you well."

Cadence watched the man closely. "What do you mean?"

"The daisy is considered the thunder flower."

Cadence shared a look with Abby, and her friend shrugged her shoulders.

"Daisy is my middle name."

The shopkeeper nodded. "Then it's even more apropos."

She cocked her head to the side. "I've never heard it called the thunder flower."

The man gestured to the daisy on the knob. "The daisy not only remains unharmed after a thunderstorm—it thrives. They're survivors."

Survivors.

Cadence swallowed hard and pasted on a grin. "Well, the place was in quite a state of disrepair when we...I purchased the paired homes. They were missing several sets of these antique daisy doorknobs when I took possession. I've been able to find most of them, but I'm still missing a few. So, thunder flower or not, I'm on the lookout for a couple more sets."

"Lucky for you, your friend got that set before Mrs. Hilderman."

"You saw that?" Abby asked, hand on her hip.

The man grimaced. "That woman's been coming here every day for the last year or so. She only sees dollar signs when she rummages through my treasures. I've found the best way to deal with her is by hiding in the back until she leaves."

Cadence glanced down at the doorknobs. "Rest assured, I certainly won't be selling these on the internet."

The man nodded. "Those doorknobs were meant for you.

Antiques are special. They connect the past to the present. They have a history, and there's true beauty in their imperfections."

Cadence gave the man what she hoped was a pleasant grin.

Her mask. Her facade.

She wore her scars on the inside, and if she'd tried to speak, her words would have defied her manufactured agreeable demeanor and come out cracked and broken.

"Let's see," the shopkeeper said, glancing at the small price tag tied to the doorknobs. "They're marked as fifty dollars. But what would you say to thirty-five?"

Relief washed over her. She had a hundred dollars left to get them through the week, until she got paid, and she could stretch sixty-five dollars like nobody's business.

And more than that—she needed these doorknobs, and if that meant she ate mac and cheese straight for the next couple of days, then put a pot on the stove and get the water boiling.

She glanced from the knobs back to the shopkeeper. "I'd say, you've got yourself a deal."

"Wonderful! Let me write up the bill of sale and wrap them up for you," the man said, taking the knobs and heading behind the counter to an antique cash register.

She turned to Abby. "I owe you big-time for finding those daisy doorknobs and for guarding them from that beady-eyed antiques bandit. How can I make it up to you?"

Abby's face lit up. "Easy! Agree to be one of my bridesmaids."

"I'd be honored," Cadence answered and embraced her friend. "And I'm happy to help out with whatever you need for the wedding."

"You mean that?" Abby asked.

"Absolutely!"

Abby sighed. "That gives me such peace of mind. Planning a Bergen wedding is no small feat. My cousin, Elle, is going to be my matron of honor, but she's pregnant with the twins, and I don't want her overextending herself."

"It must be hard with the both of you being engaged to billionaire Bergen brothers," Cadence answered with a cheeky grin.

Abby practically glowed with happiness. "Who would have thought that Elle and I would end up marrying brothers?"

Cadence squeezed her friend's hand. "I'm really happy for you both," she said when her smartphone pinged an incoming message. She pulled her cell from her pocket and smiled down at the picture of her son, grinning ear to ear and swinging at a piñata.

"Everything okay?" Abby asked.

Cadence held out her phone. "Sandy Boyd sent a picture of Bodhi. He's at Porter's birthday sleepover."

"I hope they've alerted the fire department," Abby said with a sly curl to her lips before her expression grew pensive.

Cadence frowned. "What is it?"

Her friend gestured to the phone. "Still nothing from your *Man Find*?"

"Oh, Abby," Cadence huffed.

"What?" Abby asked with a smirk. "You've *found* a nice guy online. You just can't *find* him in the real world."

Cadence shook her head, chuckling at Abby's name for... Holy pickles and relish, what would you call him? Her pen pal? Her mountain bike forum friend? Her online beau? The person —whoever he was—who made her laugh, who messaged her late into the night about things as silly as how to hard boil an egg to questions about life and the universe and what was the point of existing on this tiny rock floating through space.

Cadence pocketed her phone. "No, he's been MIA for the past week."

Abby crossed her arms. "Did you guys have a falling out?"

Cadence sighed. "I thought, just the opposite. We've been corresponding for nearly a year. Sometimes several times a day."

He made her laugh. And while she had a beautiful son and good friends, she didn't have anyone to hold her at night, and his messages filled the void that had been left the day Aaron died, and she became a widow at the age of twenty-five.

Cadence shook her head. "We've never seen each other. We don't even know each other's real name. But a week ago, I took a picture and sent it to him."

Her friend's eyes went wide. "Of yourself?"

"No, just a quick photo of my bike and the trail around Baxter Park. He's the one who helped me figure out the kind of bike to get. That's how we met on that mountain biking chat forum." She stared out the shop window. "Maybe it's for the best that he's gone silent."

"Why do you say that?" Abby asked.

Cadence swallowed hard. "Because sometimes, I feel like I'm cheating on my dead husband with a person I've never met—when what I need to be doing is putting all my energy into fulfilling Aaron's dream of fixing up the units."

Abby's expression softened. "Cadence you're putting everything you have into renovating the houses and caring for Bodhi. I never got to meet Aaron. But I can't imagine he'd be upset that you've met someone who makes you happy."

"But I haven't, Abby—not really."

Abby chewed her lip. "And you're sure your Man Find is a *he*?"

Cadence shrugged. "His handle is Mountain Mac. I guess that could be a guy or a girl."

But her heart believed it was a man. It had to be. Even though she knew nothing about Mountain Mac, she knew everything. Nights spent curled up in bed messaging back and forth, her cheeks hurting from smiling.

"What's your handle?" Abby asked.

She glanced at her phone. "Mountain Daisy."

Abby patted her arm. "Well, Mountain Daisy, I know how to get your mind off of Mountain Mac."

"And what's that?"

"Cake."

"Cake?" she echoed.

Abby glanced at her watch. "Go pay for your doorknobs. We're going to a wedding cake tasting. You're coming with me to Brennen's grandparents' house to try about six thousand different flavors of wedding cake. And if there's one sure-fire thing that can mend a broken heart—it's got to be cake."

Cadence opened her purse and handed the shopkeeper the majority of the bills in her wallet then glanced back at her friend. "Are there any extra billionaire Bergen brothers lying around at the Bergen estate? You and your cousin seem bliss-fully happy."

Abby shrugged. "Sorry, Mountain Daisy, I can't promise that. Just the cake."

Cadence sighed. "Then cake it is! Lead the way."

2

CAMDEN

Camden Bergen signaled for a cab outside Denver International Airport as the early June mountain air filled his lungs.

Christ, he'd done it. After ten long years, the runaway Bergen heir was back, and nobody knew it.

And that was just the way he needed it to stay.

A cab stopped in front of him, and he got in.

The driver glanced back, and for a second, Cam thought the man had recognized him until the cabbie's gaze traveled to the back seat where his well-used Bergen Mountain Sports backpack sat, tattered and faded, then slid to his ripped jeans and worn T-shirt.

"You better have the cash to pay, buddy," the cabbie said, taking in his dark, scruffy beard and wild tangle of hair.

Camden reached for his wallet and handed the man a fifty. "I think this should cover my fare."

He had one stop to make before starting this crazy escapade that had led him back to the place he'd sworn never to return.

The man pocketed the cash. "Where to?" he asked, still eyeing him warily.

Camden handed the man a torn piece of paper with an address.

The cabbie took the paper and entered the information into his phone. "You better not be pulling my chain, man."

"I'm not," Cam answered, voice void of emotion.

The cabbie caught his eye in the rearview mirror then looked away as he maneuvered the car into traffic. "I've been driving a cab in this city for twenty years. You look a little familiar. Are you from around here?"

"Not anymore," Cam answered. He came from Colorado's most affluent family, but nobody could know that.

The cabbie shook his head, giving him one last glance in the mirror before turning on a talk radio station.

The commentator's voice droned in the background as Cam pulled out his smartphone and opened the internet browser to the mountain sports chat forum and his pulse raced.

Mountain Daisy.

He stared at the two words on his phone then scrolled down to the picture posted on the private chat page he'd created on the forum for just the two of them, known only as Mountain Daisy and Mountain Mac.

His visits to the chat forum had started out as a form of self-imposed punishment. A punishment for failing his family.

The world may not know the real story.

But he did.

And all these years later, he could still smell the exhaust. Hear the squeal of the tires and the gut-wrenching sound of twisting metal pierce the night air just like it was yesterday.

Each time he'd logged on to the chat forum, he'd be reminded of his old life a decade ago before it all went to hell.

Days spent weaving perfect S-curves into the side of Bergen Mountain as he skied with his brothers in the winter and early spring months. Pedaling hard and catching air while mountain biking on the twisting rocky trails he and his father liked to ride during the summer and fall.

But he'd never interacted with anyone on the site until he read her post:

Colorado gal with zero mountain biking knowledge seeks advice. D-canoes need not reply.
—Mountain Daisy

Nearly a year ago, she'd been the reason he'd laughed for the first time in ages.

He'd barely recognized the sound.

He didn't own a television or a computer. His smartphone was the only connection he'd had with the outside world. His grandmother had insisted on that, and he'd used it to remind himself of everything he'd lost until Mountain Daisy's post caught his attention like a beacon of light leading him out of the darkness.

He'd replied immediately to her query—his heart overpowering his mind. Growing up as a Bergen, he'd had every opportunity to use the best mountain sports gear, and he was still an expert mountain biker. It was the only pleasure he'd allowed himself over the past decade while living hidden away in the Swiss Alps over five thousand miles from the life he'd once cherished in Denver.

He'd typed out a few lines in reply, suggested a couple of bikes, and told her to make sure whatever bike she got, it needed to have disc brakes and a detachable derailer. It was basic information she could have gotten anywhere, but he'd be lying if he said his heart hadn't skipped a beat when the gray italicized *Mountain Daisy is typing* message appeared seconds after he'd hit send.

And that's how his ascent from hell began.

One message led to two, then ten. And soon, they were corresponding every day—sometimes, several times a day. She was funny and sweet. Sure, they'd messaged about biking, but after a week or so, their conversations shifted. Sometimes they were silly and made him laugh—like when she told him about watching a vegetarian eat animal crackers and wasn't sure what to make of it. And sometimes they touched on life and happiness and the deeper questions, often easier confronted under the cloak of anonymity.

Do you believe in fate?

Did you ever imagine you'd be right where you are at this exact moment?

But the picture she'd posted a week ago to their private chat page had to be a sign.

He'd known she was in Colorado all along. She'd mentioned it in her first post. But Colorado is a big state. Mountains to the west. Plains to the east. And even a desert region to the south. Just knowing Mountain Daisy was in Colorado wasn't enough to get him to leave the place where he'd been holed up all these years.

Until she posted a picture.

It was the first image she'd ever shared with him. To the casual observer, it would have looked like a shot taken from someone sitting on a mountain bike. Nothing but handlebars and a bike trail.

But it was way more than that.

He knew her location immediately. The gravel path. The boathouse in the distance perched on the edge of a lake. And not just any lake. Smith Lake.

Mountain Daisy had taken the picture at Baxter Park in Denver. The same park he'd ridden his bike hundreds, maybe thousands of times. He knew the rise and fall of each curve. He remembered the pitch and drop of each straightaway.

And there was more.

She'd added daisy decals to her handlebars, but it was the two letters etched into the metal that caused the breath to catch in his throat.

C + B

Camden Bergen.

It popped into his head the moment the image flashed across his screen, and within seconds, he'd started checking flights back to the States.

That picture, with his initials tucked between two daisies, drove him to board a plane, fly across the ocean, and come back to Colorado—the place he'd sworn he'd never return, all to try to find Mountain Daisy, whoever she was.

He shifted forward on the seat as the cab stopped and glanced up from his phone.

"Do you want me to wait?" the cabbie asked, narrowing his eyes in the rearview mirror.

Camden grabbed his bag, opened the car door, and looked up at the entrance to Fairmount Cemetery.

"No, you can go," he answered, his voice rough like chalk scraping along a stretch of cracked pavement.

He'd spent so much time alone these past years, interacting with others as little as possible. But he wasn't a complete hermit. He'd go into town from time to time. He was a big man. A strong man. Working odd jobs on and off at the different ski resorts, shoveling snow, running the lifts, and in the summer months, building and maintaining trails had left him lean and ripped. And even with his wild hair and bushy beard, women were drawn to him. He'd lost count of the meaningless one-night stands—those times where he'd venture out when his body craved carnal release. But that empty part of his life ended the day Mountain Daisy's message flashed across his phone's screen.

He got out of the cab and clenched his jaw, remembering the last time he'd been here.

Green and lush with birds calling out to one another in the late afternoon sun, the cemetery looked different in the springtime. When they'd buried his parents, it had been cold. Damn cold. The kind of cold that seeped into the bone, unrelenting and unrepentant. The wind had whipped across his cheekbones, and the lashes had been a welcomed distraction from the two coffins lying prostrate on the snow-covered ground.

He set off down the path toward two grand headstones. He may not want the living members of his family to know he was in Denver, but he needed to pay his respects to the dead before he set out to try to find Mountain Daisy. He owed them that.

Not another soul in sight, it wasn't long before he stopped beneath a beech tree and stared at the headstones of Hannah and Griffin Bergen with *loving parents of Jasper, Brennen, and Camden* etched beneath their names.

He set his pack on the ground and scrubbed his hands down his face.

"I'm sorry it's been so long. I don't know how this works, but I'd like to think you know why I'm here. But first..." He released a pained breath. "I need you to know that I'm sorry I turned out so unworthy of the Bergen name."

He paused. Not only did he not want to live in the spotlight of being a Bergen, he didn't deserve it.

He'd cut himself off from his clan. At eighteen years old, he'd attended his parents' funeral then left this place and headed to the Alps before the first shovel-full of dirt covered their caskets.

Even now, despite being a Bergen, he had nothing to contribute to his family.

His oldest brother, Jasper, sat at the helm of Bergen Enterprises as its CEO. And Brennen, the middle child, had been a pro skier and Winter X Games champion. Moreover, he'd seen the news of Bren's engagement to a local teacher, and his brother's work with the philanthropic arm of the company had made international headlines.

His brothers had a place in this world. His brothers represented the family.

What had he done?

Starting at age twelve he'd taught ski lessons at Bergen Mountain and worked as a camp counselor during the summers for the Bergen Adventure Summer Camp. He'd been good with kids back then, but he'd spent the last decade barely breathing a word unless it was absolutely necessary.

He closed his eyes and pictured the letters carved into Mountain Daisy's handlebars. "I just thought that maybe I could be somebody different with her."

He'd never spoken the words out loud. Never verbalized what he'd been feeling this last week. Jesus! What had seemed entirely plausible now sounded almost insane. Yes, he could have sent Mountain Daisy a message. He could have asked if she wanted to meet. But then, she could have said no. She could have dashed his dreams before he'd even ventured out of his sad little cabin, and something deep within him couldn't take that chance.

He paced the length between the headstones and pressed on. "I decided to come home and give myself the summer to try to find her. We met by chance. I guess, what it comes down to is that, if I'm meant to find her, I will."

He knew she rode the trails around Smith Lake. He knew what her bike looked like. He could spend the summer in Denver. He'd lay low and stay off the radar. He'd saved up a little money. He could find a studio apartment or even rent a room nearby. He had a trust fund with millions, but he'd sworn he'd never touch a penny of the money he didn't deserve.

And maybe, if he found her, they could be together.

He'd assumed she was single from how frequently they corresponded. Despite being eight hours ahead of her, he knew her schedule. Nine p.m. for her was five a.m. for him, and he'd gotten used to being up at that early hour to message with her before she went to sleep. Surely, if she was married or with someone, she wouldn't be able to spend hours at the end of her day chatting with him, right?

He looked back and forth between the headstones. "I know I have no right to ask for your help or your blessing, but I feel like I've found something good. I think there's someone out there for me. Just like you guys and Gran and Grandad."

But that twist in his chest was back. Was he selfish? Was he breaking some unspoken agreement between himself and Mountain Daisy? Were they destined only for a long-distance pen pal relationship? Could that be all she wanted?

Cam picked up his pack and eased his arms through the straps, then stared at his father's name carved into the gleaming onyx headstone. "When we'd ride a really technical trail you'd always say, 'Look at where you want to be. Find that spot and focus on it.' I think I found it, Dad. I think that spot is my Daisy."

He kicked at a clump of grass. He wouldn't have to tell her he was a Bergen—at least, not at first. She could be his fresh start. His clean slate.

He shook his head as a thread of doubt twisted around his heart. Fuck! Was this all some crazy pipe dream? Maybe it was, but he'd come this far. He had a plan. A loose plan. The worst-case scenario was that if he didn't find her, they'd just go back to being forum buddies. But Christ, he wanted more. They'd connected. She might not know his name or his face, but she knew his heart.

He glanced between the headstones one last time when a voice caught his attention. He turned to find his cab driver running toward him while holding up his cellphone.

"I knew you looked familiar!" he called, gasping for breath. "And then when I saw you head over to where those fancy Bergens are buried, I knew I was right! You're the Bergen grandson. You're the missing heir who left town right after your parents died. I'm going to be able to sell these pics for a fortune. Nobody's seen you in years!"

Fucking hell!

It would break his grandmother's heart if she found out he was back, and he hadn't let her know.

Camden pushed the man's phone out of his face and strode up the path.

"Hey! I'm right, aren't I?" the cabbie called, trailing behind him as a *click click* sound emanated behind him.

Cam glanced over his shoulder as the paunchy, middle-aged man struggled to keep up, but he needed to get the hell out of there and out of this wannabe paparazzi's sight.

And he needed to get to his grandmother.

She'd been nothing but kind to him over the years, emailing him every week. Updating him on his brothers and grandfather.

He'd never replied. Not once.

He could send her a message. But what if she didn't get it before this jackass sold the pictures? It would kill him to hurt her any more than he already had.

He had no choice. It was time to run.

Luckily, he ran a six-minute mile and doubted the camera-happy cabbie could walk a mile, let alone keep up with him.

He looked around and got his bearings. He still knew this city like the back of his hand and headed west on Alameda Avenue. He was about four miles away from his grandparents' estate situated near the Denver Botanic Garden, and he could get there in under thirty minutes easy.

But would they be home?

Fuck if he knew, but it was his best option.

His backpack bobbed and jostled behind him as he edged by a woman pushing a stroller and rushed past a trio of power walkers to make the light. He was a little over a mile in when a car honked behind him.

"You can't outrun me, buddy!" the cabbie called from the driver's side window. "I'm gonna retire off these pictures!"

Fuck that!

Camden doubled his pace, headed north and zigzagged through the neighborhood, but the cabbie kept up.

This asshole was persistent. His brother, Brennen, had been hounded by the press for years—news of his escapades even made it all the way to Switzerland. Cam gritted his teeth. He'd be damned if he was going to fall prey to some gossip blog thirty minutes after blowing into town.

His arms sliced the air at his sides, pumping and driving him to push harder, when the rarely used south entrance to the botanic gardens came into view.

The cabbie honked his horn again. "You can run, but you can't hide! I'll find you, Bergen!"

Wanna bet?

Cam's breaths came fast, and his mind raced. He couldn't lead this jerk to his grandparents' place. That would be just the confirmation this moron would need. But he knew something this persistent prick didn't.

He glanced behind him, flipped off the cabbie, then scaled the wall surrounding the gardens like a mountain lion. He'd barely missed a bush coming down and landed with a thud on solid ground. But just when he thought he was home free, he was met with a round of gasps.

"Jesus, Joseph, and Mary!" a man blurted.

Cam brushed the dirt off his knees and looked up. A woman in a flowing white dress stood next to a man in a dark tux with a minister between them, his mouth hanging open.

A quick check of the space confirmed what he already knew. To lose the cabbie, he'd just committed a nice little bout of breaking and entering into the gardens and ended up crashing an outdoor wedding. He stepped forward and reached out toward the groom.

What the hell was he doing?

The man cocked his head to the side then seemed to remember his manners and shook Camden's hand with a glazed expression.

Cam gave the man's hand a firm shake. "Congratulations! I'm sure you'll both be very happy."

He nodded to the stunned wedding guests then weaved his way past the still slack-jawed minister and seven very confused bridesmaids, over to the path that led to a secret door.

A few stately homes backed up to the botanic gardens. His grandparents' estate happened to be one of them, and they had an even bigger perk than just being able to see the gardens in all their splendor from their backyard. They had a gate that led from their property into the gardens.

Private access.

He and his brothers had loved sneaking into the gardens, pretending they were secret agents, infiltrating whatever cops and robbers or espionage scenario they could imagine.

He slowed to almost a walk when a security guard turned the corner and charged toward him.

Cam sucked in a breath. He did not have time for this!

Adding a mugshot to the paparazzi pictures was not at all the homecoming he'd envisioned.

He cut down a path and skirted by a cluster of willows. The gardens sported little offshoots—dirt paths that led patrons off the main walkways and through the dense foliage that lined the wall dividing the gardens' property from that of the surrounding estates. All he had to do was lose this guy and get to the door.

"Stop! There's nowhere to hide," the guard called.

But the man was wrong. There were plenty of places to hide. Secluded nooks. Areas draped behind thick canopies of leaves. He remembered them all. He may have been the youngest Bergen brother, but he was the best when it came to discovering the most secluded spots. He turned down a narrow path then cursed under his breath. The once concealed nook had changed from when he'd last been here.

Shit! He was twenty-eight! It had been damn near twenty years since he and his brothers had played hide-and-seek in the gardens, and the once hidden alcove was now part of a new open garden, teeming with daisies—and nowhere to hide.

"Stop!" the guard shouted, gaining on him.

Cam had to act fast. His only hope was to make it to the gate. He cut back onto the narrow dirt trail that followed the wall and saw the rooftop of his grandparents' house peek through the trees. He was so close but cursed under his breath when he reached the door and tried to turn the knob.

Locked!

Of course, it was! What was he expecting? Denver's most influential family would leave it open for any Tom, Dick, or Harry—or runaway Bergen heir—to pop in at their leisure?

The guard's footsteps grew closer, and Cam prepared for impact. He was six five and weighed two hundred and fifty pounds. It was time to put that muscle to work. He reared back and banged his shoulder into the door. The lock gave way, and he crashed into his grandparents' backyard, tumbling onto the ground and knocking over a table.

Before he could even blink, something white slid off the surface and mushed into his face and shoulder as another round of gasps filled the air. He brushed his finger across his cheek and glanced at the substance.

Icing?

Why the hell was he covered in cake?

He didn't have time to work it out because a small man in a chef's uniform with a white puffy hat started kicking him.

"That was my chocolate raspberry truffle masterpiece!" the irate man cried in a thick French accent.

Cam put up his hands, shielding himself from the man's assault—which mirrored that of a disgruntled Pomeranian, poking and jabbing, but not doing any real harm, and tried to get up. He had to figure out why there was a cake table with a pissed off baker in his grandparents' backyard when the security guard banged through the broken gate.

"I'm sorry, Mr. and Mrs. Bergen. This vagrant just hopped the fence and disrupted a wedding in progress on the grounds. I followed him here. We need to call the police."

Cam shooed off the angry French dude and turned to find five pairs of wide eyes watching him, and his stomach dropped.

This may be the worst homecoming ever recorded in the history of homecomings.

He did a quick glance around the yard. Besides the chef-dude and the red-cheeked security guard, five people stared at him, suspended in a silent state of shock, and there was fucking cake all over the place.

His gram and grandad sat stock still next to Brennen and the woman he recognized from the pictures all over the internet as his brother's fiancée, Abby Quinn. But he didn't recognize the woman sitting next to Abby. Golden-blond hair cascaded past her shoulders like rays of sunlight, and he locked onto her gaze —her eyes such a vibrant shade of blue, they put the big Colorado sky to shame.

Maybe it was the surprise of watching someone break through a locked gate, get covered in cake, then have security charge in, but she didn't turn away. And while she was clearly shocked—

you'd have to be in a coma to not be at least a little concerned when a guy the size of a linebacker crashes your cake party—he couldn't get past the kindness in her eyes, the crazy instant connection he felt toward a woman he'd never seen before.

It didn't last long.

A beefy hand gripped his shoulder, pulling him up from the ground. He came to his feet and raised his hands defensively. He did not want to add assaulting a security guard to his list of offenses.

"You've got the wrong idea. I'm not breaking into this place," Cam said, doing his best not to look like a madman.

The guard cocked his head to the side. "Did you just bust through the door?"

"Yeah."

"That's the definition of breaking in," the man answered.

Dammit! He couldn't argue with that.

"He can't break into his own home."

Cam turned to see his grandmother. She'd risen to her feet and stood next to his grandad a few yards away on the stone patio.

Confusion marred the guard's expression. "His what?"

"Home," his grandfather reiterated, stepping off the patio and coming to his side with his grandmother close behind.

"You know this guy?" the guard pressed.

"Know him? I was there when he was born," his grandmother added.

Cam turned to his grandparents. "Sorry about the door. I was..."

"Just casually dropping by, darling?" his gram finished with a slight twist to her lips.

He nodded. "Something like that."

"There's no need to call the police, Calvin," his grandad said to the guard, walking the man back toward the gate leading to the garden. "That vagrant is my grandson."

"He is?" the guard asked, craning his neck to get another glimpse.

"He is, indeed. I'm not sure why he chose to enter the house through this unorthodox method, but I can promise you, he's not a threat to anyone."

"If you're sure?" the guard said, giving Cam one last look.

"Completely, thank you for your diligence," his grandad answered, shutting the now busted gate behind the man.

"Well, well! Look who's come home!" his gram said and wrapped him in her arms.

He melted into her embrace and inhaled her familiar rosewater scent. "Sorry about all that."

What else could he say?

She pulled back and patted his cheek. "Darling, it's so good to see your face," she said, then frowned. "The part that isn't covered with hair," she added with a wry grin.

Jesus, he'd missed her. All the *darlings* aside, she was still the sassy, speak-the-truth, Brooklyn born girl who'd set off with his grandfather more than sixty years ago with barely enough money in their pockets to last a month, holding on to the dream of leaving the concrete jungle of NYC and setting up a mountain sports shop at the foot of the Rocky Mountains in Denver, Colorado.

His grandad clapped him on the shoulder. "Why didn't you tell us you were coming home, Cam? We could have sent the jet or at least a car to pick you up at the airport."

"I wanted to surprise you," he mumbled. He needed to come up with a story damn quick.

"Surprise us?" Gram echoed.

His brother, presumably his fiancée, and the blond woman walked over and joined them in the grass.

He glanced around at all the mini wedding cakes and the small Frenchman scooping up globs of what must have been a chocolate raspberry truffle cake.

"Yeah, to surprise you about returning for Bren and Abby's wedding. It's Abby, right?" he asked, exchanging a glance with the smiling petite brunette.

She nodded. "Yes, it is. And it's so nice to meet you, Camden. I've heard so much about you. I feel like I already know you."

He tensed. How much did she know? But there was no look of derision in her eyes as she reached out and squeezed his hand affectionately.

"Flipping hell!" his brother said with a wide grin, pulling him in for a hug. "When did you turn into a Mack truck?"

"Flipping?" Cam asked with a creased brow. "When did you ever have a PG vocabulary?"

Brennen chuckled and wrapped his arm around Abby. "It's a long story, but it got me the love of my life, so I'm sticking with it," he answered, sharing a knowing glance with his fiancée.

"Well, whatever the reason," his gram began with a curious glint in her eye. "We need to get you settled and then a shower. Maybe a spa day at the Ritz? You're welcome to stay with us or take the penthouse at The Dalton."

"No, that won't work," he answered in a tight whisper.

His brother cocked his head to the side. "What do you mean, it won't work?"

"I mean, no. I won't accept any of it."

His grandfather crossed his arms. "Any of what, Cam?"

"Money."

Gram shook her head. "Like it or not, darling, you do have a trust fund and multiple properties at your disposal."

"Well, I don't want any of it."

He didn't deserve any of it. But this wasn't the time or the place for that discussion.

"Darling, the wedding is several weeks away. If you're not going to stay with us and you won't touch your trust, how are you going to live? Where are you going to stay?"

"I have a little money saved up, and I could pick up a summer job somewhere if I needed more."

"Perfect! You're hired," his grandfather said, sharing a look with his gram.

"I'm not working for you guys. I'm not qualified."

"I beg to differ, Cam. You'll be working at the Bergen Adventure Camp at Baxter Park. We've just learned that the site leader who usually heads up the program broke his leg in two places yesterday and won't be able to work this summer," his grandfather replied.

Baxter Park.

Mountain Daisy's handlebars and the carved *C* and *B* flashed through his mind.

"Okay, I'll do it."

His grandad narrowed his eyes. "Really? Just like that?"

Shit! He shouldn't have given in so quickly.

"Yeah, I'll run the Baxter Park program, but I'm finding my own place to stay."

"At least, take a car. Brennen's got twelve Mercedes sitting in the garage at The Dalton," his gram added with a wave of her hand.

"Four, Gram," Brennen corrected, biting back a grin.

"And still three too many," Gram answered, biting back a grin of her own.

Cam raised his hands defensively. "Listen, I don't want a Mercedes. I don't need a car. I'll just rent a room near the park."

His grandmother sighed. "You can stay with us tonight, darling. Or let us book you a suite at the Ritz. Where are you going to find a place to rent today? It's nearly seven o'clock in the evening."

He blew out a tight breath, paced the length of the yard, and ran his hands through his wild mass of dark hair, frustration coursing through his veins. How was he supposed to find Mountain Daisy and hide his identity now?

He was just about to say fuck it all when a woman's gentle voice pulled him from the muck inside his head.

"I have a rental unit near Baxter Park. I'm finishing up some work on the place. It's still a little rough around the edges. You could stay there for the summer—as long as you're okay with me coming in to work on the place from time to time."

Her voice was honey and sunshine, and when he looked up, all he saw were those blue eyes and everything stopped. Who the hell was this woman?

"Cadence, that's so generous of you," his grandmother said.

The woman—Cadence—nodded, giving his gram a shy smile.

His pulse kicked up, and he couldn't look away from those sky-blue eyes. He should say no. He was there to find Mountain Daisy, not to grow tongue-tied in front of this lovely wisp of a woman.

"What do you say? It's yours if you want it," Cadence added, holding his gaze.

3

What just happened?

Cadence glanced over at the bearded, brooding Bergen brother taking up most of the space in the cab of her truck as they sat stopped at a red light.

Holy pickles and relish! The universe had one heck of a sense of humor.

Are there any extra billionaire Bergen brothers lying around at the Bergen estate?

She couldn't complain. She'd gotten what she'd asked for.

She knew of Camden Bergen—the runaway Bergen heir— long before she'd even met Abby and became friendly with the Bergen family.

Everyone in Denver—no, basically everyone in Colorado and probably a good part of the world—knew of the Bergens. And young and old among them still remembered when Griffin and Hannah Bergen died tragically in a car crash a little over a decade ago. The governor had attended the funeral along with many prominent members of the business community as well as top sports figures. It made the papers. It dominated the news. She'd mourned the loss of two people she'd never met but respected for the way they'd used their wealth and influence to give back to the community.

What she didn't understand was why Camden chose to disappear.

Moreover, why was he back?

"What grade do you teach?"

She startled at his question. They'd done the whole *hi, nice to meet you* song and dance in Ray and Harriet Bergen's backyard next to a pile of smashed cakes and a disgruntled baker. It had lasted a minute or two before Camden told his family he had to leave.

No one seemed surprised by this. Granted, his entrance had set the bar pretty high when it came to shock value. Quietly mumbling that he needed to go couldn't hold a candle to busting through a solid wood door like the Incredible Hulk.

"I teach second grade," she answered, turning onto the street that ran parallel to Baxter Park.

"And you teach at Whitmore with my brother's fiancée?"

She nodded as a tingle traveled down to the base of her spine. Camden Bergen's presence was all-consuming. The heat of his body. The low rumble of his voice. Even with that out of control beard and dark locks of shaggy hair brushing past his eyelashes, he still possessed an aura of authority that made her pulse race.

She released the breath she hadn't realized she'd been holding. "Yes, that's where Abby and I met."

Silence stretched between them, and she glanced at the brooding giant. He wasn't even looking her way. His attention had been diverted to Baxter Park as the last rays of sunlight glimmered on the surface of Smith Lake.

"It's lovely this time of day," she said, but her ruminating hulk didn't answer and only gave her a slight nod.

She tapped her fingers on the steering wheel and glanced at

the man. Wearing a pair of ripped jeans and with only a worn backpack in tow, this was not how you started a visit with the family you hadn't seen in a decade. And that entrance pretty much sealed the deal that something was going on that had nothing to do with Abby and Brennen's upcoming nuptials.

She'd seen his expression when his grandfather had asked why he didn't tell them he was coming back to Denver. As a teacher, she'd developed a sixth sense that told her when someone wasn't giving her the whole story.

And there was more to Camden's story than just a surprise visit from the runaway Bergen brother.

"Have you known my family long?" Camden asked, snapping her out of teacher detective mode.

She kept her eyes on the road. "Yeah, for a couple of years. Your grandmother volunteered in my classroom two years ago for the Bergen Community Partnership, the volunteer program started by your—"

"My mom. Yes, I know my mother set up the volunteer program. I've been gone for ten years. I haven't lost my memory," he bit out.

Oh, heck no!

Cadence gripped the steering wheel. The Bergen clan may tiptoe around the youngest brother, but she didn't owe him anything. In fact, she was doing him a favor.

She turned onto Williams Street and came to an abrupt stop in front of her house.

She unbuckled her seatbelt and turned to face him. "I don't know why you're here, Camden Bergen, but I seriously doubt that it's only for Abby and Brennen's wedding."

He held her gaze, and his steel-blue eyes flashed surprise.

She lifted her chin. "And I don't know what kind of beef you've got with your family or this town, but the Bergens have done nothing but good for this community. They've shown me nothing but kindness and welcomed my good friend, Abby, into their family with open arms. I don't know why you're acting like a D-canoe, but here's a news flash for you. The Bergens are good people."

"D-canoe?" he repeated with a curious glint in his eye.

"Yes, it's short for douche canoe. It means a colossal jerk."

"I know what it means." His lips twitched beneath his wooly beard. "What kind of second-grade teacher says douche canoe?"

Was he laughing at her? What a D-canoe!

"I didn't. I said D-canoe. Perfectly child-friendly." She leaned in. "And I'll have you know, that I'm the kind of second-grade teacher who isn't scared to call it like it is. You're lucky to have a family that cares about you. Somebody needs to get that through your thick head."

He unbuckled his seatbelt and leaned in, their noses nearly touching. "And what do you know about me?"

She held his gaze, unflinching. "I know that you're lucky to have a family that loves you. Not all of us have that luxury."

"You don't get it," he whispered. "I don't deserve them. Their love. Their money. Their prestige. I'm not worthy of any of it."

Her bottom lip trembled. "How could you know that for sure?"

"I know," he answered, his words thick with emotion.

"What if you're wrong?" she breathed.

They'd just been introduced fifteen minutes ago. How the heck had this gotten so deep so quickly? And why did she care? What was it to her if Camden Bergen reunited with his family?

His knee grazed her thigh as his gaze grew dark. "I'm not wrong, Cadence."

The tingle was back, and heat surged through her body at the sound of her name coming from his lips.

When was the last time she'd felt like this?

Her answer came with a pang of shame.

It was the last time she'd heard from Mountain Mac. The last time her phone had pinged and the words, *New message from Mountain Mac,* flashed across the screen.

And what of Aaron? Her husband. She'd looked down at his lifeless body before they'd closed the casket and sworn that she'd dedicate her life to Bodhi and promised to follow through on his dream of restoring and renovating the houses.

Mountain Mac had been a comfort to her. A voice in the dark. A late-night confidant. Yes, she'd fantasized about him—wondered what it would be like to curl up in his arms. It was easy to let her imagination run wild about Mac. He was only words on a screen, making her smile...allowing her a tiny space to dream.

But Camden Bergen was right here, flesh and blood. All man and very, very real.

She sat back and released a shaky breath. She had to stop this—had to resist the magnetic pull between them. She stared out the passenger window. "We're here. This is the rental unit," she said, trying to keep her voice steady.

He glanced down at his knee, still pressed against her and shifted his body in the seat. "Sorry, I didn't mean to..."

She waved him off. "It's okay, and I should apologize. I shouldn't have come at you like that. It's got to be a lot to process, seeing your family, and I'm sure you're exhausted from your travels."

He gave her a tight nod, grabbed his pack, and got out of the truck.

She picked up her purse and the bag with the doorknobs from the backseat then joined him on the sidewalk.

She gestured to the house. "This is it."

"It's a paired house?" he asked, glancing between the connected units.

"Yeah, yours is the one on the right."

She looked up at the red brick structure with two cozy matching porches and identical chimneys, one on each side of the house. She'd taken a picture of this view to teach her students about symmetry. She'd folded the image in half as the children watched and gasped as the matching sides lined up perfectly.

"These are pretty rare for the Baxter Park neighborhood," he commented.

She relaxed a fraction, grateful to move on to a more benign topic. "Yeah, they were in pretty bad shape when I got them."

Camden frowned. "Them?"

"Yes, I own both units. I live there," she said and pointed to the porch on the left.

He frowned. "Next door?"

She glanced up at him. What was it with this guy? "Yeah, is that a problem?"

His posture went rigid. "No, it's not a problem."

She sighed. This man was an enigma. "How about I show you around?"

With another tight nod, he followed a step behind her as she pulled her keys from her purse and opened the door.

"It comes furnished, but I should warn you—"

"Holy Great Aunt Edna!" he said under his breath.

He wasn't far off.

"Actually, it's Great Aunt Gertrude," she corrected then shook her head. "No, it's just Gertrude. She never became an aunt."

Camden walked into the center of the room. "It's like going back in time."

With the low ceilings and surrounded by décor that hadn't been updated since the 1930s, he resembled a muscled comic book character written into a period piece.

She walked in and set her purse and bag of doorknobs on

the seat of a high-back chair. "I haven't had the time to go through all the personal items and furniture to decide what to keep and what to donate. I've been too busy working on the renovation." She glanced at the freshly painted walls. "You're lucky. I stripped all the wallpaper last week. You should have seen it when it was still up. Little red rosebuds surrounded by tiny green leaves. If you stared at it for too long, it was like being on an acid trip."

He cocked his head to the side.

She gasped. "Not that I do, or ever did acid, but the pattern could induce vertigo."

God, help her! Now she was the one acting like a freak.

He picked up a porcelain glass goose, one of the many figurines lining just about every flat surface. "Did you inherit this place from a family member?"

She glanced at the tiny goose in his large hand. "No, the bank said that two sisters lived here, one in each unit, for over eighty years. The property was priced to sell because it needed a lot of work, and the women who lived here passed away a day apart from each other. There was no will, and the bank couldn't find any next of kin to pass the place onto."

"Really?" he said, returning the goose before lifting a lace doily off an antique round card table.

"Yeah, from what I could piece together, they were twins and had come out to Colorado with their father. He'd hit it big and made quite a bit of money from silver mining and bought them this house. But then he left town after losing his fortune—and his daughters stayed here, never married, and from what the neighbors say, kept to themselves."

He nodded. "My dad would have gotten a kick out of this place."

She watched him closely. "Oh yeah?"

"Yeah, he was a big Colorado history buff."

Cadence glanced around. "This place certainly has that, but don't worry. It's structurally sound, and the wiring has all been updated."

"By you?"

She laughed. "No, I couldn't find a good enough tutorial on the internet, so I saved up and hired an electrician."

He walked farther into the house and peered into the bedroom.

She joined him in the doorway, looked him up and down, then glanced at the twin bed with a pastel pink duvet and frilly white bed skirt. "You may not fit on that."

"I'll make do," he said. He set his pack on the floor and gestured to the door against the wall that separated the homes. "Why is this here? It must connect to..."

"My bedroom," she supplied, a little too quickly. "Yeah, it's kind of weird. I guess the sisters were pretty close, like wear the same outfits every day and have the same hairstyle." She picked up a framed photo of the siblings resting on a dressing table and held it up. "This is Gertrude and Glenna."

"Which is which?" he asked, touching the frame.

She inhaled sharply. The very nearness of this man left her gasping for breath—her fingers tingling with the desire to touch him. It had been such a long time since she'd been this close to a man. A long time since she'd been alone in a bedroom with a man.

That had to be it. The loss of her husband. Mountain Mac vanishing like they'd never spent hours chatting back and forth. No wonder her body responded to Camden. Not to mention, it had been years since she'd felt a man's touch.

But she couldn't shake the feeling that it felt like more.

She set the picture frame on the dressing table and took a step back. "I'm not sure which is Glenna and which is Gertrude."

It was time to pull herself together. She gestured toward the bathroom. "Everything in there works. I still need to change the showerhead and tighten up a few things, but it should be fine for now. I'll get to it in a few days."

He watched her closely as the light from the window faded into a misty twilight.

"Do you want it?" she asked, her words sounding huskier than she'd anticipated.

His eyes widened.

She tried again, this time using her teacher's voice. "The house. Do you want to stay here?"

"Yeah, I'll take it," he answered, their gazes still locked.

She broke the connection, unable to read him. "I'm next door if you need anything."

"I know," he answered with a low grumble that left her off-kilter as a rush of heat surged through her body.

"Right, right," she answered, shaking her head to clear the cobwebs.

She needed to get out of there. As quick as she could, she slid the key to the unit off her keyring and handed it to him, careful not to allow her fingertips to brush against his. He had nice hands. Large hands. Strong hands.

She blinked. Snap out of it!

"I'll leave you to it," she said and headed out of the room.

"Wait," he called just as she'd made it to the front door.

She stopped, and her pulse kicked up at the sound of his footsteps coming up behind her.

"You forgot your purse and your..." He glanced in the bag. "Your doorknobs?"

"Oh, thanks. Those daisy doorknobs are not easy to find," she answered, her heartbeat slowing.

"Daisy doorknobs?" he echoed.

She took one out and held it up. "Yeah, these were the knobs that originally came with the house when it was built back in the thirties. Several sets were missing when I got the place. It's been sort of my mission to replace every missing knob. They're pretty rare."

He held out his hand, and she passed it to him. Aside from herself, she'd never seen anyone stare that closely at a doorknob.

"Do you have a thing for antique door parts?" she asked, half-joking until she saw his expression grow serious.

"No, for daisies," he answered.

She narrowed her gaze. "The flower?"

Now he was shaking his head like one of those bobbleheads. "Yeah, sure, it's a nice flower," he answered gruffly and handed her back the knob then reached past her and opened the front door, presumably for her to exit.

That certainly wasn't subtle.

She stepped onto the porch. "The fridge has some bottles of water, and there are some snacks in the cupboard. Help yourself to any of it. I leave it here for when I'm working. Rest assured, they're not from the 1930s like everything else in the house."

He stared blankly at her as her attempt at humor fell flat.

She twisted the strap of her purse. "Let me know if you need anything."

He rested his head against the side of the door. "You don't need to worry about me. I'm going to take a shower then hit the sack. It's been a long day."

"Well, welcome home," she said, unsure what the heck to say to the brooding giant.

He nodded, utilizing his bobble-headed caveman method of communication. She turned to go and hadn't even made it down the two porch steps before the door slammed shut behind her.

"And you're welcome for giving you a place to live," she said under her breath as she walked across the lawn on the uneven circular pavers that led from porch to porch. She'd need to replace the stones at some point, too. She ran a hand down her face. Just add it to the renovation to-do list. Another Post-it note. Another task to complete.

She unlocked her door then sat down in the darkened room when her phone pinged.

Could it be Mountain Mac?

She held her breath, reached into her purse for her phone, then exhaled a forlorn little sigh as the light from her phone screen illuminated an in-coming text.

Abby: Is everything okay? Is Camden going to stay in your rental? Everyone is still freaking out that he's back.

Cadence slumped in the chair.

Cadence: Yes, the brooding hulk has agreed to stay.

Abby: Did he tell you anything?

Cadence: Oh yeah, he explained his prolonged absence, and then we braided each other's hair and made friendship bracelets.

Abby: You may be doing that soon with all the time you'll be spending with him.

Cadence stared at the message with a creased brow.

Cadence: I don't see him coming over for backyard barbecues.

Abby: Maybe not, but you'll both be working at the Bergen Adventure Summer Camp at Baxter Park starting Monday.

"Shut the front door!" Cadence said, smacking her palm to her forehead.

In all the melee she hadn't connected the dots. Not only was her brooding hulk her neighbor, but she'd be working with him all summer.

Cadence: I forgot.

Abby: HOW COULD YOU FORGET?

Cadence: Between the guy breaking down the gate and watching the world's most awkward family reunion, it slipped my mind.

Abby: Looks like you've got yourself a Bergen brother.

Cadence: Ha, ha! I guess I got what I asked for.

Abby: Good luck! You know Bren and I are here if you need anything. And if it's any consolation, Bren says Camden has the biggest heart of anyone he knows.

Cadence: He's big. That's for sure.

Abby: You may find him charming.

Cadence: If charming is a barely verbal guy who could give Big Foot a run for his money, then yes, he's all sorts of charming.

Abby: You never know with these brothers. He could surprise you.

That may be true for Abby, snagging the reformed bad boy, Brennen Bergen, and Abby's cousin, Elle Reynolds, who was engaged to Jasper Bergen, the eldest brother. But she wasn't like them. Between caring for her son and working on the houses, she didn't have time for love.

She exhaled a weary breath and hammered out another text.

Cadence: Any kind of relationship would require basic communication skills. Camden Bergen nods more than one of those bobblehead figures people glue to their dashboards.

Abby: Good luck with your bobble-Bergen.

Cadence shook her head and chuckled under her breath.

Cadence: He most definitely is NOT my bobble-Bergen.

She set her phone on the arm of the chair and closed her eyes.

"You get five minutes to rest, and then it's back to painting the kitchen," she whispered when something warm brushed against her leg.

She screamed and jumped up as a blur of brown fur scampered behind the large mahogany antique secretary desk that sat in the corner of the room. The thing weighed a ton, and she hadn't been able to move it herself. She grabbed an umbrella that was propped against the wall to...

To, what? Defend herself. Try to poke the critter until it came out?

She took a step forward then screamed again when another

furry creature shot out from behind the sofa and crossed the room.

It was like a horror movie. What was next? If spiders started crawling out from under the bookshelf, she'd really lose it.

Eyes wide, she scanned the cozy living room then let out another scream as the front door burst open and a sopping wet, half-naked man wearing only a towel burst into the room.

4

CAMDEN

"Cadence! Are you okay?"

Camden scanned the room, ready to confront whatever intruder or emergency had Cadence screaming. Except, instead of finding a guy in a ski mask, he saw Cadence wielding an umbrella like a baseball bat. She swung at him, her eyes flashing surprise as he reared back and bumped into a lamp. The damn thing fell over, crashing to the ground, and extinguished the light, leaving them in a hazy darkness.

"Jesus, Cadence! It's just me. It's Camden!"

"Camden?" she called out.

"Yes, your...neighbor! The D-canoe!"

What the hell was wrong with him! *The D-canoe?*

He'd just gotten out of the shower and had seen his reflection in the mirror. With an out of control beard and a dark tangle of wild hair, he looked like he'd been stranded on a deserted island for the last decade. It was a miracle they'd let him board the plane to come home. He didn't have a mirror in his cabin back in Switzerland and hadn't given two shits about his appearance until now. He'd found a pair of scissors in the bathroom and had started hacking away at his beard when Cadence's screams spurred him into action.

"Is there somebody in the house?" he called.

A scratching sound caught his attention, and Cadence screamed again.

Camden tensed, ready to clobber the intruder. "Where is he, Cadence? Where's he hiding?"

"We have to find them!" she answered back.

"Them? There's more than one?"

Dammit! He needed a weapon, and he needed to get her out of the house.

"Yes," she whispered-shouted into the darkness. "The creatures! One of them is behind Glenna's desk!"

He stilled. *Creatures? Glenna?*

"Who's Glenna?" he whispered back.

A whooshing sound cut through the air as Cadence's dark form swung the umbrella.

"Remember? It's Gertrude's sister. The old lady who died here."

Creatures and dead old ladies? Cadence was a friend of his brother's fiancée and said she was a teacher. But was she also a lunatic?

He reached for the wall and felt for a light switch. "You think the old lady who died in this place came back as a monster?"

"No! A creature! There are two creatures in the house!" she replied, an edge of irritation to her whisper-shout.

"Not a ghost?"

He was pretty damn sure dead people came back as ghosts, not creatures.

"What?" she replied.

A click sounded, and he looked over to see Cadence standing next to another lamp, bathed in a dim pool of light.

Her jaw dropped, and she cocked her head to the side. "Where are your clothes?"

"I didn't have time to get dressed. I'm here to save you," he answered, scanning the front room.

"Why?"

He threw up his hands. "Because you were screaming. Now, where are the intruders? Are they in the back of the house?"

The place wasn't that big. They had to be close.

She frowned. "Intruders? There aren't any intruders."

"Then, why are you screaming?"

She looked at him like he had ten heads. "Because of the animals."

This was getting crazier by the second.

"What animals?"

She released an audible sigh. "A mouse or something brushed past my leg. I think it's behind the secretary desk in the corner. And then I saw another one scurry out and go behind the couch."

He dragged his hand down his face. "You were screaming because of two mice."

She pointed the umbrella at him. "What would you do if you were sitting in a chair, taking thirty seconds to unwind, when all of the sudden something warm and fuzzy brushed past your leg?"

"Probably not scream," he answered with a shrug.

Wrong answer.

She scowled and pointed the umbrella toward the door. "Well, there's no intruder, so you can—"

Her gaze slid to his feet, and she gasped.

"Holy fuck!" he screamed as fur buzzed past his ankle.

"See!" she called, raising the umbrella in triumph. "I'm not crazy! There are two creatures in my house."

He watched as the tiny blur with a bushy tail scurried behind the large desk.

"It's a squirrel."

"Thank, God! I thought it was a rat," she said, relief lacing her words as she lowered the umbrella. But she quickly raised it as the relief drained from her expression. "I can't have two wild squirrels in my house!"

He nodded. She was right. She couldn't. "I think they're both behind that cabinet."

"It's an antique secretary desk," she corrected.

What the hell did that matter?

He joined her in front of the massive piece of furniture. "Fine. They're behind the secretary desk. I'll trap them and then get rid of them."

She took a step back and pressed her hand to her chest. "Don't kill them!"

Jesus! Who did she think he was?

"I'm not going to kill them."

"I'm serious!" she replied, pointing with the umbrella.

"Cadence, I'm not going to kill a squirrel. We're going to catch them and put them outside."

She shook her head back and forth furiously. "I cannot be a squirrel killer."

"You're not going to be a squirrel killer. I promise. There will be no squirrel carnage."

She craned her head to try to see behind the desk. "What if we set them free outside, and they can't find their family?"

She was giving way too much thought to the welfare of animals that spent the majority of their lives collecting nuts. But, then again, there was no way he'd hurt an animal either—so he kind of got it.

He softened his features. "They're squirrels. As long as they can find shelter, they'll be fine."

She nodded and paced the room. "How do you think they got in?"

He glanced toward the back of the house where a thin sliver of light entered from the rear porch lamp.

"I think your back door is open."

She followed his gaze, then dropped her chin to her chest. "I opened the door for ventilation when I was painting. I must have forgotten to close it this morning. Hold on."

She jogged to the back of the house, closed and locked the door, then disappeared from his view into the kitchen.

He needed a plan. He turned on another light in the room and assessed the substantial piece of furniture. If he pulled it out a few inches from the wall, that might be enough to spook the squirrels. He'd need Cadence to be ready with a bag or a box to catch them. It shouldn't be too tricky.

"Okay, I'm ready," Cadence said, now holding a colander instead of an umbrella.

"Are you making the squirrels spaghetti?" he asked, stifling a grin.

What was she going to do? Scoop them up?

That tiny cute as hell furrow to her brow was back. "I figured, if you could move the desk, then I could scoop them up."

He had to work extra hard not to laugh. She was dead serious about the scooping. "Do you have a box or a bag? We need something that we can close fast."

She snapped her fingers. "So they don't jump out."

She ran back to the kitchen and returned with a large pot with a lid.

He gave her a sideways glance.

"For after we catch them. You know, for squirrel stew," she added, wearing the sweetest smile he'd ever seen.

His jaw dropped. Two minutes ago, she was terrified of becoming a squirrel killer.

"I'm kidding," she said with a low chuckle as her cheeks grew pink.

The sweet sound of her voice had him hard in an instant.

She laughed again. "You should see your face! Hold on. Let me get a box."

She set the pot on a side table and disappeared into the bedroom—the bedroom that shared a door with his.

He looked down. Thank Christ, Gertrude or Glenna or whoever the hell the sister was who used to live in his unit had extra-large towels. Because, holy hell, he could not be sporting an erection right now.

He closed his eyes and released a tight breath. "Try not to kill the squirrels. Try not to kill the squirrels," he whispered. He needed some kind of mantra to get his mind off the gorgeous blonde with perfect curves.

He opened his eyes to find her staring at him. "Are you okay?"

He nodded.

She held up a box. "Let's try not to kill the squirrels."

Dammit, she'd heard him. And he thought she was the lunatic.

"I'll pull the desk out, but you'll need to be right behind me with the box to catch them."

"Okay, we can do this," she answered.

They got into position, and he dragged the massive desk back a few inches.

"Do you see them?" he asked.

"We found you! You sweet little rascals!" Cadence cooed.

He edged the heavy desk back a fraction more. The squirrels sprinted out, and Cadence let out a surprised little whoop.

"I've got them! I've got them, Camden!"

He glanced behind the desk. "There's something back there. A little box."

He crouched down and reached behind the desk and pulled it out. Covered in a layer of thick dust, he held it out to show Cadence.

She shrieked as the squirrel box jostled in her arms. "Just put it in the desk. I've found all sorts of bits and bobs in the houses. It's probably nothing." She shrieked again and tightened her hold on the box. "We need to get Bonnie and Clyde Squirrel outside."

He lifted the door to the desk and set the box inside then turned to Cadence. "Here, hand me the outlaws."

"Thanks, I'll get the door," she said with a chuckle, doing a little jog that had him repeating the *try not to kill the squirrels* mantra. He was here to find Daisy, not fall ass over elbow for Cadence Lowry.

He followed her down the rear porch steps and into the yard.

He started to open the box, but she stopped him.

"Should we say something first?"

"To who?" he asked. He respected nature and wildlife, sure. But a send-off speech for two wayward squirrels seemed a little much.

She gestured toward the box and then to the starry sky. "To the squirrels? To the universe? Something to wish them well."

He glanced down at the box. "I'm glad we didn't have to kill you guys."

"Really glad," Cadence added, nodding.

He set the box on the ground and took a step back. It toppled over onto its side as the inhabitants scurried out and high-tailed it up the trunk of an old beech tree on the far side of the yard.

"Have a good life," Cadence called as the squirrel duo disappeared into the dark canopy of leaves.

They stood in silence, bathed in the dim glow of the porch light, when she turned and looked him up and down.

"Do you want some help with that?"

Holy shit! Was she talking about his erection?

She chuckled. "Your beard. There's a decent chunk missing. It looks like you were trying to trim it."

He touched the wild mass of facial hair. "Oh, my beard, right!"

Her cute frown face was back. "What did you think I was talking about?"

Not my damn beard.

"Sorry, I was still thinking about...the squirrels."

She chewed her lip like she was mulling something over. "I owe you for saving me from the squirrels. Why don't you come in? I've got everything we need to get you cleaned up inside my place."

He glanced down at his half-naked body. "Should I put on some clothes?"

She reached up and felt his face and the breath caught in his throat—blood diverting from his brain and heading south.

Try not to kill the squirrels. Try not to kill the squirrels.

"How much do you want taken off?"

He swallowed hard. "Most of it."

She held back a grin. "Done with the Hagrid look?"

He chuckled, appreciating the *Harry Potter* reference. "Yeah."

"It may get messy with that much coming off. You're better off like this, so you don't get hair all over your clothes."

He couldn't argue with that.

He followed her back into the house. He liked following her —liked watching the swing of her hips and the bounce of all that golden hair. He shook his head. He could not go down that road. She was a friend of his family. Definitely not the clean slate he'd traveled across the ocean to find.

She led him into her bedroom and into the tiny bathroom and pointed to the pink toilet. "Sit."

She opened a cabinet, pulled out scissors and electric clippers, and set them on the edge of the sink then leaned in and pressed her lips together, assessing the mess of hair.

"I think I'll start with the scissors. Take some length off and clean it up with the clippers."

He stared into her sky-blue eyes. Had she said she was going to dye his hair hot pink and sprinkle glitter on his beard, he would have agreed.

"Let's find your face," she added with a sweet smile and picked up the scissors.

She cupped his cheek in her hand, and it took everything he had not to close his eyes and melt into her touch. When was the last time he'd encountered such tenderness? Not from the women he'd been with over the years. That had only been sex. No, just fucking. Two people who needed to satisfy a primal urge. Not intimacy. Not lovemaking.

The snip of the scissors pulled him from his thoughts. Cadence stroked his beard, cutting off the scraggly length. Her face inches from his, the tip of her pink tongue peeked out from between her plump lips as she concentrated.

"Have you done this before?" he asked.

She grinned. "For my grandfather, back when I was a teenager."

"But not anymore? Do they not live around here?"

Her expression darkened. "No, I'm from Grand Junction, but he passed away a few years before my grandmother when I was a freshman in college."

"I'm sorry, Cadence. What about your parents? Are they out in Grand Junction, too?"

Her throat constricted as she swallowed. "Never knew them. My grandparents raised me."

No wonder she gave him shit about his family in the car. At least he had one.

"Now hold still. I can't be responsible for damaging the face of one of the legendary Bergen brothers."

One of the Bergen brothers.

He hadn't thought of himself as part of Denver's most prominent family in a long, long time.

A quick series of snips cut through the silence as she worked, and he couldn't take his eyes off her. His pulse quickened, and when she ran her tongue across her top lip, he balled his hands into tight fists. Christ, how he wanted to touch her! She moved in closer, straddling his leg, and filthy thoughts invaded his mind. All it would take was one tiny movement to have her on his lap. All he'd have to do was grip her hips, press his fingertips into those perfect curves and pull her close. His cock was all for that idea.

"Ground control to Major Camden," Cadence said softly.

He blinked.

"Ten inches," she added with a grin.

He glanced at his lap. Did she see his...

"I took about ten inches off your beard with the scissors. I was going to start in with the clippers to clean it up. Are you ready?" she asked, a slight crease to her brow.

Sweet baby Jesus!

He cleared his throat. "Yeah."

The sharp buzz of the blades tickled his skin, and he shifted, making damn sure the towel was still covering his hard length. Cadence set her hand on his shoulder as she worked, and her touch sent a rush of heat through his body. He couldn't take much more of this. He'd been celibate for almost a year for Daisy. He couldn't do anything to undermine his devotion to her.

The buzzing stopped, and she stepped back, assessing her work. "How about a little haircut while we're at it?"

He should say no. He should thank her for getting his beard under control and go back to his side of the house. Then he met her gaze, and he was powerless.

"Sure, a trim would be great."

She ran her fingers through his hair, and he inhaled a sharp breath.

"Am I hurting you," she asked.

"No, I just haven't had anyone..."

"It's okay," she said. "I'll be gentle."

He closed his eyes as she leaned in with the scissors. Her warm breath tickling the shell of his ear.

Try not to kill the squirrels. Try not to kill the squirrels.

"What was that?" Cadence asked.

Crap! Had he said that out loud?

"Nothing," he mumbled, keeping his eyes shut.

The snipping stopped, and Cadence pulled back.

"Open your eyes," she said softly.

He did as she asked, then took in another sharp breath. She'd held out a mirror, and if it weren't for his steel-blue eyes, he wouldn't have recognized the face in front of him. He glanced up at her.

"You clean up nicely, Camden Bergen," she said with a smile, but he'd swear there was a trace of sadness in her voice.

He ran his hands down his cheeks and paid special attention to his chin, feeling the skin that had been buried under his beard for years.

"I left a little bit of stubble. It suits you. Here, I'll give you a second to get used to your new face." She handed him the mirror and left the bathroom.

It was wild! He hadn't seen this version of himself since he was eighteen. He turned from side to side. She'd done a good job, and he was grateful she'd left a little scruff. He brushed his fingertips across his lips, no longer hidden by a mound of thick hair.

"What do you think?" she asked, returning with a small dustpan and broom.

"You do good work. Thank you."

She crouched down and started to sweep.

He joined her on the floor. "Here, let me," he said, taking the mini broom.

She glanced at him and cringed.

"What?"

She dusted off his shoulders and chest. "I got hair everywhere. You must be so itchy."

Actually, he'd been so focused on her, the thought hadn't crossed his mind until she mentioned it, and his skin started to crawl. He dumped a dustpan full of hair into the trash can then scratched at his chest.

She was right! It was like being covered in ants.

"Here," she said, reaching into the shower and turning on the water. "I'll give you some privacy, and you can rinse off."

The water trickled out, and she jiggled the handle. "That's weird?" She stepped inside the shower. "I just replaced this showerhead." She reached up and tapped it, and the showerhead came loose, squirting water in all directions.

"Oh my God!" she called, shielding her face from the spray.

"Scoot over!" He climbed into the tight space next to her and tried to reach past her to turn off the warm gush of water.

Already drenched, she batted at the spray with her hands and scowled. "I did everything the guy in the video said to do! This is supposed to work!"

"It may just need to be tightened," he replied, growing wetter by the second.

"No, I followed every step. It was working this morning!"

He tried again to reach past her. "Cadence, turn off the water!"

"No, it's going to start working. It has to!"

This was insane!

"You can't tell a showerhead to work properly! Stop being so stubborn. Turn it off, and I'll take a look."

She was soaked, and his towel was growing wetter by the second. If he didn't get this water situation under control pretty damn quick, the towel would fall, and he'd be naked.

He gripped her hips and lifted her up and out of the spray of water.

"What are you doing?" she shrieked.

He pressed her back to the wall. Rivulets of water ran down her face, and the outline of a lacy bra appeared through her wet white T-shirt.

It would take a towel the size of Texas to hide his erection now.

He leaned in as drops of water running off his face trickled onto her chest. "Showerhead 101. We have to turn off the water. You can't fix anything with it on."

She rested her hands on his chest, then parted her lips like she was about to protest, but nothing came out.

He slid his hand from her waist and tucked a strand of blond hair behind her ear, his thumb trailing along her cheek.

"But I watched a video on how to install it on the internet. The guy leading the tutorial said he was a licensed plumber," she replied as she stared into his eyes, her voice taking on a dreamy quality.

He brushed his thumb across her cheek, unable to stop himself. "You need to be careful with who you trust online. Not everybody is who they say they are."

"The guy seemed to know his stuff. He had over a thousand of those little thumbs-up on the video," she countered.

Her chest heaved with each breath as her breasts pressed against him, her body flush with his.

Cam swallowed hard. He needed to focus. Think of Daisy. Fuck! Think of the damn squirrels.

He released her body from his grip and pointed to the faulty showerhead.

"I'd give the video this." He gave her the hint of a smile and made a thumbs-down gesture.

She sighed, then nodded. "I think you're right."

They stood there like two people who weren't sure how they'd ended up in a shower together but weren't all that keen about getting out. He raised his hand, ready to tuck another lock of her golden hair behind her ear—his hands trembling with the need to touch her again.

He flexed his fingers and willed them to behave. "Do you mind if I turn off the water?"

Her eyes went wide. "Right! Go ahead!"

He turned the handle to the off position, extinguishing the spray.

She took a step back and twisted her wet hair into a bun, revealing the smooth skin and elegant curve of her neck. He glanced down at the outline of a chain with possibly a ring or some sort of round pendant. She caught his gaze, then pressed her hand over the object.

"Let me get you a dry towel," she said, her voice void of the dreamy wonder it possessed only moments ago.

She pulled her robe off the hook on the wall and quickly put it on over her wet clothes, tying it tightly, then handed him a fluffy towel from a stack on the counter, barely making eye contact.

"Just leave your wet towel. I'll take care of it."

A switch had flipped, and they were back to business. Landlord and tenant.

She left the bathroom, and he changed towels, trying to figure out what the hell had just happened in that shower.

He hadn't been that close to a woman in ages. He'd gone without physical contact for so long, and then there were the daydreams. He'd fantasized about Daisy's hands. Daisy's lips. He'd dreamed about her fingertips trailing across his body as she dropped a line of kisses down the hard plane of his abdomen. He didn't have an actual picture of her in his head. Just the sense of her. Her spirit. Her heart. He could have projected that onto anyone, right?

He secured the dry towel and glanced in the mirror. "Don't kill the squirrels," he whispered.

He'd steer clear of Cadence Lowry. He was an expert at blocking people out. He'd work. He'd play along with Bren's wedding plans, and he'd use every free moment he had to look for Daisy.

He left the bathroom and found Cadence trying to move the secretary desk back into place.

"Let me get that," he said.

She stepped back, and he slid the heavy piece of furniture into place.

She chewed her lip. "Well, thank you for helping with the squirrels."

He ran his hand down his chin then crossed his arms, suddenly feeling very half-naked. "Yeah, thanks for getting me all cleaned up."

Christ, this had become awkward.

He glanced around. "Is there anything else you need to be moved? A dresser?"

What the hell was he doing? Stick to the plan. Get the hell out of there.

She tightened the tie on her robe. "Um, not that I can think of, but thanks for offering."

He gestured toward the door. "Then I better..."

"Yeah, I'll walk you out," she said and opened the door.

He stepped onto the porch and bumped into a hanging swing which then knocked over a bike.

Jesus, Bergen! Get it together!

"Sorry about that," he said, righting the bike then froze, unable to believe his eyes.

In the dim light shining out from the front window, the white petals of delicate daisy stickers lined the bike's handlebars. He angled them toward the light and blinked, not sure he could believe his eyes.

What were the fucking chances?

He turned to her, his pulse racing. "Is this your bike?"

If he weren't still standing, he would have sworn his heart had stopped beating.

Cadence nodded and patted the seat. "Yes, this is my mountain bike."

"Have you been riding long?" he asked, gaze trained on the flowers and the unmistakable *C* and *B* glinting silver in the light.

"No, I started about a year ago. I'm still a beginner."

Cadence's voice sounded far off, like a whispered wish as blood whooshed through his ears.

"Do you ride around here? Around Baxter Park?" He bit out the words, his throat tightening with emotion.

"I do," she answered, then touched his arm. "Are you all right, Camden?"

He pulled his gaze from the handlebars to where her hand rested on his forearm.

Mountain Daisy's hand.

He took her hand in his and stared at it. She was real. She was real and beautiful and kind.

"It's you," he whispered.

"Camden, do you need to lie down? Do you want me to call one of your brothers or your grandparents?"

The bubble popped.

He released her hand and stepped back. His brothers? His grandparents? How the hell was he supposed to have a fresh start with a woman so completely entwined with his family?

Dammit! When she was Mountain Daisy, she was his. Only his. Uncomplicated. Always just a few clicks away.

He took the porch steps two at a time. "No, I'm just tired. I should get some rest."

"Well, good night. Sweetest dreams," she called from the porch.

Fuck.

Sweetest Dreams.

If the bike, daisies, and initials weren't enough, her nightly sign-off, *sweetest dreams*, sealed the damn deal. He followed the stone pavers to his unit, scaled the porch steps in one stride, and entered the house.

He paced the living room and ran his hands through his hair. His now much shorter hair thanks to a haircut from...Mountain Daisy.

Jesus! What happens now?

He closed his eyes and pictured his parents. "You two have a real sense of humor! How can I start over with Cadence? You know I can't stay in Denver with the world knowing I'm back. I can't play the part of a good Bergen son because I'm not. You both know I'm not."

He walked into the bedroom and stared at the door that led to Cadence's room. Two inches of solid oak separated him from her. Fucking hell! He'd left the safety of Switzerland. Nobody knew him there. Nobody expected anything more than a day's work. He'd hoped he'd have that same luxury with Daisy.

No expectations. Nobody relying on him.

He pictured his father next to him on the trail in mountain biking gear, gesturing to a point in the distance, and he dropped his chin to his chest, holding on to the memory. "If she's the one, you need to let me know, Dad."

Ping, ping, ping.

He glanced around the doily encrusted room and found his phone where he'd left it on a nightstand before getting into the shower.

Ping, ping, ping.

He only had an alert set for one thing.

He picked up the phone.

New message from Mountain Daisy.

He stared at the door. Was she in there? Was she curled up in bed just as he'd always imagined?

He opened the message.

Mountain Daisy: Hey Mac, I'm not sure if I'm dipping my toe into stalker zone. You didn't reply when I sent you that bike pic, but I've missed our chats, and I've had one heck of a day. So, I thought I'd try messaging you again. How are you? I hope you're doing well.

He released a slow breath.

Mountain Mac: Sorry, Daisy, I've had...

Jesus! How was he supposed to respond? *I decided to cross the ocean to track you down only to find out you're my brother's fiancée's best friend?*

He shook his head.

Mountain Mac: Sorry, Daisy, I've had some personal stuff going on. I've missed you too.

Her reply dots rippled across the screen.

Mountain Daisy: Is everything all right?

Mountain Mac: No, nothing is all right! All I want in this fucking world is you. A "you" who doesn't know I'm the runaway Bergen heir. A "you" who I could be someone new with. Someone who wasn't the cause of so much pain.

He sighed, deleted the message, and started over.

Mountain Mac: I feel like I don't know anything anymore, Daisy.

It was the damn truth.

Mountain Daisy: You have a good heart, Mac. Whatever it is you're going through, I'm always here for you. Now, do you want my two cents?

This woman.

Mountain Mac: Always.

Mountain Daisy: Focus on what's important. Once you do that, you'll find your way.

He stared at her message and could hear his father's voice: *Look at where you want to be. Find that spot and focus on it.*

The wording, nearly identical to Daisy's message. The meaning, entirely the same.

Focus on what mattered.

That's easy. It was Daisy. It was always Daisy.

A resolve he hadn't known since he was a teenager pulsed through his veins. He had to tell her. He had to take the chance. He sat down on the edge of the old lady's bed, Gertrude, Glenna, whoever, and listened as steps padded toward the joint door between the houses. It was Cadence. She was standing right there, her feet blocking the light coming from under the door.

He muted his phone.

Mountain Daisy: Mac? Are you there?

Mountain Mac: Yeah, I'm here.

Mountain Daisy: Good, I like knowing you're here.

He was more *here* than she could imagine.

Mountain Mac: How are you? You mentioned having a tough day. Are you okay?

A pang of shame cut through him. This was a slippery slope. He knew damn well what her day had been like.

Mountain Daisy: I'm good—much better now that I've talked to you.

Shit! And this is what she did. Her magic. She made him feel...useful, helpful...needed. That was it! She'd given him purpose.

Mountain Daisy: Well, Mac, I think it's time for this Daisy to get to bed.

He waited like one of Pavlov's dogs for those four words to flash across the screen. Those four words that cracked his hard exterior every damn time.

Dots rippled across the screen as she typed, and his pulse kicked up.

Mountain Daisy: Sweetest dreams, Mountain Mac.

There they were, like a salve to his broken heart.

He smiled. He couldn't help it.

Mountain Mac: Sweetest dreams, Mountain Daisy.

The muffled creak of mattress springs caught his attention and the light from beneath the door, disappeared. She'd gotten into bed. All these nights, he'd imagined her doing this, and now, he could hear her, just beyond the door, not miles and miles away but inches.

He rested his head against the door, closed his eyes, and focused on her face, Daisy's face—no, Cadence's face. He'd never considered physical attraction with her. He'd fallen for Daisy without knowing anything about her appearance. But he'd been drawn to Cadence from the moment he'd caught a glimpse of her after he'd crashed the cake party.

It made sense. The connection. The desire. It had to be because she was Daisy.

He went to the bed, pulled back the pink covers, and maneuvered his body into the snug space. Another creak came from the other side of the door. She must have shifted in her sleep, and the muscles in his chest tightened. Would she be in his arms soon? He'd pictured it. Holding her. Wrapping her in his embrace and never letting go.

He was so damn close.

He adjusted the pillows and rested his head into the pink softness and stared at the door.

"Tomorrow, Daisy," he whispered, his eyelids growing heavy. "Tomorrow, you'll be mine."

6

CAMDEN

Camden rolled over, hugging a pillow to his chest, then felt the bottom go out beneath him as he hit the floor with a sharp thud.

"What the?" he exclaimed, his voice thick from sleep.

He ran his hand down his chin and froze. This was not the bearded, woolly face he was used to. This was his new face, or maybe the revival of his old face. It didn't matter because this was the face Cadence would be looking at when he revealed his identity as Mountain Mac. He got up and went into the small adjoining bathroom and looked into the mirror.

He stared at his reflection and released a slow breath. "You're probably not going to believe this, Cadence, but I'm Mountain Mac. And I've been crazy about you from the moment I read your message on the mountain sports chat forum."

Okay. That could work. It didn't sound too crazy. She'd be surprised—that was a given. But after yesterday, after their little spat in the car and after their time spent breathless and staring at each other soaking wet in the shower, she had to have felt the connection between them.

Was it the fresh start he'd fantasized about?

No.

But he'd found Daisy. It was almost as if his parents had heard his plea and answered.

He pulled a fresh pair of jeans and a T-shirt from his pack, got dressed, then brushed his teeth.

This was the day everything was going to change.

He picked up the framed photo of Glenna and Gertrude. "I found her, ladies," he said, then stilled at the sound of a sharp knock at the front door.

It must be Daisy—Cadence—Jesus, he had to remember, they were one and the same.

He went to open the bedroom door and reached for the knob, the antique glass knob with the daisy center, and a rush of euphoria surged through him. The signs were all there. The daisies. Cadence calling him a D-canoe just like in her first message on the forum's main page. He hurried to the front door and threw it open, ready to confess everything.

But nobody was there.

He walked onto the porch and shielded his eyes. Christ! What time was it? With the sun that high in the sky, he must have slept through a decent part of the day.

"Good morning, Sleeping Beauty."

Camden descended the porch steps then stopped. "Bren?"

"Wow, Camden!"

Cam glanced over to find Abby standing next to Cadence.

"I told them to be ready for a new you," Cadence said, watching him closely.

"Cadence, I...," he began as his brother, his brother's fiancée, and Cadence stared at him. "I shouldn't have slept so late," he said, chickening out.

He couldn't tell her now—not in front of his brother and Abby. They'd need privacy.

"I told your brother to let you sleep a little longer," Cadence said with a sympathetic grin.

Brennen held up a nondescript white bag. "She tried to protect you, Cam. But then, I knew you wouldn't want this to get cold."

"You shouldn't have," Cam said, shaking his head, but his stomach had a different story and growled.

Brennen grinned. "Santiago's breakfast burritos used to be your favorite, and from the chorus coming from your belly, it sounds like they still are."

"Not a lot of breakfast burritos in Switzerland," he said, taking the bag and inhaling the heavenly scent of eggs, potatoes, and breakfast sausage.

Abby held up another larger bag. "We brought enough for all of us. And Bren and I were hoping to talk to the two of you. If you're not too busy."

Camden shared a glance with Cadence. She gave him a little shrug—her eyes telling him she was caught off guard, too.

He had to stop himself from grinning like an idiot. They already had a secret, subtle communication system. They just fit together.

Cadence gestured to her side of the house. "It's so nice out. Let's eat on my porch."

"Perfect, but first I need to grab a few things from the car," Bren said then jogged over to his Mercedes.

Camden followed the women onto Cadence's porch. Abby took a seat on the hanging swing while Cadence gestured for him to sit in one of the two patio chairs on the other side of the snug space. He settled in and stared past Abby's shoulder at Cadence's bike, propped against the side of the wall, those daisies calling to him.

He was so damn close. He'd just have to wait until Bren and his fiancée left.

Cadence sat in the chair next to him as Brennen carried a

box onto the porch, set it on the ground by his feet, and took a seat next to Abby.

Cam turned to his brother. "Are you going to tell me what's in the box?"

"Eat first. Abby and I want to ask you—well, you and Cadence something," Bren replied.

Cadence chuckled and unwrapped her burrito. "Oh no! I'm not sure how much good ever came out of the *eat this before I ask you something* scenario."

Cam unwrapped his burrito and took a bite. Sweet Christ! It was good, but unease swept through him. What could they want?

"I promise, it's nothing terrible," Abby added.

Cadence pointed her burrito at Abby. "Do you need a kidney? You know you've got dibs if you ever needed one."

She was just like this with him over chat—sweet, funny, giving.

Abby shared a look with Bren and heat rose to Cam's cheeks.

"You guys can't be asking for one of Cadence's kidneys," he said, glaring at his older brother.

Brennen bit back a grin. "It looks like you've got quite the protector living next door, Cadence. And no, bro, Abby and I decided not to add vital organs to our wedding gift registry."

Cam's anger instantly cooled when Cadence patted his arm.

"Down, boy! Nobody's losing a kidney today."

Abby leaned forward. "Well, Camden, Cadence has already kindly agreed to be one of my bridesmaids, and now that you're back, Bren and I would love for you to be a part of our wedding, too."

"Yeah, Cam, I'd like you to be my best man along with Jas," his brother added.

Holy shit! Was this for real?

He hadn't spoken one word to his brother in ten years.

He glanced between the happy couple. "Who, me?"

Brennen's eyes went wide, and he looked from his fiancée to Cadence. "Flip, dude!"

"Yes, you!" Cadence and Abby answered in unison.

"Couldn't be!" Abby sang.

"Then, who?" Cadence replied, dramatically feigning confusion.

Cam's gaze bounced between the women then settled on his brother. "What the hell was that?"

He'd been gone a long damn time. His social skills may not be up to par, but he was not at all expecting anyone to break out into song over breakfast burritos.

"It's a teacher thing," Bren said with a chuckle.

"It's the 'Cookie Jar Chant,'" Abby answered as if this was common knowledge.

"Okay?" Cam replied. Maybe he did need another hour of sleep.

"You don't have to worry about being in trouble with the 'Cookie Jar Chant.' But as soon as you hear one of them bust out the *One, Two, Three. Eyes on me.* Run for cover, brother," Bren added and shared a knowing look with his fiancée who blushed in response.

It was weird seeing Bren so smitten.

But he forgot all about his love-sick brother when Cadence patted his arm again. "The cookie jar thing is just a little game that Ms. Quinn and I play with our students." She turned to Abby. "What can Camden and I do to help?"

He held back a grin. It was all falling into place. She was already talking about them like they were a couple.

Abby's expression grew serious. "We could use your help with some of the planning. I've asked my cousin to be my matron of honor, but with her writing schedule and the pregnancy with the twins—"

"Wait, twins?" Cam interjected.

Bren frowned. "I thought Gram emailed you?"

She had. It didn't mean he'd read the message.

Cadence's hand was back on his arm, and she leaned in, conspiratorially. "Here's the Bergen brothers slash Quinn Reynolds cousins recap. Jasper and Elle Reynolds, that's Abby's cousin, are expecting twins this winter, and are both crazy busy with their careers."

"Where are they now?" he asked.

"Our place in the Caymans," Bren answered.

Cam frowned. "Working?"

"Man feasting," Bren added with a wide grin.

Abby blushed. "And that would be the opposite of working."

"Jasper's on vacation?" Cam asked.

From the emails he did glance at, it sounded like his oldest brother was a workaholic who never took an hour of downtime, let alone went on vacation.

"Jasper's come a long way. He and Elle are really happy and excited about the babies, but each has a lot on their plate. Abby and I were hoping you and Cadence could help out with the wedding stuff, too," Bren replied.

Despite the warm breeze, a chill passed through Cam's body. He hadn't even been back a day. Everything his family did garnered publicity and playing a lead role in his brother's wedding would undoubtedly attract attention...and questions.

Why is the runaway Bergen heir back? And why did he disappear right after the death of his parents?

His throat tightened. "I don't think—"

"We'd be happy to step in and help," Cadence said, cutting him off.

Abby sat back and sighed. "Thank you so much! Planning a wedding in just a few months is no easy feat."

It was hard to believe that his brother—the brother who'd

made headlines worldwide as a womanizing playboy—was sprinting to the altar.

"Why the rush to get married?" he asked.

Bren wrapped his arm around Abby and pressed a kiss to her temple. "Because there's nothing I want more in this world than to have Abigail Rose Quinn as my wife."

Cadence grinned at the happy couple. "I'm so excited for you guys. Don't worry, we'll make sure everything runs like clockwork."

Brennen's eyes went wide. "Which reminds me, I come bearing gifts."

Cam tensed. "Bren, I told you back at Gram and Grandad's place. I don't need anything."

Bren frowned. "What do you think this is? A box filled with money?"

Cam schooled his features. "I'm serious, Bren."

His brother's expression softened, and he opened the box. "One laptop—this is standard Bergen Adventure Camp issue. I'm sure you remember from your days as a counselor," he said and passed him the computer.

Cam set the laptop on a small table situated between the chairs.

Next, Bren pulled out a helmet. "This is to go along with your mountain bike. It's still in the back of my car."

"I didn't know you mountain biked, Camden?" Cadence asked, watching him closely.

"Oh yeah," his brother answered. "He and my dad used to ride the trails all over the city and up in the mountains. They especially loved to ride right over at—"

"Is that all that's in the box?" Cam asked, cutting him off.

Maybe Bren was good with discussing their parents, but he sure as hell wasn't ready to shoot the shit with his brother like nothing happened. Like it all wasn't his fault.

"There's one more thing." Bren reached into the box and pulled out a small wooden box.

Camden stood and shook his head. "No, not Dad's Patek Philippe."

"What's a *Patek Philippe*?" Cadence asked, coming to his side.

"It's a watch," Bren answered softly.

"It's not just a watch," Cam bit out and stared at the box.

It wasn't just a watch. It was a watch that was worth a quarter of a million dollars—probably even more now. A watch he'd traveled all the way to Geneva, Switzerland with his father to purchase when he was sixteen years old. A watch that his father had told him would one day be his.

He just didn't expect the day to come so soon and because of his actions.

Bren joined them. "They're some of the finest timepieces ever made. Some would argue, the finest. Each watch is hand-crafted and can take up to two years to complete. There are no off the shelf pieces. It's quite extraordinary. Cam and my dad got to visit their store in Switzerland."

"Can I have a look?" Cadence asked.

Bren nodded and handed her the box.

She traced the gold Patek Philippe emblem with her finger-tip. "It's heavy," she said, gazing down at the glossy, polished wooden box.

"They don't mess around with the packaging. It's solid wood and has metal feet. The official certificate is in there, too."

Cadence furrowed her brow. "Official certificate?"

"Yeah, for its authenticity. These timepieces are passed down from generation to generation, some going back to the eighteen hundreds, and they won't issue another certificate. It truly is a one-of-a-kind family heirloom."

Cam crossed his arms. "Why don't you keep it, Bren? Or Jas, he could take it."

Cadence smiled up at him. "Now, hold on. You should look at it before you decide you don't want it."

If it were anyone other than her, he'd tell them to fuck off.

But it was her. His Daisy.

He released a tight breath. "Okay, let's have a look."

But the day they'd picked up his father's watch was as fresh in his memory now as it was then, and he didn't need her to lift the glossy lid to know what was inside. A Patek Philippe watch with a platinum band, blue face with a small dial for the phases of the moon. He and his father had spoken with the watchmaker and witnessed the painstakingly precise work that went into creating the legendary timepieces.

Cadence opened the box and gasped. "It's beautiful."

She wasn't wrong. The watch looked as exquisite today as it had all those years ago.

She handed the box to Bren and gently removed the watch from its secure perch. "Let's try it on," she coaxed.

"I don't..." he began.

"One, two, three, Camden Bergen. Eyes on me!" Cadence said, holding his gaze.

He froze. Jesus! His brother was right! That teacher talk was Jedi level mind control.

"Hand, please," she said sweetly.

He raised his right hand.

She cocked her head to the side. "You're a lefty?"

"Yeah."

"That explains a lot," she said, biting back a grin.

Now it was his turn to cock his head to the side, but before he could protest her lefty comment, she stepped back and nodded.

"It suits you."

He looked down at his father's timepiece. It fit like a glove. It was loose when he'd tried it on his sixteen-year-old wrist. He was gangly back then. It was another six months before he started to fill out like his brothers. He nearly smiled remembering the day he'd tried the watch on, and it had fit.

This watch will be yours one day, Cam. And you'll pass it on to one of your children. We'll all be connected through time and space.

He'd been so proud after his father had told him that. Proud to be a Bergen. Proud to be the son of a man as kind and as giving as his father. Now, all he felt was shame. And children? Jesus, he'd never trust himself with the life of a child. He couldn't.

"You should keep it, Camden."

He glanced up and the overwhelming urge to come clean and tell her he was Mountain Mac welled up inside him like a river a breath away from cresting. Maybe he could be worthy of her? Maybe, with her by his side, there was a chance he could be a better man.

His mouth had gone dry. "Cadence, I'm—"

Beep! Beep!

What the hell?

Cadence broke their connection and waved to someone over his shoulder. "Hold that thought."

He watched as Abby and Cadence walked over to a BMW parked in front of Bren's Mercedes. The tinted front window rolled down to reveal a smiling woman in the passenger seat as a little boy with golden hair climbed out of the back seat and stood next to Cadence on the sidewalk.

Cam stared at the boy as Abby and Cadence spoke to the woman.

He turned to his brother. "Who's the kid?"

"That's Cadence's son, Bodhi. He's great. He spent some time with us up at the cottage. I took him out on the slopes. He skis like you—no fear and all speed."

"Her son?"

The bottom dropped, and Cam clutched the railing, his resolve draining. His heart hardening.

C and *B* did not stand for Camden Bergen—but Cadence and Bodhi.

He was a goddamn fool.

Mountain Daisy had a child, and that changed everything.

7

CADENCE

"There was a piñata, and we went swimming in their very own private swimming pool, and we roasted s'mores in their backyard."

"Slow down, Bodhi. Did you remember to bring Mr. Cuddles home?" Cadence asked, taking her son's backpack as the Boyd's car set off down the street.

Bodhi had left his beloved bear all over Denver. It was a miracle they still had him.

"I remembered him, Mom! I made a little note for myself like you make all your notes," he answered, pulling a scrap of paper from his pocket and holding it up for her to see.

Abby patted Bodhi's shoulder. "Hi, Bodhi!"

"Hey, Miss Quinn!" he said with a wide toothy grin.

The boy looked around. "And Brennen!" he called, jumping into Abby's fiancé's arms.

Brennen tossed him into the air, then set him down. "Hey, little man!"

Cadence swallowed hard as the sweetest kind of sorrow washed over her. Aaron used to play with Bodhi just like that when he was a toddler. She released a shaky breath. It would be easy to fall apart, but she pasted on a smile.

She'd gotten good at soldiering on. At acting like she had it all under control. Pretending the role of the do-it-all single working mom was enough—because it had to be.

"Who's that?" Bodhi asked and pointed toward the house.

"That's my brother, Camden," Brennen answered.

Bodhi's eyes went wide as if someone just told him he'd won ice cream for life. "You have another brother?"

"Yep, Cam, come over and meet Bodhi."

Cadence turned to find Camden with his back to her, one foot on the porch step leading to the rental unit. The hard muscles in his back tensed under his T-shirt as the man froze.

"Did you hear, Mom? Brennen has another brother!"

That was the understatement of the year.

She nodded, her pasted smile in place. Not only did Brennen have another brother, but that brother was also their neighbor who, only hours ago, had her pinned against the shower wall. She grazed her fingertips across her cheek where he'd touched her so tenderly, and all her worries had disappeared. The broken showerhead. The to-do list that was a mile long. Her dwindling bank account. Her fears. Her broken heart. They all melted away when she was lost in his steel-blue gaze.

Camden joined them in the front yard, looking a shade paler. They could be friends, right? They were going to be neighbors, coworkers at the Bergen Adventure Summer Camp, and now, they'd agreed—well, she'd agreed for them—to help with Abby and Brennen's wedding. It made sense—and it was only for the summer. He'd made that much clear in the Bergens' backyard.

Still, when she was with him in the shower under the warm spray of water, her body wasn't contemplating a platonic friendship. His hands gripping her hips. His body pressed to hers. Her lips, tingling with the desire to be kissed. Whatever that was, it wasn't friendship.

She smiled at him. But there was no warmth in Camden's eyes. The man who'd burst into her house to save her from squirrels had disappeared. Jaw set. Posture rigid. He stuffed his hands into his pockets.

Could it be the watch or memories of his parents?

But her sixth sense told her his change in mood wasn't due to his unease with his family. And it wasn't like she couldn't relate. The other day, she'd found one of Aaron's old T-shirts in a box, and it had hit her hard. His smell. His laugh. It all came rushing back.

But the hard glint in Camden's eyes wasn't there when she'd slid the watch onto his wrist.

There was something else that crushed the hopeful glint in his eyes.

Bodhi didn't seem too concerned with the brooding giant standing next to Brennen.

"How tall are you?" her son asked, assessing Camden as one would evaluate the height of a skyscraper.

"About six five," Camden answered.

"Did your mom make you eat lots of vegetables?"

The hint of a smile pulled at the corner of Camden's mouth. "Yeah."

"Bananas?" her son continued.

"Yep."

"Oatmeal?"

"All of the above," Camden said, sharing a look with Brennen.

Bodhi turned to her with a serious expression. "See, Mom! That's what's going to happen to me if you keep making me eat vegetables and oatmeal and bananas. I'll turn into a giant like Camden."

"Hey! What about me?" Brennen asked. "I'm pretty tall."

Bodhi scrunched up his face. "Not tall like him."

"I'll have you know, he's my little brother," Brennen said, feigning outrage.

"Not anymore," Bodhi replied with a certainty only bestowed on individuals who weren't quite tall enough to ride the big coasters at the amusement park.

The adults chuckled, and she glanced at Camden—only to find him watching her. The warmth was back in his expression for a fraction of a second before he resurrected his stony facade.

"Brennen, I'm going to ride my bike without the training wheels," Bodhi said, moving on to a new topic. "Want to come with us to the park and watch?"

Brennen checked his watch, then shared a look with Abby.

Abby bent down and put her hand on Bodhi's shoulder. "I'm sorry, B. Brennen and I have to go."

"Abby's right, little man. We have to leave now to meet with some really cool volunteers who help blind people ski."

"Wow!" Bodhi said, eyes wide.

"Yeah, it's pretty awesome." Brennen glanced up at his brother. "But I'm sure Cam would go with you. He's really good at riding bikes."

"Better than you?" Bodhi asked.

Brennen cocked his head to the side. "Maybe."

Camden shook his head.

"Better than Jasper?" Bodhi pressed.

Brennen's expression grew serious. "Absolutely." He turned to Camden. "We do need to head out. Can you help me get your mountain bike out of the car?"

"Can I help, too?" Bodhi asked.

"Sure," Brennen said, taking Bodhi's hand as the men headed to the Mercedes.

"How are things with Camden?" Abby asked, lowering her voice. "You guys looked..."

Cadence frowned. "What?"

"In sync. He seemed ready to chuck that watch in the garbage before you stepped in."

"I didn't step in."

Abby raised an eyebrow. "You busted out one, two three. Eyes on me."

Cadence sighed and watched as Camden lifted the bike out of the back of the car. "I don't get him, Abby. I'm hoping we can be friends or at least act civil toward one another."

"I think it'll be good having him here," Abby replied.

Cadence leaned into her friend. "Good to have a brooding bobble-headed Bergen next door?"

"Good that you won't be alone," Abby said with a sympathetic grin.

Cadence closed her eyes and pictured Camden, dripping wet, his thumb caressing her cheek, then crossed her arms. She had to put a stop to thoughts like that. Between the guilt over her feelings for a man she'd met online and wanting to honor the commitment she'd made to her deceased husband, adding in a crush on the brooding Bergen just wasn't in the cards—at least, that's what her head said. Her body, and maybe even her heart, were still in that shower.

"It's just for the summer," she said, trying to sound indifferent.

"Then I'm glad you'll have someone close by for the summer. Plus, I may have you guys on hot glue gun duty to make the wedding favors," Abby added.

Cadence reared back. "Abby, you're marrying a billionaire with a *B*. All you'd have to do is drop the Bergen name, and you'd have vendors throwing themselves at you."

Abby hooked their arms together. "I want to do a little something myself. And you know I love my glue sticks. I'm all about the glue."

Cadence chuckled and rested her head on Abby's shoulder.

"Abby Rose, we better hit the road," Brennen called.

"We'll talk soon," Abby said with a hug, then joined Brennen at their car.

She and Bodhi waved as the Mercedes pulled out, then glanced around the yard and didn't see the brooding Bergen.

"Wait, Camden!" Bodhi called.

The man had already made it to his porch—again!

Bodhi ran to him. "Will you come to the park with us? Mom said we could take off my training wheels, and I could try riding without them."

Cadence joined them and put a hand on her son's shoulder. "Honey, Camden might be busy."

Doing what, she had no idea, but she'd never seen a man retreat so quickly.

"But, Mom, you still get nervous when we ride bikes, and if Camden's really good—maybe better than Brennen—he could help us."

The breath caught in her throat, and she pasted on her plastic grin. "Why would you say that?"

He pointed between his eyebrows. "You get a line right here when we're about to ride bikes."

"No, I don't!"

"It's there right now," Bodhi answered.

She touched her forehead. Hello, premature frown lines.

Her son looked up at the stoic giant. "Please, Camden. Will you come with us to Baxter Park?"

He nodded. "Okay, for a little bit."

Bodhi jumped with a hoot of excitement. "I'll get my bike," he said and set out for the little shed on the side of the house.

"Here." She handed Bodhi his backpack. "Set this on the porch, and don't forget your helmet."

And then it was quiet. She and Camden stood there, neither saying a word, before she broke the muted stalemate.

She glanced at his mountain bike, leaning against the side of his porch. "It's easier if we walk and just let Bodhi ride. The training wheels slow him down, and once they come off, I usually run alongside him. He's still a little wobbly."

"I know," Camden answered.

"How would you know?"

"Experience. I spent my childhood summers in the Bergen Adventure Camp. When I was old enough, I became a high school counselor. I taught tons of kids how to ride a bike up until the summer before..." he trailed off.

"Before what?"

He shook his head. "It's not important."

But the sadness in his eyes contradicted his statement.

"I've got the wrench for you, Mom," Bodhi called from his bike, pumping his little legs with the socket wrench clutched in his hand.

The squeak and rattle of the training wheels came to a stop, and she took the tool from her son.

She held it up. "It's to remove the—"

"Training wheels," Camden finished.

"Yeah, I guess you already know that."

Her Bergen bobblehead nodded.

This may be the longest summer of her life.

"Can we go?" Bodhi asked.

Cadence glanced up the street. No cars. "Okay, but remember to stop and look before you cross over to the park."

"Got it, Mom!"

Bodhi set off, and she and Camden followed behind. Luckily, they only lived a block away from the park.

"I didn't know mountain biking still made you nervous."

He speaks.

She glanced up at Camden. "Why would you know that?"

"I mean, your son mentioned it."

"It still does a bit, but I'm getting better. A friend's helping me with that," she answered.

She wasn't about to get into the past with a man who seemed to be ruled by his.

"A friend?" he asked.

She smiled, thinking of Mountain Mac.

"Just someone I met online."

He tensed.

"I know what you're thinking. It sounds creepy—the whole, meeting someone online—but it's not. We met on a mountain biking forum. And it's not like we've shared any personal information. I don't even know where he lives or what his real name is. He's just..."

"Just what?" Camden coaxed.

Cadence smiled. She couldn't help herself. "Kind."

"And you know it's a guy?"

She shrugged. "I think so, but it's never come up."

This was the most talkative he'd been all day, and why the heck was she telling him—this brooding giant who couldn't wait to get away from her—about Mountain Mac?

"How does he help you?" Camden asked, cutting into her thoughts.

She watched as Bodhi looked both ways then crossed the street. "It started with the basics: what type of bike to get and all the necessary gear. But then, it changed."

"And now you're friends, that's it?"

She glanced at him. "What do you mean 'that's it'?"

"Forget it," he said, hands in his pockets, head down.

"Mom!" Bodhi called, waving to her next to one of the willows lining Smith Lake.

She walked over to her son with Camden a half a step behind her, crouched down and started to loosen the bolt on the training wheels.

"I can get those off for you," Camden offered.

"I got it," she said. She'd lost count of how many times they'd taken off—and then put right back on—the training wheels.

"I'm going to do it, Camden! I'm going to ride around the whole lake," Bodhi said.

The brooding bobblehead nodded.

"Just take it nice and—" she began, setting the training wheels and wrench next to the tree when Bodhi took off.

"I'm a race car!" the boy shouted, tearing down the paved path.

She shot up and started running. "Slow down, B! Wait for me!"

He didn't. Building speed, he cruised down the slight incline. He was fine on the straightaways. It was the turns that got him.

"The curve, Bodhi! Slow down for the—"

"I got him."

Camden's long legs consumed the pavement as he sprinted down the path and passed her.

Her heart jumped into her throat. With the curve in sight, Bodhi's little shoulders twisted, overcorrecting. He bumped off the path and tore through the grass.

"The lake!" she yelled, pushing her body as hard as she could.

Bodhi had never kept going once he'd hit the grass. He usually bailed and tumbled off the bike, adding another scrape to his knees. But today, her determined boy wasn't stopping.

Neither was Camden.

Arms slicing through the air as he ran, he hurdled over a poodle then weaved between a group of power walkers before hitting the grass and grabbing the seat of Bodhi's runaway bicycle.

"Whoa, there," Camden said, taking a few steps as he slowed the bike to a stop.

She ran to her son, heart pounding. "Are you hurt?"

"That was awesome!" Bodhi cheered.

She schooled her features. "Bodhi Lowry, that was not awesome. That was very unsafe. You could have hurt yourself or someone else."

He dropped his chin to his chest. "Sorry, Mommy."

She glanced up at Camden. "Thank you. I don't know what I'd do if..."

If what? If she lost her son, too? It was too painful to imagine.

She released a shaky breath. "Let's walk your bike to the tree, and I'll put the training wheels back on."

"Mommy, why are you crying?"

Oh no! She could not cry—especially in front of Camden Bergen.

She brushed away the tears. "I'm just glad you're okay, that's all. Come on, we'll try again tomorrow."

"You should let him try now."

She glared at Camden. "How could you suggest that? You saw what happened. If it wasn't for you..."

She swallowed past the lump in her throat. She had to push past her fears. Push past Aaron's death. She knew this. But it didn't make the pain any less real or the apprehension any easier to bear.

"Yeah, he went off the trail," Camden answered calmly.

"And almost ended up in the lake," she countered.

Camden got down on one knee to Bodhi's level. "What were

you looking at when you jumped the path and started plowing the grass?"

Her son pointed toward the lake and a line of three ducklings trailing behind the mother duck. "The baby ducks. They're so cute!"

"That's what happened," Camden said, looking up at her.

"Ducks?" Cadence shot back.

"No, focus."

"I looked at the ducks, and then I went that way," Bodhi said, connecting the dots.

Camden held Bodhi's gaze. "Do you think you could try again and focus on the things I tell you to look at?"

"Will that help me ride without training wheels?" the boy asked.

"Yes, it should," Camden answered.

Bodhi's expression darkened. "My friends don't need training wheels. I was the only kid who had them during the end of the school year Whitmore bike parade."

Cadence's heart sank, but everything stopped when a large, warm hand touched her arm.

"I'll stay next to Bodhi the entire time, Day—I mean, Cadence."

Could he not remember her name? It didn't matter. What did matter was Bodhi and his safety.

She frowned. "What if he heads for the lake again?"

"Then I guess we're both going for a swim," he answered with the same warmth she'd seen in his eyes when he'd helped her with the squirrel removal.

Who was this Camden Bergen? One minute the man couldn't get away from them fast enough. The next, he was volunteering to teach her son to ride a bike.

"Please, Mom!"

She crossed her arms, holding herself tightly. "Okay. One more try."

"I won't look at the ducks when I'm riding my bike. I promise, Mommy."

Or birds or people or flowers or insects. Distractions were everywhere.

She gripped the bike seat, lifting it from where it came to rest on the ground, then stilled as Camden's hand covered hers.

She tried not to focus on the warmth of his touch. "I really don't want my son crashing into a lake."

"That's reasonable."

She swallowed hard. "Or a tree or a bench or a person."

"Those are all good things to avoid," he answered, the low rumble of his voice calming her frayed nerves.

Bodhi had walked to the edge of the lake and started throwing pebbles into the serene water. The soft, *plop, plop* of the stones rippling through the placid surface faded away when she met Camden's gaze.

"Why are you doing this for Bodhi?"

Pain flashed in his eyes. "Because I can. Because I owe it to you for all the things that I can't give you."

She studied him closely. "I don't understand. What can't you give me? We just met."

Sadness marred his features. "Let me help, Bodhi. If he's not circling the lake in ten minutes, we can call it a day."

"Okay," she answered, hardly believing she'd uttered the word.

He lifted his hand from where it had rested on top of hers and gripped the handlebars. "Let's give it another try, Bodhi," he called.

She stood, her body buzzing from his touch, and watched as Camden helped Bodhi onto the bike.

"Okay, Bodhi, look at where you want to go. Find that spot and focus on it."

Her son nodded.

"Start with the trees that line the path. Pick one, and after you pass it, pick another."

Camden gestured around the lake, pointing to the largest trees.

"Like landmarks?" Bodhi asked.

"Exactly like landmarks. Are you ready?"

"Will you stay next to me?"

Camden patted Bodhi's back. "Yes."

The boy nodded. "Then, I'm ready."

Camden pointed to a tree a good twenty yards away. "Do you see that tree with the curve in its trunk? That's your first landmark."

Bodhi craned his neck. "Mommy, are you watching?"

She smiled at her son. "Always."

"Mommy, can we..." He reached out his hand.

Warmth filled her chest as she took it in hers and gave it three pumps.

I love you.

He squeezed back four.

I love you, too.

Bodhi leaned in toward Camden. "That's our secret code for saying I love you. It's how we said goodbye every day before I went to kindergarten. Want me to teach it to you, Camden?"

"If your mom doesn't mind," Camden replied, his gaze flicking to her.

"It's fine," she said, not sure what to make of her son wanting to teach their secret *I love you* handshake to someone he'd just met.

Bodhi took Camden's hand in his and gave it three quick pumps. "That's the *I love you* part. Now it's your turn. You squeeze my hand four times and think, *I love you, too.* But don't say it. Pretend you're a secret agent."

Camden glanced up at her, a quick movement, but she caught it, then gave Bodhi's hand four quick pumps.

"Did you think the words?" Bodhi asked.

"I did."

"Now you know how to do it! You're a secret agent like me and my mom."

Camden cleared his throat. "Okay, Secret Agent Bodhi, it's time to focus on your first landmark."

Her son gripped the handlebars and stared at the willow. "Here we go!"

"How many times did I go around the lake, Mommy?"

"I stopped counting at eleven," she answered and handed Bodhi another slice of pizza.

"And remember when that group of runners went by, and I had to move all over the path so I wouldn't hit them, Camden?"

Cadence looked across the table and didn't see an empty chair and watched as Camden swallowed a mouthful of pizza.

"That was some expert-level maneuvering, buddy," the man answered.

Bodhi yawned. "I did what you said. I picked a spot and focused on it—and I got through them without crashing into anything!"

Camden had done it. In less than ten minutes, he'd had Bodhi pedaling past people walking their dogs, parents pushing strollers, and even slicing and dicing his way through a pack of joggers.

She'd watched the first wobbly lap ease into the second, then third. And with every pass, Bodhi improved, his chin raised with a determined expression as he concentrated on the landmarks. And something amazing happened. As Bodhi's confidence grew, her anxiety tapered off, and she'd stopped neurotically counting the laps and watching her son and let her focus drift to the man running alongside him.

His strong, muscular body never more than a few feet away from Bodhi. His gaze darting between her son and the bike path. They went around and around for almost two hours.

"Thanks for the pizza," Camden said from across the table.

"It's the least we could do, right, B? Camden was kind enough to teach you how to ride all around the park," she said, but when she looked over at her son, his eyelids fluttered.

"It looks like Secret Agent Bodhi may be falling asleep," Camden said with a chuckle.

"I'm not tired," the little boy answered, chin dipping then coming up again.

She bit back a grin. "Are you sure, sweetie? You look a little tired."

"I'm going to ride around the park ten more times," Bodhi said, his words running together.

"Ten?" she asked, sharing a look with Camden.

"Twenty," Bodhi countered, before falling forward.

She and Camden reached out at the same time and braced the sleepy boy from using his slice of pizza as a pillow.

Bodhi opened his eyes a fraction then slid in his chair toward Camden. In one fluid movement, the man stood and had her son in his arms, Bodhi's head resting on his shoulder.

"Sweetest dreams, Camden," Bodhi mumbled.

Camden's eyes went wide. "What did he say?"

Cadence smoothed her son's hair. "Sweetest dreams. It's just what I tell Bodhi when I kiss him goodnight before bed."

And Mountain Mac—but she wasn't about to tell him that.

She'd typed the words that very first night when they'd spent hours messaging back and forth.

"Do you want me to put him to bed?" Camden asked.

She stared at them. It had been years since anyone besides herself had carried a sleeping Bodhi. He'd gotten so big. When Aaron used to hold him, he was just a tiny little thing, all rosy cheeks and chubby toddler thighs. Now his lanky legs dangled, one shoelace untied swaying back and forth as he shifted his weight in Camden's arms.

"Cadence?"

She pulled her gaze from her son. "Yes, let's get him to bed. He had a sleepover birthday party last night, and then with all those laps this afternoon, I think he's pretty tuckered out."

She led Camden down the hall and opened the door to Bodhi's room. She turned on a rotating lamp and stars and planets began to circle the room in a cozy blue glow.

"I had one of those lamps as a kid, too," Camden whispered and surveyed the room.

"He likes to think he's a big boy, but he still gets a little frightened of the dark."

Bodhi shifted again, and Camden adjusted his hold.

"Here," she said and pulled back the covers.

Camden gently set Bodhi on the bed. He stepped back, and she went to work, taking off the boy's shoes and socks then pulled up the covers.

Bodhi yawned. "Mr. Cuddles?"

"He's right here," she answered, tucking the bear in next to her son.

"Sweetest dreams," she whispered and kissed his forehead.

"Sweetest dreams, Mommy," Bodhi murmured, hugging the bear to his chest.

She turned to find Camden watching her, the blue light casting him in an ethereal glow that highlighted his strong jaw and broad shoulders, making him look like some other-world superhero.

He followed her out of Bodhi's room, and she closed the door with a soft click.

"Is that a new one?" he asked.

She cocked her head to the side.

"The doorknob," he said.

She touched the glass knob. "Yes. I found this one in an antique shop not far from Bergen Mountain."

His expression dimmed a fraction. "I better—"

Something inside her wasn't about to let him finish that sentence.

"Would you like a beer? I think you earned it after today. You must have run ten miles," she blurted, hoping that she didn't come off as desperate for company as it sounded.

She didn't want him to go. Not yet.

"Sure, a beer would be great."

She pointed to the front door. "Why don't we sit on the front porch?"

"Okay."

"I'll meet you out there," she said, holding his gaze before heading to the kitchen.

She opened the refrigerator door and inhaled the crisp air, hoping it would cool her down.

What was she doing?

She was having a beer. She'd had beers with Brennen plenty of times. Granted, Abby was there, and she and Brennen had no...

No, what?

Attraction?

Shower escapades?

She grabbed two bottles of Left Hand Brewing Company's Sawtooth Ale and closed the fridge and popped the tops off the bottles. Wisps of the last rays of the late spring sun shined in through her kitchen window, setting off the amber ale in a warm glow.

"We're just two people having beers," she whispered, leaving the kitchen.

But that didn't stop her body from buzzing with anticipation when she caught sight of him on the porch.

He'd left the front door propped open, his long legs moving as he rocked back and forth on the swing. She stepped onto the porch, and he stilled.

She handed him the bottle and sat down on the swing beside him. "I hope this is okay?"

Camden glanced at the label, and the ghost of a smile pulled at the corners of his mouth. "I haven't had this in years. Bren used to sneak them for us when we were teenagers." He pointed to the label of a simple red left hand, and his smile morphed into a frown. "I distinctly remember you making a lefty comment."

She glanced at the Patek Philippe watch on his right wrist. "Bodhi's left-handed, too. He used to get frustrated with scissors and hated writing in those spiral notebooks."

Camden leaned back. "I don't blame him. I spent a good part of high school with the side of my left hand covered with ink."

She chuckled. "Well, I'll have you know, you're in good company."

"Oh yeah?"

She set her beer down by her feet and started counting on her fingers. "Albert Einstein, Isaac Newton, Charles Darwin, and Benjamin Franklin were all lefties who did great things for this world."

He took a long pull off the bottle and glanced away, but she saw the pain in his eyes.

She leaned in. "Can I ask you something?"

He nodded.

"What's Switzerland like? That's where you've been all these years, right?"

He took another sip, then held his beer in his lap. "It's quiet."

"What do you do there?"

He cocked his head to the side.

"When you busted into your grandparents' backyard like the Incredible Hulk and demolished that poor cake," she began.

Camden looked into the beer bottle, shook his head, and chuckled. "The Hulk?"

"Well, yeah or like that old commercial where the giant pitcher of Kool-Aid busts through walls. I figured you'd prefer the Hulk."

"Good call," he answered and took another sip.

She bit back a grin. "Well, I couldn't help hearing you say that you haven't touched your trust and didn't want any of your inheritance. I just wondered how you made it work?"

He leaned forward and stared out at the street. "I do a lot of seasonal work at nearby ski resorts. It didn't hurt that I grew up a Bergen and already knew everything about them. I can do basic maintenance on just about anything. I can fix snowmobiles and chair lifts. I've shoveled snow. Ran the snowcats. In the summers, I build and tune-up mountain bikes and help out with any of the water sports. I have a little cabin, and it doesn't cost much. That's all I need."

She relaxed into the rocking rhythm. "But doesn't everyone know you're...you?"

He grinned. "People care a lot more about me being a Bergen here than they ever did over there."

"So, nobody knows?"

"Not really. Staff turnover is high. People come and go. It's very international. Lots of languages. Nobody really sticks out. Big guys with burly beards grooming the ski runs are a dime a dozen. I've kept to myself. I rarely engage with anyone. Years passed, and I faded into the daily grind."

"Is it lonely?" she asked, the words escaping before she could stop them.

He glanced back at the bottle and sighed. "Sometimes, what about you?"

She stiffened. "What about me?"

"Are you ever lonely?"

She closed her eyes and sighed. "Would it be weird to say yes? The funny thing is, I'm hardly ever alone."

He gave her a sweet smile. "That doesn't mean you can't be lonely."

"I have good friends—Abby and her cousin, Elle, are great, but I..." she trailed off.

"You're not like them?" he pressed.

She stared at the night sky. "They're like sisters to me. But we're different. I have a child."

He nodded. "What about other friends?"

She opened her eyes. "My online friend. But he's been..."

The rocking stopped.

"What?" Camden asked.

"A little distant."

Camden studied his beer bottle. "I'm sorry."

She waved him off. "It's not your fault. Maybe it's just the ebb and flow of an online friendship, or maybe he's found a real person to talk to. I've never known anyone like this."

A muscle twitched in his cheek as he set his empty bottle on the ground.

She toyed with the hem of her skirt. "Do you think you'll go back to Switzerland at the end of the summer?"

"I have to."

"Why?"

He shifted to face her when his foot hit her beer and the

clank of the bottle cut through the air.

"Oh, shit!" he said, bending over.

She leaned over. "It's okay. I've got it."

Nose to nose with Camden Bergen, she stilled, no longer concerned with a little spilled beer. Without breaking their connection, he reached down and righted the bottle.

"Can I tell you something?" she whispered.

"Anything."

Her breaths grew shallow. "I'm not lonely right now."

He cupped her cheek in his hand. "I'm not either."

Their breaths mingled together. The sun had set, and in the darkness, it was like how she felt with Mac. Hidden. A sweet secret just for her. But this was real. Camden's touch. The heat radiating off his body. She pressed her hand to his chest, and his heartbeat quickened—or maybe that was hers. At this point, she didn't know where she ended and he began. She gathered the fabric of his T-shirt in her hand and pulled him a breath closer.

"Maybe we could *not* be lonely together this summer," she whispered.

He rested his forehead against hers. "Is that what you want?"

A summer being *not lonely*—whatever that meant—with this man would eventually come to an end. It was temporary, and it didn't have to mean that she cared any less for Aaron or that Mac wasn't an important part of her life. It just meant...

He stroked his thumb across her lips, and her mind stopped spinning. Stopped weighing and assessing and evaluating. Stopped projecting and planning and budgeting, and everything became crystal clear. Cloaked in the twilight, she pulled back and met his gaze in the hazy darkness.

"Kiss me, Camden," she half-whispered, half-pleaded, then held her breath, not sure if the heat coursing through her body was from the apprehension that he'd deny her request or the excitement that he'd grant it.

He could barely believe his ears. Had Mountain Daisy asked him to kiss her?

This day and this woman had him reeling.

He slid his hand into her golden hair and trembled.

"Are you cold?" she whispered against his lips.

Not cold. Completely and utterly mesmerized and completely and utterly lost. The fresh start he'd dreamed of had disappeared, evaporated when Bodhi Lowry got out of that car. He couldn't tell her he was her Mountain Mac—because Mountain Mac couldn't be anything more than a message in a chat room.

Or could he be more...for the summer?

He could give her that. And Christ, he wanted her! Last night, she'd transformed his appearance—cut off the layers he'd hidden behind for years. Today, she'd transformed his heart, loosening the grip of the pain and guilt that tormented his soul.

But it was only temporary.

He barely trusted himself enough to find Mountain Daisy. A child changed everything. It was hard enough to carry the pain of what he'd done to his parents. But to hurt a child? That was the line in the sand he couldn't cross. He'd failed the two people he'd loved the most in this world. He couldn't bear the responsibility of ever doing that to a child—especially to Mountain Daisy's son.

Still, he couldn't deny the joy that coursed through his body today. Running alongside Bodhi as he rode his bike had been exhilarating, but the look on Cadence's face—the gratitude and relief, ignited a tiny part of him that dreamed he was worthy of a real life. That tiny part that wanted so badly to quiet the voices in his head and believe that he could keep Cadence and Bodhi safe.

Cadence released her grip on his shirt and slid her fingertips up to his collarbone, and her touch sent a rush of heat to his belly as lust edged out his anxiety.

He could give her the summer as Camden and Cadence. And when it ended, they'd go back to Daisy and Mac—and she'd never have to know.

He tangled his fingers in her hair. "Do you know how much I want to kiss you?" he said, lips barely a breath away from hers.

"How much?" she answered.

He slid his hands down her back, and just as he'd done in the shower, he gripped her hips. Except for this time, instead of pressing her lithe frame into the wall, he lifted her onto his lap. She gasped as the swing jostled, his hard length pressed between her straddled thighs. Her skirt rode up her legs, and he slid his hands underneath, palming her ass, his fingers tracing the outline of a lacy G-string.

"Wow!" he whispered.

She wrapped her arms around his neck. "I kind of have a thing for pretty panties."

No sweeter words had ever been spoken.

She threaded her fingers into the hair at the nape of his neck, and a fresh rush of desire overtook him as she swiveled her hips. He could spend eternity here—in this space, a heart-beat away from his first kiss with Mountain Daisy. Want and need building, layer upon layer, his desire intensified. He'd denied himself for so long waiting for her, dreaming of her. And now he had her.

"Camden," she said, her breath tickling the corner of his mouth.

Daisy.

He cupped her face in his hands. "Let me look at you."

She pulled back. "You don't want to kiss me?"

He stroked her plump bottom lip. "I've wanted to kiss you from the moment we met, but I need to look at you, so I know this is real. So I know you're real. I don't want to close my eyes and have you disappear."

"I'm not just some voice in the dark, Camden. I'm right here, and I'm not going anywhere."

The muscles in his chest tightened as he stared at the real Mountain Daisy.

She gave him a sweet smile, and her eyelids fluttered closed. "I'll go first."

A strand of her blond hair caught the wind in the cool night breeze as a pair of headlights from a passing car illuminated her face.

He tucked the hair behind her ear. "I never imagined you'd be so beautiful."

He needed to be careful. Talk like that could get him in trouble. He couldn't reveal he was Mac. It was just so damn hard not to tell her she was the reason for...Christ! For everything. For giving him the courage to step out of the safety of seclusion.

"I'm not going to disappear, Camden. I'm real, and I might explode into a million tiny pieces if you don't kiss me," she whispered with a sexy curve to her lips.

He sighed, hovering on the precipice with Daisy on one side

and Cadence on the other, hardly able to believe they were one and the same and that he'd been given both of them. He tilted his head and dusted her lips with a whisper-soft kiss.

Their first kiss—and his fantasies couldn't hold a candle to the reality. Like the first drops of rain falling from the sky on the verge of a summer storm, the kiss started slowly; the air buzzing with expectancy and giddy with anticipation.

Cadence released a sweet, breathless moan as her lips parted, and what started as merely the hint of a kiss morphed into a whirlwind dance of passion. One hand cupping her cheek as the other gripped her ass, their tongues met, heat building between them.

"You taste so good," he said between kisses.

He could feel her smile. "I must taste like pizza."

"No, you taste like..."

Home.

She tasted like home. Her touch was shelter. Her scent, the air, fragrant with wildflowers.

She was everything he'd loved about his life in Colorado before he'd exiled himself to Switzerland, and she was his —for now.

He guided her body against him in slow, delicious strokes, his cock straining against his jeans as her sweet center rubbed his hard length through the fabric. He slipped his fingers inside her G-string and took in a sharp breath. Hot and wet, he teased her entrance. Her arousal had him thrusting his hips, desperate to make her come.

The hanging swing rocked beneath them, the wood creaking and the chains jangling, but he kept her close, kept the rhythm of their bodies steady, and slid his fingertips over her tight bundle of nerves.

She gasped and thrust her hips, tightening her hold around him, and twisted the hair at the nape of his neck.

Her chest heaved against him. "Camden!" she whispered against his lips.

Fire scorched his veins, and another wave of heat washed over him. This was no detached, purely physical encounter like he'd grown used to before he'd met Daisy. This was a connection, a fusing of minds. He'd never touched her, but he already knew her heart. A carnal triumph surged as he took her higher. He dialed up his pace, increasing the pressure on her sweet bud. The rocking of the swing and the rhythm of his touch had her riding his hand, swiveling her hips and bucking against him. She was close.

He kissed a trail to her earlobe, grazing it with his teeth. He would own every ounce of her pleasure. He pressed a kiss to the delicate skin. "I'm going to make you come so hard."

She twisted her fingers into his hair—every tug amping up his desire.

"I—" she gasped, then stilled.

"*Here, boy!*"

They pulled apart; the swing swaying as she slid off his lap, their gazes meeting in the darkness.

"Did you hear that?" she whispered.

"*Here, boy!*"

There it was again along with the slap of shoe meeting pavement.

"Rufus! There you are! Were you chasing those squirrels again?" the man said as the dog's excited yelps peppered the night air.

Cadence leaned in. "I recognize the voice. It's just a neighbor from a few blocks away."

Camden glanced over his shoulder. Had Rufus made it a few more houses, they would have been caught making out like horny teenagers.

"Looks like those squirrels are causing mayhem in the neighborhood," she said, a nervous lilt to her voice that wasn't there before.

He turned to her to say what, he didn't know, but she spoke first.

"Is this crazy?" she asked.

A pang of guilt shot through him. Was this not only crazy but was it also selfish—him knowing he'd found her while she still believed Mountain Mac was just some message on her phone?

"Maybe," he answered.

She nodded. "Should we call it a night? Camp starts tomorrow."

"For me," he said.

She nodded. "Yeah, me too. It's my summer job. I'm the certified teacher for Baxter Park's Bergen Adventure Summer Camp."

Jesus Christ! Not only was he going to live next door to her this summer, but they'd also be working together.

She frowned, clearly reading his disbelief. "I figured you knew."

He hadn't checked his email or opened the laptop Bren had dropped off. Dammit! He needed to get his shit together.

"I didn't."

"Bodhi will be there, too, in the primary grades group." She ran her index finger down his jawline. "You're going to do a good job as site leader, Camden."

"Why would you say that?" he asked.

He'd barely interacted with anyone besides her in years— and none of them children.

"You were great with Bodhi today. I know you've been on your own a long time, but you're a natural with kids."

"That was one afternoon," he answered, feeling the weight of agreeing to work for his family's company this summer.

She rocked the swing. "Call it a professional hunch, but I bet you were one of the best high school counselors back before..."

"Before I ran away?" he supplied.

Her expression grew pained, and she felt for her necklace underneath her shirt. "We don't know what life's going to throw at us. Sometimes, all we can do is try to get through it the best we can."

"Is that what you're doing?" he asked, the words spilling out before he could stop himself.

She rolled the pendant between her thumb and index finger, almost as if she were trying to soothe herself.

He touched her hand. "Can I see your pendant?"

He ran his fingertips across her collarbone. This was the second time he'd noticed her touch the necklace in what looked like an involuntary response anytime that sad, faraway expression marred her features. Cadence dropped her hand, and he pulled the chain and pendant from where it lay hidden beneath her shirt.

But it wasn't a pendant.

"It's my husband's ring," she answered, a thread of sadness woven into the words.

He stilled, the weight of the cool metal multiplying with her admission.

"I became a widow at twenty-five."

"I'm sorry, I didn't..."

She'd never mentioned this in any of their chats. But why would she? He sure as hell didn't know she had a child. Why would she have disclosed she'd had a husband? They never got into specifics. In fact, with her, he could be the unbroken version of himself. Not the runaway Bergen heir. Not the son who'd failed his parents.

Had she done the same?

Had she found solace in their friendship, sharing the best

parts of herself, too? Had she also longed for someone to confide her hidden dreams and deep contemplations? Had he been her guiding light in the dark just as she'd been his?

It blew his mind.

He'd never assumed she carried the kind of pain he shouldered.

She touched the ring as their fingertips overlapped and he let go, allowing her to tuck the gold band back into her shirt.

She gestured to the houses. "This was our dream: leave Grand Junction and move to the big city. Aaron, that was my husband's name, he worked construction when we were teenagers and studied engineering when we were in college. He was always taking something apart and putting it back together. He loved the idea of renovating these historic houses."

"You guys grew up together?" Cam asked, surprised at how much he wanted to know about her life to fill in the gaps left between two people who'd shared both everything and nothing with each other.

She nodded. "Our grandmothers met in a support group."

"A support group?" he echoed.

"For grandparents who were given custody of their grand-children. Aaron and I never knew our birth parents."

His brows knit together. "What happened to them?"

She was back to toying with the ring. "Methamphetamine, oxycodone, heroin. They died of drug overdoses."

"Jesus, Cadence," he said, and took her hand.

She gave his hand a light squeeze. "We were both taken away from our parents when we were still in diapers. Neither of us had any memories of that time." She paused. "That's strange."

"What?" he asked, watching her hand fall from the pendant.

"You're the first person I've told in Denver about my parents."

"Brennen's fiancée doesn't know?"

She shook her head. "No, I don't really have a reason to talk about it. Aaron's gone. My grandparents are gone. If anyone asks, I just say my parents passed away." She smiled up at him. "You're very easy to talk to, you know that?"

Of course, he knew.

He stilled, and she took his silence as an opening to go on.

"Our grandmothers became friends, and Aaron and I grew up together. Holidays, summer breaks—we were always together. We got married right after college, and Bodhi came along soon after."

"And then you moved here?"

The streetlight lit her in a silvery glow as her hand went back to the ring.

"Bodhi and I drove up a day early to start going through the houses. Aaron was wrapping things up at his job and getting the rental we'd been living in all cleared out. He called me before he left for his last day of work. He'd biked to work every day for two years. He loved biking. Mountain biking. Road biking. He loved it all. Well, that day—his last day in Grand Junction—a car hit him on the way to work and fled the scene. Someone drove by and saw him and called nine-one-one. But he died right there on the side of the road. It wasn't until a police officer knocked on our door a day later that I learned he'd been in an accident."

"How do you do it?" he asked, again, the words escaping before he could stop them.

"Do what?"

He exhaled slowly. "Keep going?"

"Bodhi, my job, and this place—these houses. At Aaron's funeral, I promised him I'd follow our plan to fix them up. We buried him close by at the Fairmount Cemetery. We didn't have any family left in Grand Junction, and I wanted him to be close so we could visit him."

"That's where my parents are," he said softly.

Cadence stroked his palm with her thumb. "See, we're just two people doing the best we can."

He shook his head. "You sure as hell are. Me, not so much. You stayed and built a life."

"You could, too. It's like what you said to Bodhi today. Look at where you want to be and focus on that spot."

"My dad used to tell me that," he replied.

She leaned against him. "Maybe you just need to find your focus."

He'd found it. He just couldn't have it.

They sat there, listening to the hum of the city at night, when she released his hand and stood.

"Can we try something?"

"Sure," he answered, clueless as to what she had in mind but on board with whatever she wanted.

"I think we could use a little redirection."

"*Redirection*?" he echoed.

"Yes, it's a teaching term. It means we need to shift our behavior and get back on track."

"Oh," he answered, remembering Bren's warning about when Abby and Cadence busted out the teacher talk.

She lifted her chin. "I'd like you to go home."

He was not expecting that.

He came to his feet. "What? Back to Switzerland?"

"No, back to Glenna's," she replied with a laugh.

He couldn't keep the sisters straight.

"That's next door? My place?"

"Yes," she answered.

"Did I do something wrong?"

Shit! Was it the kiss or talk of her past? He couldn't read her. She didn't seem upset. In fact, that twist to her lips said she was the opposite of angry.

She touched his face. "No, you've done everything right. That's why I want you to go home and go into your bedroom."

"Glenna's bedroom?" he asked again.

"Yes."

"For *redirection*?"

"Yes, follow the doilies, Bobble-Bergen."

Bobble-what?

"What did you just call me?"

She glanced away, but she was still smiling. "Bobble-Bergen. I named you that because when you got here, all you seemed to do was nod."

He nodded. He couldn't argue with that.

She chuckled. "Now go. If there were ever two people who needed a little redirection, it's us."

Cadence picked up the beer bottles and went inside, leaving him on the porch without a backward glance.

He ran his hands through his hair. What the hell was going on?

Dazed, he crossed the yard and entered Glenna's Doily-land domain.

"Camden, are you there?"

He looked around. "Glenna?"

Jesus! Was it the dead doily lady haunting him?

"No, it's Cadence. I'm at the door that connects our bedrooms."

"You are?" he called.

"Yes."

He entered the bedroom and saw the outline of her feet underneath the door.

"I'm here," he said and pressed his hand to the cool oak.

"Things got pretty deep out there. Redirection is a way to... get back on track," she said.

He could hear the smile in her voice, but he was still

confused. "Is this redirection? You want to talk through the door? Don't get me wrong. I'm totally down for that," he answered, mentally punching himself in the mouth.

If she wanted to tie tin cans to a string and chat that way, he'd make a mad dash for the can opener.

He waited, but she didn't answer.

"Cadence—"

"Did you like kissing me?" she asked softly, cutting him off.

Was the sky fucking blue?

"Yes."

"Did you like touching me?"

The thought of her riding his hand got him hard instantly.

"If I were standing next to you, I wouldn't be able to keep my hands off of you," he said, his tone infused with a primal rumble.

"What would you do first?"

He rested his forehead on the door. "I'd get a real look at those sexy as hell panties you've got on."

"You could see them now."

Holy hell!

"Yeah?" he answered.

"I'm right here."

He gripped the knob. "I don't have a key to open the door."

She chuckled. "There's no lock."

He took a step back and looked at the glass daisy doorknob. "I could come in there right now?"

"We'd have to be quiet," she whispered.

"I could be quiet."

He could be anything she wanted.

"This would have to stay between us, I wouldn't want Bodhi to..."

She didn't have to say the words.

"I understand."

The light shifted under the door. "I could use a little redirection—a shift away from all the obligations and worries. I need this summer, Camden. I need..."

Someone to take her mind off all her responsibilities. Someone to hold. Someone to ease the loneliness.

He couldn't give her Mac, but he could give her this. In the blink of an eye, the need to have her in his arms consumed him. He turned the daisy knob and charged through the door.

She reared back and gasped. "Oh! You really know how to make an entrance."

He'd busted into his grandparents' backyard, charged through her front door last night, and he nearly knocked her over, overcome with the need to get to her now. He should have knocked or at least let her know he was coming, but that thought evaporated when his gaze landed on the temptress standing in front of him.

"You're still dressed," she said with a sexy twist to her lips.

In nothing but a lacy bra and that G-string he'd been dying to see, she rendered him speechless—all that blood heading south.

His jaw dropped, but he willed himself to speak. "Is this redirection?"

"Yes."

"You, standing here in your underwear looking like a goddess, is redirection?" he asked. He needed to be sure.

"Yes, we needed to find a productive focus."

He held her gaze. "I like redirection."

She ran a finger slowly down her bra strap. "I thought you might."

"You're stunning," he said.

"And, again...you're still dressed."

She bit her lip, and his cock took over. He kicked off his shoes, got his shirt stuck on his head, and almost fell over trying to take off his pants. He stood in front of her in his boxer briefs.

"Wow," she breathed. "I mean, I knew. I mean, I figured. I mean...you are really big and pretty built and when I was on your lap..."

At least he wasn't the only one here totally botching the sexy talk.

She glanced away. "If it's not completely obvious, it's been a while for me."

"Me too," he confided.

"I'm on the pill if you don't have any *condoms*," she said with a little cringe.

"Oh, I have some!" he blurted out like it was the winning answer on *Jeopardy*.

She cocked her head to the side. "You do?"

"I do, but not because I thought..."

I thought in some fantasy world I'd find you and start instantly fucking you into next week.

"You know, safety," he said, thankful his brain was capable of basic rational thought.

She nodded. "That's smart."

"Hold on!" He went into his bedroom and pulled a condom from his backpack.

He hurried back and held it up. "Got it!" he whispered-shouted.

Shit! He needed to pull it together. He set the foil packet on her nightstand.

She went to touch the ring, but she'd taken it off, and her hands fell to her sides. "Thank you, Camden. I know you're not here to stay, and I know the arrangement between us is a little unorthodox. But I'm really glad you're here."

No longer ruled by nervous energy, he closed the distance

between them and cupped her face in his hands. This was Daisy. His Daisy.

It was time for some redirection.

"Tell me what you need."

She smiled up at him. "I'd like you to kiss me again and..."

"And, what?" he asked.

She turned away. "And...I like knowing that you want me. I liked feeling you between my thighs. Just for a little while, I'd like to be more than a mom and a widow and a teacher. I'd like to be...desired."

Jesus, if she only knew.

"Cadence, look at me," he said gently.

She released a shaky breath and met his gaze. A dim lamp in the corner of the room lit her features, and in the hazy glow, her bottom lip trembled.

He brushed his thumb across it, trying to smooth out any apprehension. "I can do that. But I need you to know, I see all of you, and you're perfect. I'm going to show you exactly what it feels like to be desired."

He leaned in and pressed his lips to hers, and she melted into the kiss, her hands coming to rest on his chest. She sighed as he deepened the connection, his tongue finding hers, as his hands skimmed down, past her shoulders, and brought her body flush with his.

Her hands didn't rise to the nape of his neck as they had when they were on the swing. Instead, they glided down his back, feeling the muscles ripple and contract as he shifted his hold on her body and lifted her into his arms.

She released a surprised gasp. "Are we going somewhere?"

"Redirection," he said with a naughty bend to the word. He glanced down at her queen-sized bed. "How come you don't have a tiny Glenna bed?"

"I guess, Gertrude liked having more space."

He gave her a wolfish grin. "Do you want to know what I'm going to do to you on that old lady's bed?" he whispered into her ear.

He liked finding his focus.

The concern in her eyes vanished and was replaced with a sultry spark that had him ready to peel the lacy undergarments from her body.

She licked her lips and closed her eyes. "I'm listening."

He'd never been a talkative person. Growing up as the youngest Bergen, his brothers were either telling him what to do or finishing his sentences. Reading and writing hadn't come easy to him as a child. As he'd gotten older, he'd preferred hands-on, kinesthetic learning. He'd written words backward, forgotten vowels, and was often at a loss for the right word. It wasn't until third grade or so when written and oral language clicked, but he'd remained quiet. As the oldest, Jasper called the shots. Bren was always hot-dogging it, showing off or being silly. He'd become the observer—quietly assessing and contemplating.

But when he'd message back and forth with Daisy, he'd found himself talking aloud as if she were right there.

He set her on the bed, resting her head on the pillow. Her hair fanned out across the pale pink bedding, bringing out the color of the kissable rosy plumpness of her lips. Like a present set out before him, he prowled the length of her body, dropping kisses as he moved from her ankles to knees to thighs before stopping at the lacy panties.

"I'm going to slide your panties down your legs so slowly you'll be begging me to tear them off."

A shiver passed over her body as her hips lifted a fraction.

"See, you already want them off," he said, a low primal edge to his voice.

He hooked his index fingers into the slim band and slid the G-string down, one delicious inch at a time.

He stood at the foot of her bed. She was a goddess. All golden hair and sweet curves. She propped herself up on an elbow and stared at the bulge in his boxer briefs. "Your turn."

He took off the garment, revealing his rock-hard cock. He took his hard length into his hand and gave it one slow pump. This wasn't him. He wasn't an exhibitionist, but he liked having her eyes on him.

"Come here," she whispered, beckoning him.

He ran his fingertips up her legs as another shiver passed through her when he stopped at the apex of her thighs. He gripped her hips and licked a trail across the smooth skin of her inner thigh all the way to her sweet center.

Her body trembled beneath his touch, and as much as he wanted to drive his thick shaft into her, fill her completely, and feel her tighten around him, he wasn't about to let this end in a matter of a few hard, sweaty thrusts.

He worked her sweet bundle of nerves with his tongue. Her fingers tangled in his hair as she twisted and writhed beneath him. And Christ! She tasted good. Sweet, warm, and slick with arousal, he drove her higher and higher, her breaths coming fast, her moans intensifying.

He released her hips and raised his hand to her lips, muffling the cries as she took his middle finger into her mouth and sucked. The sensation rocketed to his already weeping cock, emboldening him, focusing him on one thing and one thing only...her sweet release.

She gripped his hand and pressed it to her lips as a shudder passed through her, meeting her orgasm. Carnal conquest swept through him. He worked her, licking and sucking her sweet bud until her body relaxed beneath his touch.

She sighed. "I want you inside of me."

"I want that, too," he said in a heated rumble of breath with her sweet taste lingering on his lips.

She picked up the condom and handed it to him.

He tore open the packet and rolled it onto his cock.

She watched him closely, then met his gaze. "Why does it feel like we've been waiting for ages to do this?"

Because we have. Because I've dreamed of this, of you, so many nights, you felt more like a memory to me than just a dream.

He covered her body with his and positioned his hard length at her entrance. "Because we both really need some redirection," he said instead.

She smiled up at him. "All the redirection."

"Hours of redirection," he countered and thrust inside her.

She gasped, and he stilled.

"Am I hurting you?"

"No, it feels so very..."

He pushed in farther, filling her completely. "So very, what?"

"So very right," she whispered, rolling her hips and grinding against him.

It was more than right. It was everything. He glided his cock back and forth, their bodies growing slick with sweat as friction between them built. He laced one hand with hers, her fingers entwined with his. Their bodies came together in a perfect harmony that had him dangling on the edge of release. He wasn't sure he could hold back until Cadence tightened around him, meeting her second orgasm as he buried his face in the crook of her neck and met his.

Holding back the roar of his release intensified the sexual sensations. Every thrust, every feverish buck of their hips, every breathy sigh, and the carnal scent of sex in the air all amplified. He pressed a kiss beneath her ear, and she tightened her grip on his hand.

"Camden?"

His name had never sounded sweeter.

He closed his eyes and breathed her in. "Yes."

"Would you stay until I fell asleep?"

He pushed up onto his elbow. "I can do that," he said gently.

He took care of the condom then joined her back in bed, wrapping her in his arms. She hummed her contentment and snuggled into him. Her breaths grew rhythmic, their legs tangled together as her body relaxed into his embrace.

"Sweetest dreams, Camden," she said in a dreamy sigh.

He held her and stared at the ceiling and listened as she fell into a deep sleep. He pressed a kiss to the crown of her head, then slid out of bed, careful not to make a sound, and pulled on his jeans. He glanced around her room and found a picture of her and Bodhi. The necklace with her late husband's ring hung off the corner, the dim light glinting off the gold surface.

A protective impulse swept through him. And he couldn't leave—not yet.

He glanced at Cadence, sleeping soundly, then opened the door—not to his side of the house—but into Cadence and Bodhi's side. He checked their front door, making sure it was locked then went to the rear of the house. The back porch light was on, and just as he was about to turn it off, he caught the shadow of something moving. He opened the door as two critters sprang from a nearby bush and scampered across the yard.

He chuckled and shook his head. "Don't kill the squirrels."

He turned to go inside when a cluster of flowers caught his attention. Even in the dim light, he could make out the slim, rounded petals and the button centers.

Daisies.

He picked one and grinned.

Locking the door behind him, he made his way down the hall and stopped at Bodhi's door. He turned the knob and quietly looked in as the hazy blue light serenely circled around the sleeping boy.

The muscles in his chest tightened.

"I can give you the summer," he whispered, closing the door as the boy shifted in his sleep.

Cam entered Cadence's room and picked up the notepad and pen on her nightstand. He glanced from her to the daisy and scribbled out a note.

He collected his clothing, then leaned over her peaceful form.

"I can't believe I found you. Sweetest dreams, Mountain Daisy," he said, leaving the daisy and the note on the pillow next to her before closing the door and retreating to Glenna's bed.

9

CADENCE

"Mommy, you have a big, big smile on your face."

Cadence closed and locked the door behind them and adjusted her backpack. "It must be because I'm so excited for Bergen Adventure Camp."

Or—that I spent a good part of last night having my body ravaged by the sexiest man on the planet.

If she hadn't woken up to the scent of him on her sheets, she might have thought she'd had an erotic dream. But when she'd opened her eyes, the first thing that came into focus was a daisy on the pillow next to her along with a folded piece of paper.

You look like an angel in your sleep.

Eight words.

One simple line of text that put a smile on her face as the sweet ache between her thighs left no doubt that she'd spent the night with Camden Bergen.

What was even more shocking was that she'd suggested it.

She'd asked him for the summer.

She'd asked him to kiss her.

She'd played the part of the naughty schoolteacher and had given him a lesson in the X-rated version of redirection.

She'd never been bold in the naughty department. She'd been with Aaron. All their firsts happened together. There was never a chase or even seduction. Not that she didn't enjoy being intimate with her late husband. She did. But it was never...unexpected. She'd never known the rush of anticipation.

What had given her the push?

Well, everyone around her was falling ass over elbow in love.

She'd been surrounded by her friends finding their forever with a Bergen brother.

And even though she couldn't have the all-encompassing happily ever after they'd found—Camden was only here for the summer and Bodhi and her commitment to Aaron ensured that—maybe she could have a little piece of that happiness with the youngest Bergen brother.

A taste of being truly desired.

When she'd hit pause on the internal ticker tape inside her head before she'd asked him to kiss her, she'd felt lighter. At that moment, she didn't see herself as merely a widow and a mother. She was just a woman with needs. A woman who craved the touch and attention of a man.

A woman in need of a secret summer liaison.

Nobody would have to know. It would be like summer break—all the more sweeter because you knew the hours would roll into days and the days into weeks. And then, it would be over, and like the seasons, life would move on.

She might be left longing and possibly heartbroken, but those truths couldn't outweigh her desire to squeeze every drop out of this summer fling.

A delicious tingle danced down her spine and settled between her thighs at the thought of Camden's hands, gripping her hips. His mouth working her most sensitive place and his hard length thrusting deep inside her.

But it wasn't just the sex and mind-blowing orgasms that had her smiling like a Disney princess at a Character Breakfast.

Drifting off to sleep in Camden's arms was sweeter than any lullaby. It had been years since she'd allowed herself to fall into such a peaceful slumber. As a single parent, she'd grown used to sleeping lightly. Ready to react to any crisis. Always on-call to respond to her son's needs.

It was like she'd been walking a tightrope without a safety net for years. She was Bodhi's sole protector. His sole provider. And she didn't take that lightly.

But last night she wasn't alone. The man who'd crashed through her door to save her from a pair of squirrels was there, and her body—and maybe her heart—sensed, in his arms, she'd be safe.

"Camden!" Bodhi cried as the door to Glenna's house opened.

Her son ran across the stone pavers.

"You have a big, big smile just like Mommy does. Did you find a treasure?"

Camden cocked his head to the side and caught her eye from across the yard.

Bodhi pressed on. "Sometimes, I find treasure under my bed like a toy or a sticker or a cookie. That's when I smile big like that."

Camden ruffled Bodhi's hair then met her gaze. "Yes, you could say I found a treasure."

Holy pickles and relish! Her heart skipped a beat.

"Guess what Mommy slept with last night?" Bodhi said, hopping from stone to stone.

Camden's eyes went wide, and her heart stopped skipping and sprang into her throat.

No! There was no way Bodhi could have known about her

naughty rendezvous with Camden. They barely made a sound, and her son would have mentioned something over breakfast.

Mom, were you doing jumping jacks last night?

Or, Mom, were you humming a lot because you were eating chocolate cake in bed?

Camden's tanned skin turned ghost white. "A Teddy bear?"

Bodhi stopped hopping and shook his head. "No, I'm the one who sleeps with a Teddy bear," Bodhi answered, then patted the top of Mr. Cuddle's head from where it jutted out of his backpack.

Camden stood there, his mouth opening and closing like a flounder.

"A flower!" Bodhi supplied, going back to his hops. "She had a flower on her pillow when I went in to cuddle. I told her the Flower Fairy must have brought it."

Relief washed over Camden's features, and she held back a grin.

"Maybe it was a Flower Gladiator or a Flower Warrior," Camden suggested.

Bodhi wasn't having it. "Nope, it was a fairy. A Flower Fairy."

Now it was Camden's turn to bite back a grin.

Bodhi turned and waved to her. "Can I run ahead, Mom?"

She loved the raw honesty of children. When they were done with a conversation, they moved on. Sometimes, literally.

"Go ahead, B," she called, coming down the porch steps.

Bodhi headed to Baxter Park as Camden Bergen, looking like the exact opposite of a Flower Fairy, all broad chest and tanned forearms, strode toward her.

He glanced over his shoulder at Bodhi, skipping down the sidewalk then took the tail of her braid between his thumb and index finger, twisting the hair. "Good morning."

Heat swelled between her thighs. That voice. His voice. That low rumble sent her pulse racing as if he spoke so little to save that gravelly, sex-coated sound all for her.

"Good morning," she echoed, unable to say more when Camden's thumb grazed her collarbone.

"I hope the flower wasn't too much."

She smiled up at him. "It wasn't. And the note..."

He blushed. And heaven help her, to see this mountain of a man's cheeks grow pink made her weak in the knees.

They were doing this. The summer fling was on.

A tiny part of her had worried that he'd see her this morning, and the brooding Bergen bobblehead—now, at least minus the Hagrid beard—would have taken the place of the man who'd taken her over the edge last night.

She pushed up onto her tiptoes, pressed her hands to his solid chest, and...

And nothing.

She still had a good six inches to go.

"I'm going to need a little help."

Those steel-blue eyes darkened as he leaned in and twisted the braid around his fingers. The tug of her hair paired with the brush of his lips sent a shiver down her spine. How had they fallen into a rhythm so quickly?

Then it hit her.

They didn't have a choice. This wasn't forever. There wasn't even the possibility of forever. Maybe all those *beginning of a relationship* jitters people spoke about didn't apply to them because, A, there was no possibility of a relationship and, B, time was ticking away.

She hummed her contentment, and he smiled against her lips.

"I've been counting the minutes until I could hear you make that sound again," he said, just as his stomach decided to join the party with a growl.

She lowered herself back down, unzipped her pack, and handed him a breakfast burrito. "Here, I know there's nothing of substance in the cupboard at Glenna's. Bodhi and I got up early and got this for you."

"That was really thoughtful," he answered with a pained expression.

"If you don't want it—"

"No, I do. These are my favorite. It's just like you to be so kind," he said, unwrapping the burrito and taking a bite.

She gave him a devilish smile. "Well, you've only known me for two days. I may not be as sweet as I look."

He swallowed and matched her grin. "Oh, I know how sweet you are."

Clench.

She'd be the Queen of Kegels after this summer.

"What color panties are you wearing?" he asked.

She watched him through her eyelashes. "Pink."

Now it was her turn to blush.

He took another bite through a wolfish grin. "Lacy like the ones you had on last night?"

She nodded.

"How long is camp?"

"Nine until three."

"I have to wait six hours to see them?" he asked with a naughty gleam in his eyes.

She grinned up at him. So, this is what it's like to start something new. The little presents. The excitement of anticipation. This feeling with Camden was like....

Her stomach twisted.

Like the first days of messaging with Mountain Mac.

She blinked as her phone pinged.

Could it be him?

She pulled her phone from her pocket.

Camden frowned. "Everything okay?"

She stared at the screen. "It's just Carrie. She's texting to say Bodhi made it to Baxter Park."

Camden nodded. "She's a college student. One of the senior camp counselors, right?"

Cadence raised an eyebrow. "Yes, how'd you know that?"

He gestured to the sidewalk, and they set off for the park.

"After you fell asleep, I went through the camp things Bren dropped off."

"Really?"

She didn't mean for it to come out as astonished as it sounded.

He bumped his shoulder against hers playfully. "What? Did you think I'd show up completely unprepared?"

She shook her head. "No, I'm sorry. I shouldn't have reacted like that. It's just..."

"It's just that you were expecting the Bergen brooding bobblehead? Did I get that right?"

She chuckled. "Maybe I was—but I'm happily surprised to have you instead."

The park came into view, and she was about to cross the street when Camden stopped, and a pained looked marred his features.

"Cadence, I meant what I said. I want to give you this summer. I know you have a lot on your plate with Bodhi and your job and the houses. I don't want to be a burden to you. And last night..." His expression softened, pain morphing into wistfulness. "Last night was the closest thing to perfection I've ever experienced."

She touched his arm. "It's okay, Camden. I know what this is, and I want it, too. You don't have to jump through any hoops for me. I just like you, and I think you like me." She gave him a teasing grin. "And helping Brennen and Abby choose between white and ecru tablecloths will be a lot more fun if we enjoy each other's company."

He frowned. "What's ecru?"

"It's like white but not white."

He rubbed his chin. "How about we agree that you get to take the lead on that."

She chuckled as they continued on toward the park. "Don't worry. After all the paint samples I've shuffled through over the years, I'm fully qualified to field any white versus ecru questions if and when they come up."

He chuckled then pulled a small notepad from his pocket. "Okay, now that we've got that all squared away, let's get to camp business. We should call the staff together when we get to Baxter Park, do a quick team meeting, then assign all the high school counselors to groups."

Cadence chewed her lip. "Yeah...about that..."

They crossed the street, and the park came into view— already set up for the day's events—with counselors buzzing around the lakefront prepping canoes and another group setting up cones on the perimeter of the large multipurpose sports field.

Camden stared out at the orderly activity. "Did you do this?"

She nodded. "This is my third summer as the certified teacher. The first year was a little chaotic. The old site leader..."

Camden glanced at his notes. "Curt, right? I saw his name all over the materials."

"Yes, and let's just say Curt was more interested in bragging about being a Bergen Adventure site leader than doing any actual work. So, I stepped in and..."

"And organized the hell out of it. It never looked this good even when I was a kid," he said, a thread of awe in his voice.

She'd met with the high school and college-aged counselors weeks ago. Everyone knew their assigned group and duties. Being a single mother and a full-time teacher meant she'd had to learn to be efficient and regimented in every facet of her life.

Long story short—she did not have the time or the energy to mess around with camp chaos. And nothing irked her more than Curt's lack of preparedness that left her gathering up all the loose ends and running the show on a wing and a prayer.

She scanned the park, pleased with the fruits of her labor.

"Curt checked out, and I checked in. I made a few changes that improved transition efficiency and bolstered the curriculum. You and I aren't assigned to any group. We're floaters and can fill in where needed. We'll act in an advisory role—except with water sports due to the student to teacher ratio requirements."

"Jesus, Cadence! What you've done sounds amazing. Does anyone at Bergen Adventure or the Bergen Mountain Education Department know about this?"

She shook her head. "I don't think so."

She didn't want to rock the boat or throw Curt under a bus, but changes needed to be made, and just like an effective teacher, she made them.

Camden took in the scene. "So, what do *we* need to do?"

She looked at her watch. "We should check-in at the rec center. That's where you and I will share a little office. We could make sure all the activity waivers have been signed, but I had the college kids do that last week."

"And Bodhi?" he asked, gesturing toward her son working alongside Camp Counselor Carrie.

"Oh, he's fine. He adores Carrie. She's been a counselor with the Bergen Adventure Summer Camp for as long as I've been here. She's studying to be a teacher, and she's great at giving him little jobs to help out."

Camden's steel-blue gaze darkened. "If I hear you right, you're telling me we basically have nothing to do for the next thirty minutes because of your insanely amazing managerial skills."

"More like classroom management on a larger scale. But, yeah, we're free for..." She checked her watch. "Twenty-eight minutes."

He pressed his hand to the small of her back and guided her toward the rec center. "Is the Bergen Adventure Summer Camp office still that supply closet they clear out in the back corner of the building?"

She grinned. "Yep, and it still smells like old sneakers and the sweat of those who'd lost the Dodgeball Battle of 1982."

He chuckled. "You."

"What do you mean, you?"

"It's just like you to say something like that."

She frowned. He was doing it again. That weird thing like they'd known each other for ages.

He shook his head. "I just mean...you're really funny."

They followed the path to the rec center, settled between the park and the waterfront, as the hint of a smile pulled at the corners of his mouth. "We better go check out the office. I have a few things I'd like to go over with you before camp starts."

"Sure," she said and waved to Carrie, then gestured to the building. The counselor pointed to Bodhi and gave her a thumbs-up.

She and Camden entered the building, bustling with the sounds of fitness instructors cueing directions and the clank and bang of free weights hitting the ground. They picked up the key to their office from a teen running the check-in desk who'd barely looked up from her phone.

"It's this way," Cadence said, leading Camden down a long hall that snaked back to the tucked away forgotten supply closet otherwise known as the Baxter Park Bergen Adventure Summer Camp office.

Racks of partially deflated basketballs lined the wall outside their door as a fluorescent light hummed a rickety tune above them.

"Here we are, under the oldest light bulb on the planet and next to the home for decrepit basketballs," she said, staring down the long corridor when Camden unlocked the door and pulled her inside.

Like a super-sized ninja, he had their packs off before the latch even clicked and pressed her back against the door.

He tilted her head up. "I know exactly how I want to spend twenty-eight minutes," he said, then leaned in for a scorching kiss.

She melted into his touch. Kumbaya! She could get used to summer camp starting like this.

"We only have twenty-four minutes," she breathed as he dropped kisses along her jawline.

Crap! This was not the time to worry about...*time!*

Camden pulled back a fraction and checked his watch. The Patek Philippe watch.

She touched the metal band, hardly believing she hadn't noticed he'd been wearing it. "You kept it?"

He tucked a loose strand of hair behind her ear. "You helped me find a reason to keep it."

She smiled up at this enigma of a man.

He stroked her cheek. "You've helped me find a lot of things."

Her smile faded. All these weird cryptic comments were starting to pile up. But her train of thought came to a screeching halt when he leaned and pressed his lips to the shell of her ear.

"Right now, I'm going to find those pink panties, slide them down your legs, and make you come against the door."

That snapped her back, and her eyes went wide. "You can do all that in twenty-four minutes?"

He glanced at his watch. "Twenty-three minutes now. We better stop talking and get down to business."

She ran her tongue across her top lip. "Official camp business."

"What else?" he answered with a wolfish grin that made her want to be the naughtiest Little Red Riding Hood in a very dirty version of the fairy tale.

He dropped to his knees. "I love these skirts, Cadence."

"It's a sports skirt," she replied—like a total idiot.

He reached between her thighs then stilled. "Why are there pants connected to this skirt?"

She held back a grin. "I told you. It's a sports skirt. Do you think I'd get into a canoe in a regular skirt?"

"You had on a regular skirt last night."

"I didn't ride in a canoe last night," she answered, gazing into his eyes.

A panty-melting grin graced his perfect features.

"No, you rode me."

Holy pickles and relish!

She gasped as he pulled down the garment. She wiggled her feet free from the hidden Lycra mini shorts.

"Hello," he said to her panties.

She twisted a lock of his hair between her fingers. "I wouldn't have taken you for a panty-man."

He cocked his head to the side. "We have to have our thing, right? Mine is any pair of panties you're wearing."

She bit her lip. This was fun. Being with this man was fun. Crazy and outrageous and core-clenchingly fun.

She schooled her features. "What if I had on granny panties?"

"I'd still tear them off with my teeth," he said, the gravelly tone deliciously raking its way through her body.

"Holy pickles and double the relish!"

He smiled up at her. "What was that?"

"Did I say that out loud? The whole pickles and—"

"Relish? Yeah, you did."

But he wasn't laughing at her. In fact, just the opposite.

His gaze darkened as he hooked his index fingers in the band of her G-string and slowly removed them.

"Do you have protection? I mean, I'm on the pill and all but—"

He shook his head. "We don't need it."

"We don't? But aren't we..." she trailed off as he hooked her leg over his shoulder.

Heat rushed between her thighs as a tingle of wanton anticipation traveled down her spine.

"Oh...we're doing this."

He pressed a kiss below her navel. "I said I was going to make *you* come."

"Holy p—"

She stopped herself. Darn her second-grade vocabulary!

"But what about you, Camden? Don't you want to..."

He stopped her mid-sentence with a kiss to her inner thigh.

"Do you know what it's like listening to you get turned on?"

She shook her head.

He licked a slow hot trail to her most sensitive place, his breath hot against her throbbing bud.

"It's like a symphony. There's no sweeter sound."

She moaned then pressed her hand to her mouth.

He slid his hand up her thigh and gripped her ass. "Cadence?"

"Yeah?" she breathed.

That wolfish grin twisted at the corner of his mouth. "You don't have to do that. Nobody can hear you back here."

She stilled. Between the low bass beats coming from the spin class and the mechanical grind of the treadmills and rowing machines, their little hovel in the bowels of the rec center was soundproof.

She looked down at him. "Then what are you waiting for?"

Clearly...nothing.

Camden's grip on her hip and ass tightened, and the man went to work. She steadied herself, one hand on his shoulder, the other clenching the doorknob as she bucked against him, her gasps growing louder with each stroke of his tongue.

"Yes, Camden, don't stop!"

Letting go never felt so good. And she hadn't been able to let loose in years. Even when she touched herself, she had to stay quiet. There was no way she was going to have her son telling a therapist twenty years from now how he'd heard his mom getting off alone in her bedroom.

Camden set a punishing pace, increasing the pressure on her tight bundle of nerves, and within the space of two carnal cries, she flew over the edge. Giving herself over to the sensations, she pumped her hips and threaded her fingers into his hair, riding out the sweet, pulsing waves of ecstasy.

He squeezed her thigh. "I'm keeping these," he said, pocketing her underwear.

"You are?"

"I am."

"I like those panties!"

"You know where I live. You can always get them back and..." He held up the sports skirt. "These have built-in underwear already."

She plucked the skirt from his hand and got dressed. "You'd think someone whose family owns a sporting goods and apparel empire would have heard of skirts with built-in shorts."

He stood, and that pained expression was back.

She reached up and stroked his cheek. "Whatever you may think, you're a good man."

"I don't know if that's true, but when I'm with you, I feel like maybe I could be."

The pain he carried broke her heart, and all she wanted to do was gather the pieces of this kind, broken man and make him whole. But that wasn't what this summer was about.

She glanced down at her watch. "Well, we have four minutes left, and I'd really like to spend that time with your lips attached to mine."

The sadness in his eyes disappeared as he lifted her into his arms. She wrapped her legs around his waist and tangled her fingers into his hair as their mouths met in a toe-curling kiss.

He pressed her back to the door. "Do you know all the things I'm going to do to your body tonight," he said, the heat of his breath scorching each word until a knock at the door brought their make-out session to a screeching halt.

10

Cadence's eyes went wide as they stared at each other.

"That was the door, right?" he whispered.

She nodded, panic flashing in her eyes.

They did not need this. He'd already been chased by that nosy taxi driver looking to cash-in on his identity. They didn't need whoever the hell this was getting in on the Bergen dirt bandwagon, too.

Enough shit would hit the fan when the staff and camp families learned he'd taken Curt's place as the site leader.

And more than that, he didn't want anything to get in the way of what he'd found with Cadence. This perfect respite. This place where he wasn't the runaway failure of a Bergen brother, but a man giving the woman he'd fallen for the chance to be someone different from the cards life had dealt her.

He couldn't give her forever, but he wasn't about to let anyone take this summer from them.

"You better put me down," she whispered.

"Yeah."

He gently lowered her, and she smoothed her T-shirt.

Time to put on his game face. "Ready?"

She glanced at him and gasped. "Panties."

Shit! The lace trim of her G-string peeked out from his cargo shorts.

He shoved the sexy scrap of fabric deep into his pocket. "Thanks! Good catch!"

She nodded, then reached for the doorknob.

Worst-case scenario, it was a parent or a counselor. Jesus! What did he just say to Cadence? Something about all the things he was going to do to her body? He tensed as she gripped the knob.

They could play it off like she needed a massage for a pulled muscle. That might be a reasonable explanation.

Or not.

Christ, he was a fucking idiot!

He held his breath as Cadence opened the door.

"Yes...hello?" she said and stepped into the hall.

He pulled the door open to see the teen from the front desk, staring at her phone and wearing—thank the technology gods —wireless earbuds.

Cadence tapped the girl's shoulder and the teen startled.

"You knocked?" Cadence asked and gestured over her shoulder to the door.

The girl pulled out the earbuds, exploding with a techno beat. "What?"

"Was that you, knocking on the door?" Cadence tried again.

The teen tugged on her earlobe, probably still vibrating from the booming music. It was a miracle she could hear at all.

"What can we help you with?" Cadence asked, a little louder.

The teen wrinkled her nose. "It smells like my brother's jock-strap down here."

Cadence glanced back at him, gaze brimming with relief. They could have been setting off bottle rockets while blasting heavy metal music and the poster girl for teen hearing loss wouldn't have noticed a thing.

Cadence glanced at her watch. "Is there a problem? We need to leave to meet with the Bergen Adventure Summer Camp counselors."

"No problem," the girl answered, her eyes glued to her phone.

"Then...how can we help you?" Cadence asked with a placating smile.

He pressed his lips together and smothered a grin. He knew this smile. It was the one she'd given him on the drive back to her place right after she'd laid down the law about her perceptions of his family. It was her *I don't have time for your shit* smile, and he loved watching her use it on someone other than himself.

The teen swiped her thumb across her phone's screen and a muscle ticked in Cadence's jaw.

"One, two, three! Eyes on me!"

He took a step back. This girl better pull it together. Cadence Lowry was about to lose all the Miss Honey and drop some Trunchbull.

The girl's head whipped up like Cadence's teacher chant had temporarily activated the attention center of her brain.

"Oh yeah, some delivery guy came in and said he left a bunch of corrugated cardboard next to the boathouse. He told me to tell you and Curt." She glanced his way. "Hey! You're not Curt!"

He crossed his arms. "Curt broke his leg. I'm taking his place this summer."

The girl's shoulders drooped. "Damn, that's too bad. Curt always had the best weed and was the bomb to chill out with. We'd shoot the shit for hours under the boathouse," she said, inserting the earbuds then heading down the hall, the effect of the One, Two, Three charm wearing off.

"That Curt sounds like a peach," he said.

Cadence snapped her fingers. "So that's where he'd go all day! He'd disappear for hours at a time."

They started down the hall behind Miss Teen Hearing Loss USA.

He opened the door for Cadence and joined her outside.

Camper drop-off was in full effect, and he surveyed the circular drive, manned with counselors in Bergen T-shirts. One by one, cars drove up, and kids wearing backpacks hopped out. Small groups of children sat clustered together with their counselors, waiting for the activities to begin—everything running seamlessly.

"I wonder how Curt got hired in the first place?" he mused.

Bergen Adventure Summer Camp was his parents' idea. Before their deaths, they'd headed up the Bergen Mountain Education division which, under their leadership, had progressed from winter educational programming at their nineteen mountain resorts worldwide to summer activities. And then, onto the summer multi-activity day camps in Denver and across the state. They'd been working on implementing camps like this in Vermont and California near their resorts when...

He swallowed hard as his hands clenched into fists, his jaw tightening.

"Hey," Cadence said, touching his arm. "We need to go check-in with our lead counselors. And I'm pretty sure Curt is the idiot brother or screw-up nephew of some important Colorado someone or other. You know how it goes. These D-canoes always get a pass," she added with a teasing grin.

He met her sky-blue gaze, and he was back.

She brought him back.

This summer was about her, not brooding and licking the open wounds of the runaway Bergen brother.

"Right," he said, walking in step with her toward Carrie and a young man holding a clipboard.

"Hey, guys! I wanted to introduce you both to the new site leader," Cadence said when the young man turned to face them.

Camden's jaw dropped. "Lucas Parker?"

"Cam?" the counselor replied.

"Yeah, it's me. It's been a long time."

"Holy..." Lucas began, then glanced at Cadence. "Moly."

Cadence chuckled. "You two know each other?"

Lucas' wide grin nearly spanned his face. "Do we know each other? Cam was the only one out of all the Bergen and Parker brothers who'd actually put up with me on the slopes."

Camden clapped the kid on the shoulder. "The last time I saw you, you must have been..."

"Thirteen. All gangly legs and braces," Lucas supplied.

Camden turned to Cadence. "Lucas is the youngest son of our family friends, the Parkers."

"Yep, I was the oops baby, five years younger than Cam. And it's just Luke now," *Luke-now* said, his cheeks growing pink.

Camden took a step back and shook his head. Jesus! Lucas—no, Luke Parker—had gone from a boy to a man in the time he'd been gone.

Cadence glanced between the men and grinned. "It's wonderful you two know each other. It's Luke's first year with us. And let's not forget Carrie Mackendorfer, our other college-aged lead counselor.

"Nice to meet you, Carrie. I'm Camden Bergen," he said and shook the girl's hand.

She turned to Cadence. "What happened to Curt?"

Cadence bit back a grin. "Broken leg. Poor thing."

Carrie seemed to be holding back a grin of her own.

"That's...too bad. I really hope he's on the mend soon—but not too soon."

"He won't be with us at all this summer," Cadence said, lowering her voice.

Carrie's grin broke free as she glanced his way. "You're one of the Bergen brothers, right?"

He gave her a tight nod.

Carrie released a relieved sigh. "Thank God! You'll know what you're doing. Last summer, I had to stop Curt from piling a bunch of five-year-olds into a canoe without an instructor. He was about to push them off into the lake and hadn't even given them a paddle."

Cadence shook her head. "Curt was the worst."

"Totally, the worst! It was easier when he'd disappear." Carrie added.

Camden watched the women's exchange—flabbergasted. This Carrie not only didn't seem steeped in the runaway Bergen folklore, but she was also happy to have him there for his qualifications.

Granted, the qualification was that he wasn't a pot-smoking child endangerer—but, hell, he'd take that.

"All right," Cadence said and glanced at the empty circular drive. "Why don't you give Camden and me an update."

Carrie and Luke nodded.

"Drop-off went smoothly. The campers are with their group leaders going over behavior expectations and camp safety," Carrie replied.

Luke tapped his clipboard. "And we've got all the morning outdoor activities set up and ready to go. Here's the rotation schedule," he added and handed over a sheet of paper.

Cadence scanned the park. "Good work, guys. Any issues come up, Camden and I will be on the waterfront this morning. As the groups cycle through, we'll be telling the campers about the upcoming events and the end of the summer cardboard boat regatta here at Smith Lake."

Camden stilled as memories of the regatta flashed through his mind.

He'd spent so much time these past ten years focusing on his mom and dad's death, he hadn't allowed any happy memories to break through the barrier of guilt and shame he'd built around his heart.

But those special summer days when he, Bren, and Jas would push their boats to the edge of the sparkling lake and wait for the start whistle, like cats preparing to pounce, came back to him.

The Cardboard Boat Regatta at Smith Lake had been one of the highlights of his summers growing up. More than the mountain biking, the rock climbing, the canoeing, and the hiking, he loved laying out his giant sheets of cardboard next to his brothers' and planning their boat designs alongside their parents. Jas, with every ruler and protractor scattered about, and Bren, going at the cardboard without making one mark or measurement.

He fell in the middle, allowing creativity and thoughtful design to guide his boat crafting. Then again, as the youngest, he got to learn from his big brothers' mistakes and got a little extra attention from his parents.

Those were good memories—his mother and father, waving their hats and cheering for them as they paddled with their hands, splashing and laughing, zigzagging across the lake. He could almost feel the spray of water and hear his mother's cheers.

"Keep going, my brightest stars!"

"Were you able to distribute the flyers to the parents?" Cadence asked, snapping him back.

Carrie nodded. "This morning at drop off we provided each

family with a copy of the cardboard boat building rules and let them know the cardboard is ready for pick up."

"Nice work! You're really on top of it. Now, let's get this day started," Cadence said with a warm grin as Carrie and Luke set off toward the clusters of children seated in the shade.

She looked up at him. "Is it coming back to you, Cam?"

Cam.

Christ, how he liked the sound of that.

He thought of his mother's smiling face. "Yeah, it is."

"See, you've got this," she said as they made their way down to the waterfront.

"No, you've got this," he answered in awe of this petite powerhouse of a woman. "How do you do it all? Bodhi, teaching, the houses?"

"Lots of Post-it notes and chatting with my online friend is a real stress reliever."

"Mac, right?" he asked, careful to keep his voice even.

He was doing it again. Pressing, pushing, fishing for information. Why did he need to hear her confirm what he already knew? She cared for Mac. Anytime her phone made a sound, he knew she was hoping it was a message from Mountain Mac because that was the face, the exact expression, he had when her messages would come in.

That zing of anticipation. That hopeful thread, weaving its way through his broken heart.

She tucked a loose strand of blond hair back into her braid. "Yeah, but he's had stuff going on, and we haven't chatted much lately."

"And he's helped you? This Mac?"

She grinned up at him with a smile so genuine, it made the breath catch in his throat. "Mac gave me the courage to get on a bike again to help my son learn to ride. So yeah, I'd say he helped."

"But you're not chatting now?"

A playful glint sparkled in her eyes. "Are you jealous of Mac?"

His gaze darkened. "I'm jealous of anyone who makes you smile like that."

And Christ, how he wanted to tell her, it was him.

She touched her lips. "Like what?"

"Like you're smiling with your whole heart."

Her expression softened. "What kind of smile do I give you?"

The kind I could wake up to every day for the rest of my life.

The kind that's brighter than the sun.

The kind that deserves the man I could never be.

The errant lock of blond hair came loose again, and he tucked it back into place. "You give me the kind of smile that makes me want to press you up against the boathouse, pull down that skirt contraption you're wearing, and listen to you beg me to make you come."

"Wow," she said on a breathy sigh. "That's quite a smile."

"You're quite a woman."

The moment hung in the air, sweet and fragrant. He took a step toward her when a little hand grasped onto his.

"Hi, Camden! My group gets to be with you and Mommy first!"

"Hey, sweet boy!" Cadence said and went to give Bodhi a hug, but the boy pulled back.

"Mom!" he whisper-shouted then extended his hand.

"I almost forgot," she said, squeezing his hand three times.

I love you.

He squeezed back, *I love you, too.*

"Camden?" Bodhi said, holding out his hand.

"Let's bump it," he replied, not sure what he'd do if Bodhi gave his hand three little squeezes.

"Bump explosion?" Bodhi asked with a wide, toothy grin.

"Sure!"

They bumped fists then each made a pretty spectacular explosion sound.

"I'm going to go sit with Porter, but Mommy..."

"What is it, honey?" Cadence asked.

"Logan Klein is in my group, and he's kind of being mean."

Camden scanned the pint-sized campers, heat rising to his cheeks at the thought of some bully picking on Bodhi.

"You stick with Porter. I'll keep an eye out and let your counselor know," she answered.

Bodhi nodded and sat down next to a little boy holding a toy firetruck.

Camden leaned in. "Who's this Logan kid?" he whispered into Cadence's ear.

She pursed her lips. "He's the one with the freckles. He goes to Whitmore. I know the family and let's just say, I don't think little Logan gets many hugs at home."

"Really? I was ready to pummel the kid."

She chuckled and shook her head. "Try not to do that. We like to keep the kids pummel-free here at Bergen Adventure Summer Camp."

He gave her a wry grin. "I guess I can see how pummeling kids may become problematic."

She glanced at the children, all sitting with their legs crossed, in a neat row. "How about I introduce us to the kids, and we'll go from there."

He nodded, excited to see her in teacher mode.

"One, two, three," she called, in a much sweeter tone than she'd used with the teen this morning.

"Eyes on me!" the children replied in unison.

Cadence clapped her hands. "Good morning, boys and girls, I'm Ms. Lowry and this is Mr. Bergen. We're the people in charge of the Bergen Adventure Summer Camp. If you see us walking around, just know we're always here to help you stay safe and have fun. Now, we've got two big activities coming up this summer. The Bergen Cardboard Boat Regatta the first week in August and the Father's Day Bike Parade coming up very soon!"

"Bodhi doesn't have a dad. Last year, he did the bike parade with his mom and he still had training wheels on his bike," blurted the kid with freckles.

Logan Klein.

All the kids except Bodhi and his little fire truck buddy laughed. Cadence started to speak when Bodhi cut in.

"I don't have training wheels anymore, Logan. Camden Bergen taught me how to ride without them, and he's going to do the Father's Day bike parade with me, right?" Bodhi said, meeting his gaze, his little lip trembling.

Camden glanced from Bodhi to Cadence. Her posture had gone rigid. Her expression, one of stunned silence.

He looked at Bodhi as a protective instinct as fierce as any emotion he'd ever known coursed through his veins. "Absolutely, Bodhi, I wouldn't miss it for the world."

Little Logan Klein hugged his knees to his chest and sulked.

Scoreboard: Bully, zero. Nice kid without a dad, one.

"Okay, campers!" Cadence said, finding her voice. "Your counselor is going to help you put on a life jacket. I'll be right back. There's something I need to check on in the boathouse, and then we'll get a look at an example of a cardboard boat just like the one you'll be making at home this summer for the regatta."

Cadence smiled at the children and gestured toward a rack of orange life vests then high-tailed it through the doors leading to the storage space below the boathouse.

He turned to the camp counselors. "I'm going to see if Ms. Lowry needs any help. Don't touch the canoes until we get back."

The teens nodded, and he strode past them and entered the darkened space.

Arms crossed tightly, Cadence paced along the worn wooden planks. "I want to pummel that kid."

"You just told me that was a big no-no here at camp," he replied gently.

"I've changed my mind. At the Baxter Park location, we pummel the creepy kids."

He stood in front of her, stopping her frantic movements, and rested his hands on her shoulders. "Okay, wait here. I'll go kick that seven-year-old's ass right now."

She met his gaze, held it for a beat, then started laughing. It was a tired little laugh, but at least the sadness had vanished from her eyes. She rested her forehead on his chest, and he wrapped his arms around her.

"I knew there would be days like this. I know kids can be cruel. I figured, I'm a teacher. If this happens, I'll be measured and composed. I'll treat it as if Bodhi was just my student."

He stroked her back. "But he's not."

"He's not," she echoed. "He's my baby. I'd do anything for him."

Cam tightened his hold as the realization hit him.

So would he.

He pressed a kiss to the crown of her head. "What can I do to make it better, Daisy?"

She pulled back and looked up at him. "What did you call me?"

Oh shit!

"Daisy," he said, both wanting her to know that he was Mac and terrified about the prospect at the same time.

"Did Bodhi tell you that Daisy is my middle name?"

His heart dislodged from his throat. "Yeah, and you've got

daisies growing all over your yard, and then there are the stickers I saw on your bike. It's a pretty name, Cadence Daisy."

She sighed against his chest. "The shopkeeper who sold me those glass daisy doorknobs I had with me that first day we met told me that the daisy was one of the strongest flowers. He called it a thunder flower because they're able to survive terrible storms."

"Then it suits you perfectly," he whispered.

All that time they'd talked, he'd never realized the pain and worry she shouldered all on her own.

"I'm glad you're here, Camden. I know that you can't stay. But, I'm grateful to have you here now."

With her words, he felt the weight of his father's watch, and he was transported back in time. He could hear his father's footsteps, checking the house before he went to bed. The creek of his bedroom door as his father went from room to room, looking in on him and his brothers.

Could he be that kind of man? A good man. A responsible man. A man worthy of Cadence and Bodhi?

He closed his eyes.

He'd never be that man. He proved that ten years ago.

He pulled back.

"What is it, Cam?"

"Cadence, I need to tell you something."

"You can tell me anything."

He tried to think of where to begin when cries and screams from the waterfront stopped him from speaking, and he heard the counselor yell five words that sent adrenaline rushing through his body.

"Bodhi, Porter, stop! You'll drown!"

"What's happened?" he yelled, bursting out of the boathouse with Cadence by his side.

A terrified camp counselor turned to face him. "The squirrels!" she shrieked.

Squirrels?

Jesus! Not again!

"What are you talking about?" he asked as two squirrels darted past him.

"I told them not to get into the boat!" the frantic counselor continued.

He frowned. There were no boats, only canoes. "You mean, canoe? Take a breath. Just tell us what's going on."

"Not a canoe," the counselor replied, shoulders slumping just as Cadence gasped and pointed toward the lake.

"Camden, they're in the sample cardboard boat. It's the one they send over for the kids to look at. It's just an example, and it's not waterproofed," she said, panic lacing her words.

"Should I call nine-one-one?" the counselor asked.

He watched the two boys jostling around inside the cardboard boat—without life jackets.

What the hell were they doing?

"There's no time!" He turned to Cadence. "Grab a paddle."

She nodded as he lifted a canoe from the rack and set it in the water.

He got in and checked the cardboard boat's location. It hadn't started to sink yet, but with the boys flailing around, they didn't have much time.

"Here," Cadence said, throwing him a life jacket as she strapped one on. "I'm going with you."

He glanced from her to the cardboard boat. "All right! Come on."

She hurried onto the canoe, and within seconds, they paddled in quick punctuated strokes, gliding through the water.

"Bodhi! Porter! We're coming!" she called, panic replaced with determination.

"We'll pull up alongside them. You can hold onto the cardboard boat, and I'll lift them into the canoe," he called to her.

"Got it! I just can't imagine why Bodhi would do something like this?" she answered.

He increased his pace. "The counselor mentioned squirrels."

"Squirrels?" she repeated.

"Yeah, I don't know," he answered.

"It couldn't be the same squirrels we caught in my house, could it?" she asked just as he was thinking the same damn thing.

Maybe he should have killed those squirrels. Ahh shit! No, he shouldn't have! But if the same two squirrels had something to do with this catastrophe, they were seriously pushing the limits of his squirrel patience—if that was even a real thing!

"Camden! Mommy!" Bodhi called.

"Sit tight! We're going to pull up alongside you," he called.

"Mommy, Porter and I had to save the squirrels!" the boy called back.

"We'll worry about the squirrels later," Cadence answered, reaching out and clutching the side of the soggy boat.

Camden set his paddle in the canoe.

"Mommy, it's sinking!"

"We don't have time. You grab Bodhi. I'll get Porter!"

He hooked his arm around the little boy, still clutching a fire truck, as Cadence pulled Bodhi onto the canoe, and cheers erupted from the waterfront.

"Are you a fireman?" the boy asked.

"No, I'm the campsite leader."

The boy grinned. "Is your job to save people?"

Cam released a relieved sigh. "It certainly is today."

The boat, now just a heap of soggy cardboard, floated in pieces around them. He turned to Cadence.

"Is Bodhi okay?"

She cradled her son in her lap and nodded.

"What happened, Bodhi?" he asked. "Why would you and Porter get in the cardboard boat, especially without a life jacket?"

"The squirrels," the boys answered in unison.

"Squirrels told you to get into the boat?" Camden asked, picking up his paddle and steering the canoe toward the shoreline.

"No! Two squirrels jumped into the boat. Porter and I didn't want them to get hurt or float out onto the lake, so we tried to get them out. But when we got in, they jumped out, and the boat started drifting."

Camden chuckled under his breath.

Damn squirrels.

He paddled with measured strokes toward the children, cheering and jumping up and down in front of the boathouse. It wasn't long before they hit shallow waters and he hopped out of the canoe and dragged it safely to shore.

Cadence helped the boys out, then handed him her paddle. "I'm going to take the boys to change into dry clothes. I'll be back as soon as I get them situated with their group."

"Are you okay?" he asked.

She gave him a weary yet grateful grin. "Yeah, it looks like you saved the day again."

"I'm good with bikes and rodents."

She chuckled. "It's more than that, and you know it. Thank you, Cam." She turned to the boys. "All right, you two, let's grab your backpacks and get you changed into your spare set of clothes. You've got extra shorts in your bag, right, Porter?"

"Yep, they've got fire engines on them," the boy answered.

"Perfect," Cadence said, ushering the boys toward the rec center.

Camden took a deep breath and exhaled slowly as the adrenaline surge tapered away.

"You're like a superhero, Mr. Bergen!" a boy called as the counselors led the children away from the waterfront.

He nodded and went to work, placing the canoe back on the stand when a pair of squirrels darted out from under the rack.

He watched the bushy-tailed bandits skitter up a tree. "This is your last warning, squirrels! You cause any more trouble, and you can say goodbye to your stash of acorns!"

"Yelling at squirrels. So that's what happens when you live alone in a secluded cabin for a decade."

Camden stilled. He'd know that voice anywhere. The voice that taught him how to tie his shoes. The voice that guided him down the trickiest ski runs when he was just a boy.

The voice of his oldest brother, Jasper.

"It's not that odd, Jas. I met a shaman who regularly sought out the counsel of his spirit animal, and many cultures believe in the connection between man and beast. You should try it," came a woman's voice.

"What's my spirit animal?"

The woman laughed—a warm, flowery sound. "No, my love, you're the beast."

Camden turned to find his brother standing next to a woman who looked remarkably like Brennen's fiancée.

"I'm Elle Reynolds," she said and shook his hand.

Jasper cleared his throat, and the woman bit back a grin.

"I'm Elle Reynolds-Bergen. I'm your sister-in-law."

Camden glanced from Elle's hand to Jasper's. They were both wearing wedding bands.

"You're married, Jas?"

"It was a spur-of-the-moment decision we made yesterday."

Camden frowned. "You made a spur-of-the-moment decision?"

Jesus! A lot had happened since he'd been gone!

It had been years since he'd seen his brother, but the last phrase he'd ever use to describe the oldest Bergen was *spur of the moment*. Jas was the most methodical person he'd ever known.

Elle looked up at Jasper. "It would literally take a two-hundred-and-fifty-page book for me to explain everything I had to do to turn your brother into a human, but we don't have time for that. We have a more pressing item to address."

Cam frowned. "What pressing item?"

"Public relations," his brother answered, pulling a piece of paper from his pocket. "And by the way, welcome home. I see Gram put you right to work."

Camden glanced between the pair, his head spinning. "It's just for the summer."

"Well, summer or not. We're here so we can get ahead of the story," Elle replied.

"The story?" he parroted back.

"Yes, the story of your return," Jas replied.

"But I'm not staying. I made that clear to Gram and Grandad."

Jas glanced at the piece of paper. "But two days ago, you returned, looking like someone who'd lived on a deserted island, visited Mom and Dad's graves, ran through Denver like a madman, broke into the botanic gardens, then crashed a wedding before busting through the gate of a local residence— otherwise known as the Bergen estate. Oh...and you demolished a cake."

Camden parted his lips to speak.

Shit! That was exactly what happened.

"I could eat a cake," Elle said and rubbed her belly.

Double shit! He forgot she was pregnant.

He gestured to a bench. "Would you like to sit? I know you're..."

"Knocked up with twins?" she supplied with a wry grin.

"Twins?" He glanced at his brother.

"If you're going to do something, you might as well do it right," Jas said, sharing a look with Elle.

She glanced at her husband and shook her head. "Listen, Camden, I'm a writer, and I've done some work with Bergen Enterprises, helping them with their recent rebranding efforts. There are pictures of you floating around out there. People looking to cash in on your name. I have some experience with this."

He nodded. "I know who you are. I've read your books."

Elle shot a pointed glare at Jasper.

He put up his hands. "I'm reading your books now, babe!"

"Between board meetings and ogling over spreadsheets," she replied with a teasing grin.

"Still counts," he answered.

Elle sighed. "Damn, he's right. It does."

"Hey!" came Cadence's voice as she joined them. "I wasn't expecting to see you both here. How are you feeling, Elle?"

"Great! Good enough to go skydiving. But, of course, I wouldn't do that with these two on board."

Cadence chuckled. "What brings you to camp? Did Camden tell you about our exciting morning?"

Jas shook his head. "No, when we found him, he was yelling at rodents."

"What happened this morning?" Elle asked.

"A little squirrel mishap, that turned into a cardboard boat rescue, then Camden saved the day."

"Is everyone all right?" Jasper asked.

"Absolutely, we're ready for anything here at Baxter Park," Cadence added with a wide grin.

Jasper glanced at the park. "I can tell. I've visited several of the camp locations over the years. None of them are as organized as this one."

Elle patted Jasper's arm. "Leave it to my husband to zero in on the logistics."

"Are you following the camp protocol?" Jas pressed.

Cadence blushed. "Yes, but I've tweaked a few things here and there. I hope you don't mind."

"Mind? This place is run with military precision. I want to know how you do it. We've had some personnel turnover in our Mountain Education Department. It's not as robust as it used to be."

That sweet blush still colored Cadence's cheeks. "I'd be happy to share the changes I've implemented."

"Do you have time now?" Jasper asked.

Cadence checked her watch. "We have about twenty minutes until the next group of campers cycles through to the waterfront."

Camden watched the exchange between his brother and

Cadence and felt...pride. He was so damned proud of Mountain Daisy—of who she was, of everything she was.

"Jas, you chat with Cadence, and I'll take Camden," Elle said, cutting into his thoughts as she threaded her arm with his.

He glanced down at the no-nonsense woman who had clearly smoothed out his brother's rough edges.

"How about a walk? Jas and I just got back from the Caymans last night, and I could do with some exercise," Elle offered.

"Sure," he answered, five steps into their walk.

This woman didn't mess around.

"Tell me about Switzerland."

Lonely. Isolated. Walled off from hurting anyone. Daisy was my only joy.

He cleared his throat. "I worked at several of the local resorts."

"But not the Bergen Resort."

"No."

"Did you have any Bergen gear? Coats, gloves, boots, snow pants..."

"Yeah, that's all I had."

"Your bike? Your skis?"

"All the Bergen in-house brand," he answered.

"How'd it hold up?"

"Great, that's why I had it."

Elle chuckled. "There's the angle."

"Bergen gear and equipment?" he asked.

"Yep, you've been testing it and making sure it held up under rugged conditions."

"But I wasn't."

"No, Camden, you were. Maybe you didn't know it, but you were."

Damn! He might have left Colorado, left the only home he'd

ever known, but he'd kept it with him. He'd purchased every piece of gear he owned from the sporting goods shop at the Bergen Resort in Switzerland. The resort he'd buzzed around for a decade, telling himself he was only going there to purchase the gear because he was familiar with it.

But could it have been more?

Could it have been that piece of him longing for home? Like Bodhi's stuffed bear, Mr. Cuddles, was all that gear his safety, his connection, his comfort?

They continued around the lake.

"I've kind of blown your mind, haven't I?" Elle asked.

"Even my boxer briefs are the Bergen Mountain Sports brand," he added, everything in his life going sideways.

She chuckled. "I don't know if we need to get that in-depth, but thanks for the info."

Jesus! He'd just met this woman—his brother's wife—and he'd just revealed his choice of underwear.

They rounded the bend, and the boathouse came into view with Jasper and Cadence parked on one of the benches, chatting away. The breeze lifted golden wisps of hair across her cheek, and the urge to tuck them behind her ear surged through him. And instantly, he wanted to be the man sitting beside her. He wasn't jealous of his brother. It wasn't that. It was clear the man was crazy about his wife, but he was jealous of anyone in Cadence's orbit.

"So, you're back...for just the summer?" Elle asked with a twist of suspicion in her tone.

He pulled his gaze from Cadence. "Yes, for Brennen and Abby's wedding."

"When's your return flight back to Switzerland?"

He frowned. "Return flight?"

"You said you were only staying the summer. I need to know when you're going back...for the piece I'm writing on you."

"I didn't book a return flight."

He'd been so sure of finding Mountain Daisy, the thought hadn't even crossed his mind.

"And you're staying with Cadence?" Elle continued.

"Yeah, in the house next door."

"And you're also working with her."

He could hear the wry twist to her words.

"Yes, it's kind of a funny coincidence it worked out that way," he answered carefully.

She was onto him. He'd read her travel guides. She saw everything. Observed everything. Her writing was infused with tiny idiosyncrasies of the people she met and the hidden characteristics of the places she'd visited.

"Do you believe in coincidences?" she asked.

That stopped him in his tracks.

"What do you mean?"

"You can either believe everything that happens in this life is completely random, or you can take the position that, sometimes, things fall into our path for a reason."

What did he believe?

"Cadence is a good person, Camden. My cousin and I have grown close to her and to Bodhi. They're easy to love."

He watched the blond beauty seated next to his brother and swallowed past the lump in his throat. "I'm fond of them both."

"I can tell. I think you're good for her."

He remained silent, not about to reveal their summer pact.

"She doesn't let anyone help her, not really," Elle continued. "She takes it all on and never asks for anything in return."

That was his Daisy.

"She's been very kind to me," he answered, going for a benign response.

Cadence looked away from Jas and caught him watching her.

She smiled and gave him a little wave. A quick hello. A quick, *I see you*, that sent his pulse racing.

Elle sighed. "I wouldn't doubt her kindness. That's what worries me."

"Why would it worry you?"

Elle frowned. "She's got some online pen pal. My cousin calls him her *Man Find*."

"Man Find?"

"Yeah, like Cadence has found a man, but she knows very little about him, so she can't actually find him."

Jesus! If Elle only knew! Cadence's *Man Find* was standing next to her.

"She's mentioned this friend to me," he said, treading lightly.

"I'm convinced he's a total creeper," Elle added.

That got his attention.

"Why would you say that?"

"She seems very taken with this person, but I worry he's not who he says he is."

"I thought he hadn't said much of anything. You know... about his identity," he replied, the muscles in his chest tightening.

"Well, whatever he's said, it's done something to her. She stares at his messages like she's falling in love."

Love?

Elle patted his arm. "I'm glad you're here, Camden. I'm glad she's got a friend close by—even if it is just for the summer."

"I'm happy to help. She's doing me quite a favor letting me crash in her rental unit."

He had to play this smart.

"That's right! Abby said you didn't want to stay in any of the Bergen properties."

"It's not who I am."

She held his gaze. "It's exactly who you are."

He shook his head.

"Oh, I almost forgot," she said and pulled out a Bergen Enterprises envelope. "Here."

"What's this?" he asked.

"It's for when you figure out who you are," she said with another wry twist of her lips.

He opened the envelope and found two credit cards and a checkbook.

Access to his trust.

He went to hand it back. "I can't accept this."

Elle crossed her arms. "Are you refusing your pregnant sister-in-law, standing here incubating two humans—your nieces or nephews or a combination of the two?"

Christ! She pulled the pregnancy card. How the hell was he supposed to argue with that without looking like a total D-canoe?

"I don't plan on touching any of the money, Elle."

"Then what's the harm in having it? It's not like it would be doing anything different locked in a safe-deposit box?"

Christ! Elle was just as crafty as his grandmother. Both women could bend a situation to their whim in the blink of an eye.

"Fair enough," he answered and slid the envelope into his pocket.

The same pocket containing Cadence's sexy as hell panties.

A week ago, he'd fantasized of a life hidden away with Mountain Daisy. He'd wanted to remain the runaway heir and have the woman who'd pulled him from his exile.

Was it a coincidence that she'd led him here—straight into the heart of his family?

Could this be where he belonged?

The gut-wrenching sound of metal twisting and the heavy

pound of his footsteps disappearing into the darkness told him the answer.

He removed his hand from his pocket.

The summer. That was all he had to give. That was as far as he could trust himself. And all he wanted to do was get through today, so he could hold Cadence in his arms tonight. Her scent. Her touch. He'd lose himself in her breathy cries and sweet muffled moans and forget that he was the runaway heir with each thrust of his cock, filling her, fucking her until he wasn't Camden or Mac and she wasn't Cadence or Daisy. Until they flew over the edge and were simply two lonely souls desperate for a sliver of comfort.

"Camden!"

He looked up to see Cadence coming toward him, smiling like he was enough.

That smile was his escape and his punishment.

She watched him closely. "Is everything okay?"

He pushed the dark thoughts away, letting in her light. "Yeah, we were just chatting about..."

What the hell was he supposed to say?

Nothing much. Just discussing you and how you may or may not be in love with me—the me that's Mac. You know, your online BFF.

Christ! This had gotten convoluted.

Elle glanced over at him. "About how we'll have to plan a time to get everyone together," Elle said as the women embraced.

"Then I have great news," Cadence began, glancing between them. "Jasper saw the cardboard delivery for the Bergen Cardboard Boat Regatta and suggested we get together tonight to help Bodhi with his design. I texted with Abby. Everyone's coming to my place—well, our place tonight for a barbecue. Are you up for it, Cam?"

Fucking Cam.

No one had ever made his name sound sweeter.

The last thing he wanted was to be surrounded by his brothers, by the memories. Then he caught the caring glint in her eyes. That glimmer of hope that touched somewhere deep inside of him.

He slid his hand into his pocket, past the envelope, and brushed his fingertips across the lace of her G-string. They had the summer. With her by his side, he could make it through a barbecue with his brothers.

He met her gaze and smiled. "A barbecue sounds like a great idea."

Cadence reached across the patio table. "Pass me the glue stick, Abby."

"I still can't believe you brought a craft project to a barbecue," Elle added, striking a match to light one of the outdoor candles as the sunset melted into the mountains to the west.

Cadence picked up the matches and lit two more candles with the scent of grilled hamburgers still in the air. She glanced over at her son, sitting in the grass next to the three Bergen brothers, their heads bent over a sheet of corrugated cardboard, plotting and planning Bodhi's boat design with the assistance of an outdoor lantern in the waning light.

"Hush, Elle!" Abby replied. "Keep punching holes in those hearts."

"I kind of resent you relegating me to the hole punching when you and Cadence get to use the glue sticks," Elle answered, wielding the hole puncher like a Wild West bandit.

Cadence grinned at the women. It warmed her heart to have them here, but that familiar twinge of sadness lurked just below the surface.

Barbecues in the backyard with friends. Summer nights

spent out on the patio, listening to the wind rustle through the aspen leaves.

This was the life she'd thought she'd have with Aaron.

She glued a tiny paper heart into the center of a larger one and handed it to Elle. "What are these things for again?"

Abby swirled her glue stick around the outline of the smaller heart. "For the joint bachelor and bachelorette party. Ray and Harriet are hosting it in their backyard and having it professionally catered and decorated. I should have guessed it, but Brennen's grandparents are party planning machines. There's really nothing for me to do, but I wanted to contribute something. So, I figured we could make a heart garland to hang on the pergola."

Elle punched a hole in the heart and set it on the pile. "Do you have any other projects up your sleeve that you need Cadence and I to help out with? Because I may have hit my crafting limit with this," she added with a wry grin.

"Yeah, you were worried there would be a ton to do with it coming up so quickly. How's it going?" Cadence asked.

Abby sat back in her chair. "Really well. Like so well there's hardly anything for me to worry about. We're having the wedding up at the lodge at Bergen Mountain, and Brennen and I went up this morning to meet with the event coordinator. Everyone there is so excited for a Bergen wedding. Plus, they cater and plan so many events that the last thing I'd want to do is ask them to reinvent the wheel." She glanced over at the men. "And I've never dreamed of an elaborate wedding. All I want is to be Brennen's wife."

Cadence glued another heart as the image of Aaron, smiling at her from the altar flashed before her eyes.

Abby glanced over at the men then lowered her voice. "How's it going with your bobblehead?"

"Bobblehead?" Elle repeated.

Cadence tucked Aaron's memory away. "It's what I called

Camden when he first arrived. He basically grunted and nodded, so I called him a brooding Bergen bobblehead."

"That's a good one," Elle replied.

"And?" Abby pressed.

Cadence looked over at the men and found Bodhi, leaning his head on Cam's shoulder. "And not so bobble-heady anymore. He taught Bodhi how to ride his bike without training wheels yesterday."

Elle took a tortilla chip from the bowl on the table. "So, not only are you working with him, you're also hanging out with him?"

Hanging out with him. Having mind-blowing orgasms. Sneaking in a little oral before work.

Cadence felt her cheeks heat. "Yeah, we're hanging out a bit."

"Is that why you're not wearing your necklace?" Abby asked gently.

Cadence's hand went to her neck. She hadn't put it back on since...

Since the night of her naughty redirection lesson.

"I take it off for camp. We're so active, playing games and taking the canoes out on the lake, I didn't want to lose it."

The cousins shared a look.

"Camden's just a friend," she added.

A friend with the best kind of benefits—but she needed to quash whatever plans her friends were cooking up.

"And your online creeper boyfriend doesn't mind a hot mountain man living next door?" Elle asked.

Cadence shook her head. "Mountain Mac isn't my boyfriend. He's just a friend, too."

"A friend who you know nothing about," Elle added.

Cadence glued another heart. "I know enough, but I haven't heard from him much lately."

Elle popped another chip into her mouth. "The police probably found all the bodies he has buried in his backyard or his mother stopped paying for his cellphone."

Cadence shook her head but stayed silent. It wasn't that. Whoever Mountain Mac was, this person had helped her—had shown her real kindness.

"You're terrible, Elle!" Abby said, chucking a paper heart at her cousin.

Elle snagged it and clicked the hole puncher. "It's my writer's brain. This morning, I had a whole story going in my head about the barista at my coffee shop. Long story, short: she's a domina-trix on the down-low when she's not whipping up nonfat decaf fraps."

Cadence laughed then stole another glance at Camden, catching him ruffle Bodhi's hair. He was good with kids. Calm during their morning rescue. Sweet to a little girl with a scraped knee this afternoon. The fierce bearded mountain man who'd mowed down the gate to Ray and Harriet's home had been replaced with a gentle, handsome giant who, at this very moment, had her panties in his pocket.

"I'm sorry to disappoint you, Elle, but there's no story here," she answered, focusing far too intently on her glue stick application.

"Oh, Cadence Lowry, there's always a story. Everyone has a secret life—probably even that barista," Elle added.

Elle had traveled the world as a writer. Met people from all over the globe and brought their stories to life. She was a keen observer, and if anyone was going to suss out the sexy times summer pact she had with Camden, it would be Elle.

Cadence doubled her focus on the glue stick. "You know whose lives I'd be interested in learning more about?" she began, shifting the conversation.

Abby leaned in. "Who?"

"Glenna and Gertrude's."

Elle punched a hole into a heart then added it to the pile. "The old ladies who used to live in the houses?"

"Yeah, they lived here for their entire adult lives, and they've got all sorts of strange antiques and little knickknacks."

Elle took another tortilla chip. "My schedule is pretty crazy. I leave tomorrow for New York to meet with my agent, but one of these days, I'd love to go through the houses with you. I did a whole piece on antiquing with a well-respected appraiser a few years ago. If we find anything good, we can always run it by her."

"That would be great," Cadence answered.

"What would be great?" Brennen asked, sitting down next to Abby as Jasper settled in next to Elle and Bodhi plopped down on the loveseat.

"Sit with me and Mommy, Camden!" Bodhi called, scooting in closer to her to make room for the man.

Camden maneuvered his large frame onto the loveseat with Bodhi squeezed in between them. He rested his arm across the back, giving Bodhi a little more room and allowing his fingertips to brush against her neck. The sensation sent a shiver down her spine that went straight to her core. His hidden touch sent a sweet buzz of anticipation through her body at the thought of his hands gripping her hips, his lips kissing a trail down her jawline, and his perfect cock buried deep inside her.

What would they do tonight?

She released a shaky breath.

What wouldn't they do tonight?

"Hey," he said to her, the candlelight framing his face in a warm glow.

"Hey," she echoed as the breath caught in her throat when his hand found the end of her braid, and he twisted his fingers in her hair.

Thanks to the blanket of darkness, no one could see this covert exchange. This tiny touch that sent her pulse racing.

"We were discussing Cadence's houses and the old ladies who used to live here. They left all sorts of little trinkets and treasures," Abby replied, cuddling into her fiancé.

Brennen wrapped his arm around her. "Speaking of the houses, are you still on the hunt for those daisy doorknobs?"

"I am. I only need one more set," she answered, working hard to keep her tone even as Camden continued twisting her hair.

"I might have a lead for you. I was up visiting with a group on the land my family owns about ten miles away from Bergen Mountain. We're going to allow them to use it for a charity camping event. It's pretty rugged out there—not much more than a whole lotta nature and an old cabin."

Camden's hand stilled.

"Anyway," Brennen continued. "On the way back to the city, I had to stop for gas, and there was a little antique shop next door. I went in and started chatting with the owner and asked about the daisy doorknobs Abby mentioned you've been trying to find."

"Did they have any?" she asked, waiting for Camden to resume twisting her hair, but he didn't move a muscle.

What had set him off? He'd been fine throughout the evening. Quiet, but the waves of anger and pain that had radiated off the man the first day she'd met him had disappeared...until now.

Brennen shook his head. "No, but I asked the shop owner about them, and he said his partner was hitting a bunch of flea markets around the state and thinks there's a decent possibility he may come across some."

"I'll have to add going up there to my to-do list."

Bodhi groaned. "Mommy has lots of lists. Teacher lists, house lists, camp lists, Bodhi chore lists."

She nudged her son. "I just thought of another list: All the things we'll need for the cardboard boat regatta." She turned to Camden. "Did you guys decide on a design?"

He started twisting her hair again. "There's still some discussion on the type of hull."

"The hull's the bottom, right? Isn't it just flat?" Abby asked.

"Here we go," Camden murmured, the smile back in his voice.

Jasper leaned forward and steepled his fingers. "There are several types of hulls—all of which should be considered when designing a boat. Then you need to factor in water displacement."

Brennen shook his head. "That's crazy! Bodhi's not crossing the ocean on this thing, Jas! It's a cardboard boat. He needs speed. The less time spent on the lake, the better."

"And that's why I suggested doing some stability calculations," Jasper added as Elle shook her head.

Camden grinned. "As you can tell, we didn't get very far settling on a final design. But we did decide one thing," he added, giving another twist to the tail of her braid.

Bodhi perked up. "Yeah, I'm going to name the boat Daisy."

"You are?" she said, sharing a look with Camden.

"Yeah, after you, Mommy, because it's your favorite flower."

She patted her son's leg. "And I'll be in the boat with you. Regatta rules. Kids under nine need an adult with them."

Bodhi shoulders drooped. "But I want Camden to do the regatta with me."

"Oh, well..." she stuttered.

Camden already agreed to do the Father's Day bike parade with Bodhi. It was clear as day that her son adored the man. But he adored Jasper and Brennen, too. These people were their friends. Camden was their friend, too, right?

But there was one caveat: Jasper and Brennen weren't scheduled to disappear back to Switzerland at the end of the summer.

What would it do to Bodhi when he left? What would it do to her?

She swallowed past the lump in her throat.

"Will you do it, Camden? With you paddling, we'll zoom across the lake," Bodhi said, rocketing his fist into the air.

"I could paddle quickly, B," she said.

Bodhi frowned. "Give me your hand, Mom."

She held out her hand, and Bodhi took it.

"Give me your hand, Camden," her son said next.

Camden complied, and Bodhi pressed their hands together. She inhaled sharply as the charge of his touch sent a shiver through her body.

"See! Look at how big Camden's hands are. Just think what he could do with them! We'll fly across Smith Lake."

Oh, she knew quite a bit about Camden's hands. They'd ravaged every inch of her body.

Bodhi released his grip on their hands, but Camden didn't pull away. Like magnets, the attraction kept them together. He curled his hand around hers as his thumb brushed her index finger, sending another round of tingles through her body. She met his gaze, under his spell and unable to speak. Unable to do anything but sit there with his rough, large hand wrapped protectively around hers.

"Why shouldn't he do it? You'll still be here, right, Camden?" Elle chimed in, breaking their trance.

"I could do it," Camden answered, tightening his hold on her hand.

"Okay." She nodded.

Why did this feel like he was agreeing to more than simply riding in a cardboard boat with her son?

She couldn't let her heart go there. She couldn't let her heart have a say in anything that happened that summer.

"Thanks, Cam!" Bodhi said, wiggling with excitement.

The movement broke her connection with Camden, and she glanced at her friends—all watching them closely.

Even Jasper.

She had to shift gears.

She folded her hands in her lap. "I like your idea of naming the cardboard boat. We could turn that into a camp activity. The campers could brainstorm ideas this week, and we could list the names on a big sheet of paper then hang it next to the boathouse."

Camden followed her lead, folding his hands in his lap like a schoolboy. "It would be a constant reminder about the regatta and keep the kids excited about it even though it's weeks away."

She breathed a sigh of relief. Good! He understood they needed to do something to take the focus off their little hand moment.

"Have you ever considered consulting, Cadence?" Jasper asked.

She cocked her head to the side. "What do you mean?"

"Our mother was a teacher, but she never taught in a classroom," Jasper continued.

Brennen nodded. "She and my dad ran the Mountain Education Department of the company."

"And Jasper couldn't stop talking about all the improvements you've implemented with the Bergen Adventure Summer Camp," Elle said, looking suspiciously between their folded hands.

"Those changes on a larger scale could improve our education programs significantly," Jasper added.

Cadence leaned forward. "You're interested in how I'd run mountain sports education?"

"I am."

"I could write something up for you," she replied.

"Just add it to your list, Mommy," Bodhi said and yawned.

The adults chuckled, and she stroked her son's golden hair. "We should get you to bed, little one."

"Where's Mr. Cuddles?" Bodhi asked, his sleepy words trailing together.

Camden leaned over and retrieved the bear from the ground. "Here he is," he answered, tucking Mr. Cuddles under Bodhi's arm.

Bodhi shifted and crawled onto Camden's lap. "Thank you, Cam."

Cam.

She'd caught herself calling him that today, too. The ease of being with this man had worked its way into her speech—and Bodhi's.

Brennen took Abby's hand and came to his feet. "I think it's time we called it a night."

"I agree!" Elle replied, grabbing a handful of chips. "It's a miracle if I make it to nine o'clock. These babies are killing my late-night writing sessions, but luckily, not my Oreos and tortilla chip cravings," she added, exchanging a look with Jasper and popping a chip into her mouth.

"I can put Bodhi to bed," Camden said, cradling her son on his lap.

She patted his little back, rising and falling with his rhythmic breaths. "Are you sure? I can take him."

Bodhi looked so peaceful in Camden's strong embrace with his muscled arms wrapped tightly around him.

"I'm good," he said, rising to his feet when the smack of something hitting the ground caught her attention.

"It looks like you dropped an envelope and is that a pair of..." Abby trailed off.

Oh crap!

Her panties.

Camden stood stock still.

"Laundry!" she blurted out.

"Laundry?" he parroted back.

"Laundry?" Elle, Abby, Jasper, and Brennen repeated.

"Laundry," Bodhi yawned then nuzzled his head into the crook of Camden's neck.

"Yes," she said, snagging her G-string off the ground. "This happens all the time with Bodhi and me. Our washer and dryer are ancient, and every once in a while, I'll get one of his socks tucked inside my jeans." She turned to Camden. "You did some laundry last night at my place because there's not a washer and dryer in yours, remember?"

Please, please, Camden! Just nod! If she ever needed the brooding Bergen bobblehead, it was right freaking now.

"Yes?" he answered.

"Yes!" she replied, praying her resolute yes would cancel out his perplexed one.

"Yeah, we did all the laundry last night," he continued, totally in contention to win the award for the worst liar on earth.

"Loads and loads," she added, now the one nodding like a bobblehead.

"It's a good thing we're leaving. I'm sure you two have lots more laundry to do," Elle added, eyeing them closely.

Cadence waved her panties in the air. "There is always laundry to do with a little boy in the house. So many messes!"

Double crap!

She stuffed the panties in her pocket. "How about I show you all to the door?"

Abby picked up the envelope from the ground and handed it to Camden. "We're good. We know the way."

Cadence plastered on a smile. Of course, they did. Why was she going all *Downton Abbey, let me show you out,* on her friends?

"Don't forget to email me your modifications and proposed changes to the summer camp curriculum," Jasper added.

"I'll be sure to put it on the list," she answered a little too emphatically.

"And I'll make sure she gets to it right after the laundry," Camden added, shrugging his shoulders.

She tried not to cringe and waved as her friends left through the gate. She glanced up at Camden and silently held his gaze until the sound of two car engines cut through the quiet.

"I think we may be the two biggest idiots on the planet," she said, dropping her chin to her chest.

Camden shifted Bodhi's weight to one arm and lifted her chin. "I think we covered pretty well."

"My panties fell out of your pocket, Cam."

Cam.

She was doing it again, but it just felt so right.

"They're pretty panties," he said as the glow of the candle-light caught his hooded gaze.

"I don't think anyone else was thinking that."

He cupped her cheek in his hand. "I was."

"You were?"

"But I was mostly thinking about how you weren't wearing them."

"Holy pickles and relish!" she whispered.

Bodhi sighed in his sleep, and Camden glanced down at him. "We should get him to bed."

She stared up at him. "We should. It's late."

How had it only been a couple of days since they'd met? And how had she settled into a rhythm so comfortably with this hulk of a man?

She blew out the candles, listening to the creak of the back door. Cam held it for her, and she followed him inside.

She pulled the hairband from her braid and let her hair hang loose around her shoulders. "The funny thing is, is that I really do have laundry to do."

"Oh yeah?"

"Yep, little boys do make lots of messes."

"I can put him down if you want to get started on that. Maybe I could throw a thing or two in with yours."

"Sure," she replied then chuckled.

"What is it?"

"Maybe we aren't the world's worst liars."

He smiled, but it didn't reach his eyes, then turned to take Bodhi to his room.

"Hold on." She pressed a kiss to her son's cheek. "Sweetest dreams, little one."

"Where's the laundry room?" he asked.

She pointed to a door off the kitchen. "Right there. It's more of a glorified closet."

"Will the sound of the washing machine wake Bodhi?"

She patted her son's back. "No, it's loud, but it's white noise. He may even sleep better with it going."

Camden nodded then disappeared down the hall with Bodhi's legs dangling side to side.

She smiled as a sliver of blue light escaped from the boy's room. Camden remembered to turn on the nightlight. She sighed and opened the door to the tiny torture room otherwise known as the laundry room and pulled the string to turn on the dangling light bulb. Loading the machine with Bodhi's T-shirts, she hummed to herself and reached for the detergent when two strong hands gripped her hips from behind.

"He's all tucked in, and the house is locked up," Camden whispered in her ear.

She leaned into him. "Did you grab what you needed to throw into the wash?"

He pulled the G-string from her pocket and dangled the panties in front of her. "These came from a very dirty girl."

Her nipples tightened into hard peaks at the low rumble of his voice.

"Then I suggest the heavy-duty cycle," she replied.

"Is it the longest cycle?"

"Yep, and it has an extra rinse."

He dropped her G-string into the washer, lowered the lid, then closed the door to the tight space.

"There's no daisy doorknob on this door," he murmured against her neck, pressing his hard body against hers.

She gasped and gripped the sides of the washing machine as the motor clicked on and the washer began to fill with water. The sensation of his cock pressed against her ass and the vibrations of the machine sent a delicious rush of heat between her thighs.

"Nope, I still need to replace it," she managed.

"Is it on the list?" he asked with a sexy, teasing bend to the words.

"Oh, yes," she breathed.

"I have an item to add to your list."

"What's that?"

He slid his hand inside her shirt and massaged her breasts. "Mind-blowing orgasms in the laundry room."

"You don't have anything else to go in with this load?" she asked.

What the hell was wrong with her? The answer to I'm going to screw your brains out in the laundry room is not inquiring about what's left in the laundry basket.

"There are a few more things that could go in. Raise your arms."

She did as he asked, and he peeled off her shirt, unclasped her bra, then went to work removing her sports skirt.

Camden pressed a kiss to the back of her neck then palmed her ass. "You're more perfect than I could have ever imagined."

She turned to face him. He'd done it again—made another strange comment as if they'd known each other before Saturday. But her train of thought evaporated when he reached for the collar of his T-shirt and pulled it over his head, exposing a wall of hard muscle.

She slid her hands down his chest, feeling the chiseled plain of his abdomen. "I don't think I mind doing laundry anymore."

He hummed a little laugh as she unbuttoned his cargo shorts then stilled when she felt the envelope in his pocket.

She pulled it out. "Is this important?"

He shook his head. "No," he answered and set the envelope on the shelf next to the detergent, his expression growing heated.

In the space of a breath, he gripped her hips, lifted her up, and rested her ass on the edge of the washing machine. The rhythmic purr of the appliance vibrated beneath her as Camden slid his hand into her hair, tilting her head up to meet his lips in a fevered kiss.

"I wanted to do this all day," he growled.

"Laundry?" she asked, smiling against his lips.

"No, you," he answered, pulling her body flush with his. "Ever since I got to taste you this morning, all I could think about was thrusting my cock inside you and making you come so hard you forget everything on those to-do lists."

For starting out as a barely verbal brooding bobblehead, her Bergen brother had quite the dirty talk game.

He stilled with his cock poised at her entrance. "Do we need protection? I can run back to my room and get a condom."

She rolled her hips, rubbing against his hard length. "I'm on the pill and as long as you're..."

"I am. I got tested right after we..." he supplied, then shook his head. "I'm clean."

"Okay, I trust you," she whispered, wanting desperately to know what was going on in this man's mind.

He tightened his grip on her body as pain and lust and longing flashed wild and heated in his eyes. "You do?"

"Yes," she whispered.

"You hardly know me."

She smiled up at him. "I've always been able to tell if a person has a good heart. You do, Cam. You're decent and kind, and I'm grateful you're here."

The machine clicked and switched to the wash cycle, ratcheting up its vibration. She arched into him, and he captured her mouth, kissing her deeply as he thrust his cock inside her wet heat.

She braced herself, one hand gripping the edge of the appliance while the other held tight to his forearm. But he had her solidly in his embrace. Their bodies met, moving together, his hard length filling her, his pelvis stroking her sweet bundle of nerves with each roll of their hips.

He twisted his fingers in her hair, and the titillating throb of their naked bodies coming together fused with the buzz and vibrations from the washing machine had her moaning with desire.

He buried his head in the crook of her neck and kissed the delicate skin below her earlobe. "I love fucking you bare. I love how wet you are. I want you greedy. I want you begging for me to make you come."

As the machine dialed up its pace, so did they. The sensations coursed through her like a runaway freight train, barreling down the track and headed for one hell of a crash.

"Camden," she gasped and wrapped her arms around him.

Then everything collapsed into this man, this moment, their bodies.

She surrendered to the pump and grind of their connection.

To his heated breaths. To his primal growls as he wound her tighter and tighter until she stood on the edge of desire and plummeted off the cliff. She collided with her release, her body writhing with his. Skin meeting skin and breath meeting breath.

He cupped her cheek, and she grazed her teeth across his thumb as he watched her, his steel-blue eyes burning with lust. He slid his hand between them and massaged her pulsing bundle of nerves, stretching out her orgasm and heightening the surge of pleasure roaring through her body. And in this moment, when nothing existed except the two of them, she saw every raw part of Camden Bergen. His pain, his desire, his agony all bound tightly together as he joined her, succumbing to the friction of their lovemaking.

"I found you," he bit out before swallowing her cries of pleasure with a kiss.

Their sweat-slick bodies slowed, and she rested her head on his shoulder as the whirl of the washing machine died down, the cycle completed.

Camden hummed a contented sigh against her temple, and she caught her breath.

"Why do you keep saying you found me?"

He swallowed hard. "Because I did. I found a beautiful woman, and all I want..."

He tensed, his features growing tight as if it took every ounce of strength to stop his words from tumbling out.

"What do you want?" she asked.

He pressed a whisper-soft kiss to her lips then released a slow breath. "All I want is to spend every minute of this summer with you."

Those were the words that came out, but somewhere inside her, she knew that it wasn't what he'd intended to say.

Did he want more? Did he want her? And what did she want?

Yes, they were playing house. But it couldn't be more than that. The school year would start. She needed to get Glenna's unit prepped to be rented. She was stretched financially as it was. She had to take this for what it was. Two people who'd agreed to enjoy each other's company for the summer.

Her heart might want more, but her head would win. With her lists and plans, it always did.

She stroked his cheek. "I think we're going to be doing a lot of laundry this summer."

He grinned, a sweet, grateful smile that nearly broke her heart.

"Loads and loads," he replied with a naughty glint in his eyes. "Now, let's get you on top of that dryer. We're not done with the laundry yet."

13

CAMDEN

"Can we do one more lap, Cam?" Bodhi called over his shoulder.

Camden grinned, maneuvering his mountain bike on the path to pass a little girl on a tricycle as he rode along with the other families celebrating Father's Day at Baxter Park.

He glanced over at Cadence, pedaling on her bike beside him. "What do you say?"

She smiled at him. That beautiful, sweet twist of her lips he'd grown to love over the last few weeks. And he got to see it every day, all day, and every night until she drifted off to sleep in his arms.

They'd been doing lots of *laundry* these past two weeks. He'd kissed every inch of her body and caressed every sweet curve. He'd even moved Glenna's bed from where it sat on the far wall to rest against the wall that separated his bedroom from hers just to be that much closer to her when he couldn't have her in his arms.

All that—and he still wanted more.

Her sexy sighs and breathy moans set his pulse racing, but when she'd whispered *sweetest dreams, Cam*, before falling asleep, his heart would swell—near to bursting—at the sound of Mountain Daisy's sign off.

He'd died and gone to heaven. He just couldn't let anyone know.

And they weren't just good at laundry.

They'd made a great team as site leaders at Baxter Park's Bergen Adventure Summer Camp. She'd set the structure in place that made it run like clockwork, which allowed him to tweak how they approached teaching each activity. But more than that, working year-round at the different resorts in Switzerland over the past decade had exposed him to different ways of breaking down and teaching each skill to master winter and summer mountain sports.

All that time he'd spent as part of the background, shoveling snow and building trails, had given him a front-row seat to observe different teaching methods, and in turn, he now had the knowledge and skills to improve how they did things at Baxter Park's Bergen Adventure Summer Camp.

Switzerland was his prison—his self-inflicted punishment.

He'd never assumed that his exile had garnered value. But it had. And he only knew that because Mountain Daisy had brought him back.

"Let's do it! After all those pancakes, I should do fifty more laps," she answered with a smile that made him want to move mountains to keep her happy.

The Father's Day celebration at Baxter Park started with a midmorning pancake breakfast. The same pancake breakfast he'd attended with his family every Father's Day. It had a been a Bergen tradition: pancakes at the firehouse followed by the bike parade.

But for the last decade, Father's Day had been one of his worst days. He wasn't a big drinker, but on the second Sunday in

June, he'd open a bottle of whiskey and start pouring until it became the third Monday.

But not today.

Today, Bodhi had burst through the door that connected his room to Cadence's, brimming with excitement. They'd ridden their bikes around the park each evening after dinner, and the determined six-year-old grew more confident with every ride.

Look at where you want to be. Find that spot and focus on it.

Each time he borrowed his father's words and offered them up to Bodhi, the sting of regret dulled a little.

He and Cadence came around the bend and found Bodhi stopped and talking with another little boy.

Bodhi waved them over, and Camden immediately recognized the other child.

Logan Klein.

"Can Logan and I play on the playground for a few minutes?"

Camden shared a glance with Cadence.

"Are you here with your family, Logan?" she asked.

The boy kicked at a clump of grass and shook his head. "My mom and dad are on vacation. Miss Carrie is babysitting me for the weekend."

Poor kid to have his parents check out on Father's Day weekend. Even though the freckled boy was unkind to Bodhi on the first day, the kid had dropped his bully facade thanks to the nurturing camp environment. He'd turned out to be a good kid who craved attention and seemed to be raised by a slew of nannies and babysitters.

Camden looked over to see their Bergen Adventure head counselor, Carrie Mackendorfer, walking over.

"It's so great to see you guys! I was just about to take Logan over to the playground," she said and patted Logan's slumped shoulder.

Cadence started to answer when a man's voice cut her off.

"Excuse me, Mr. Bergen, would this be a good time for a photo?"

He glanced over and saw a young man with a camera coming toward them.

Press.

But he didn't have to run thanks to Elle Reynolds-Bergen.

She'd written a piece on him for the Bergen Mountain Sports website, highlighting his use of Bergen gear over the years. Several outdoor blogs and adventure sports magazines had picked it up. And just like that, Elle had shaped the narrative of his return.

He glanced at Cadence. "Do you mind?"

"Actually, could we get a photo of all of you?" the photographer asked.

Carrie shook her head. "I'm only Logan's babysitter. I can't give you permission."

The photographer turned to him. "Then, how about the three of you?"

He and Cadence had spoken with a reporter earlier in the week for a piece the local paper was running on summer activities for families in Denver. The Bergen Mountain Sports PR department had set it up, and he could hardly believe that just a handful of weeks ago, he'd been holed up in a cabin, unrecognizable with a scraggly beard and a hollow disposition desperate to escape being a Bergen.

"Sure, that would be fine," Cadence answered.

The photographer pointed toward Smith Lake. "Why don't you all stand next to that willow. We can get the lake in the background."

They took off their helmets, leaned their bikes against a bench, then followed a skipping Bodhi to the spot next to the tree.

"Thanks for putting up with this," he said softly.

She waved him off. "I'm the one who should be thanking you for doing the Father's Day Parade with Bodhi. I know it means everything to him."

He smiled as Bodhi jumped up and grabbed onto a tree branch, his long, gangly legs swinging beneath him.

"He's a good kid, Cadence."

"Yeah, he is."

Bodhi dropped and ran over and took his hand. "Can I be in the middle?"

"I can't see why not," Cadence answered.

Bodhi reached for his mother's hand, and the three of them stood together, smiling and holding hands as the photographer snapped away.

"Just look natural. Talk amongst yourselves. I'd like to get some non-posed shots," the man said, adjusting the lens.

He glanced down at Cadence as Bodhi twisted from side to side, still holding onto them. They didn't have to try to look natural. They'd fallen into it easily.

"You're good at this," Cadence said.

His brows knit together. "At what?"

She reached up and smoothed his collar. "Being you."

"It's only thanks to you."

She shook her head. "I didn't bring you back to Denver. You did that all on your own."

The muscles in his throat tightened. She had no idea all this was because of her. He'd screwed up a few times and gotten damn close to letting the cat out of the bag. Lost in a haze of dreamy disbelief, he'd called her Daisy and alluded to knowing her, to finding her.

But thank Christ, she hadn't connected him to Mac.

She still jumped every time her phone pinged with that

hopeful glint in her eye, but she hadn't heard from her online friend in weeks.

He couldn't be both Mountain Mac and Camden Bergen to her. He felt bad enough when that spark in her eye would disappear, and she'd tuck her phone back into her pocket.

The photographer came in closer and gestured to the ground. "How about a seated shot?"

Bodhi dropped onto the grass then climbed onto his lap once he and Cadence were seated.

"Perfect! Ms. Lowry, would you mind leaning in?" the photographer asked.

Her shoulder pressed into his, and he glanced down at her. With those sky-blue eyes and golden hair blowing in the breeze, she looked like every perfect summer day all wrapped into one stunning woman.

"Look, Mommy," Bodhi said, climbing off his lap. "Daisies!"

The boy ran over and picked one of the flowers growing in a clump next to a cluster of other wildflowers.

Bodhi handed her the daisy as the photographer kept clicking away. "It's like the ones I always find on your pillow from the Flower Fairy."

Cadence bit her lip, and her cheeks grew pink.

"You mean the Flower Ninja," Camden replied as Cadence held back a grin.

The boy crinkled his nose and sat back on the ground. "Nope, it's still a fairy, Cam."

He held Cadence's gaze then glanced at the flower in her hand. "Here, let me," he said, taking the daisy and sliding it into her hair.

She touched the bloom delicately. "How do I look?"

If beauty, kindness, and grace had a face—it would be hers.

He stared at her. This would be the image he'd return to

when he was back in Switzerland, far away from this perfect summer.

"You look like every dream I never knew I had."

She smiled up at him. "That might be the sweetest thing anyone's ever said to me."

"What about when I told you that you smelled good—like the cafeteria at school?" Bodhi asked.

Cadence held back a chuckle. "That's right, B. That was by far the sweetest thing anyone's ever said to me."

"Cam's can be the second sweetest," Bodhi added with a resolute nod.

"I'm good with second place," he said, staring into her eyes.

The photographer took a step back. "I think I've got plenty."

"Can I go play with Logan now?" Bodhi asked, gesturing toward Carrie who was pushing Logan on a swing.

Cadence checked her watch. "I don't think so, sweetheart. I didn't realize how late it had gotten, and we still need to go visit Daddy today."

Daddy.

A lump formed in his throat. It was so damned easy playing house with Cadence and Bodhi. Easy because it wasn't permanent. Easy because it was just pretend.

A father should be reliable and steadfast—the kind of man who put his family first.

A father didn't run away.

Cadence handed him his helmet. "Are you ready to go home?"

Home. Christ, where was his home?

He pasted on a smile. "Yeah, let's go."

"Can I ride over and say goodbye to Carrie and Logan?" Bodhi asked.

Cadence nodded. "Sure! And would you ask Carrie if she can

still babysit you on Friday night? Camden and I have Abby and Brennen's joint bachelor and bachelorette party."

That lump in his throat doubled in size. Bren and his fiancée had decided to forgo the traditional—and often rowdy—bachelor and bachelorette fetes for a small, intimate gathering of friends to celebrate their upcoming nuptials. And as much as he was happy for his brother—both of his brothers—it still served as a glaring reminder of what he couldn't have. What he couldn't be.

A husband.

A father.

He could pretend, but that could never be his life.

"Sure, Mom, I'll ask her," Bodhi answered then strapped on his helmet and biked the short distance to the playground.

"Cam?" Cadence said and touched his arm. "Are you okay?"

He nodded.

"Are you thinking of your father?"

He nodded again.

"Are you going all bobblehead on me?" she asked with a teasing grin.

He chuckled. "No."

Her expression warmed. "Good."

He stared down at the handlebars on her bike and traced the C+B scratched into the metal.

"*C* and *B*," she said with an air of surprise. "Those are your initials."

"Yeah," he answered, staring down at the letters that had called him back.

"Maybe it's a sign," she said.

The breath caught in his throat. "What do you mean?"

"Maybe you were destined to spend the summer with us."

His gaze slid to the daisy stickers. "I thought it might be more."

She cocked her head to the side. "More than what?"

"Carrie says she can still babysit me on Friday night," Bodhi called, riding up to them.

Cadence watched him a beat before turning to her son. "Thanks, B. Are you ready to head home?"

"The last one back is a rotten egg!" he called, setting off down the path.

"We better..." Camden began, feeling the heat of her gaze burning into him.

"Yeah, we don't want Bodhi getting too far ahead of us," she finished.

Shit! He had to stop. But Christ, in those moments where the dream of a life with her felt so close, it was like he was injected with a truth serum and could barely hold the words back from tumbling out.

I'm here because of you. It's always been you. It will always be you.

She started off, and he followed, looking past the park patrons to keep Bodhi in his sights. The boy veered off the park path and stopped before crossing the street. But thanks to the holiday, the sidewalk was blocked with cars parked in the driveways.

"Just stay on the road and keep to the right," Cadence called to her son.

The boy nodded and crossed, maneuvering his bike onto the street when Camden caught sight of a Jeep speeding down the road.

Music blared from the car's stereo as the Jeep edged out of its lane—the driver's head bent as she stared at her phone and unknowingly, headed straight for Bodhi.

"Bodhi, get on the sidewalk!" Cadence called.

But the boy kept pedaling down the road.

The vehicle got closer, veering, inch by inch, into the wrong lane onto a collision course with Cadence's son.

"Cam! He doesn't hear me. And that car!" Cadence cried, panic lacing each word, and his body took over.

Pumping his legs, he pedaled hard and passed Cadence. With Bodhi in his sights, he assessed the situation as the boom of the car's bass thumped out a rhythmic beat, getting closer with each second.

In the space of a breath, he made it to Bodhi just as the driver glanced up. The Jeep swerved, and he reached out his arm, hooking it around Bodhi's waist and plucking the boy off the bike. A metallic scraping cut through the air as Bodhi's bike hit the ground, and he maneuvered them past a parked car to crash onto the safety of the grassy strip that separated the street from the sidewalk.

The vehicle screeched to a halt and the sickening scent of burning rubber lingered in the air.

"Is he okay?" the young woman asked over the thumping bass.

"Get off your phone and pay attention to the road," he called, clutching the boy in his arms.

The woman blinked and grew pale as the gravity of her situation sank in. She nodded, turned off the music, then slowly continued down the road just as Cadence jumped off her bike and joined them in the grass.

"Bodhi! Baby! Are you hurt?"

The boy shook his head. "I'm sorry, Mommy! There are so many cars, and I couldn't find a place to get onto the sidewalk."

Tears streamed down her cheeks as she held Bodhi's face in her hands. "I can't lose you, too. I can't!"

"You won't, Mommy. See, I'm okay. I didn't even scrape my knee."

Cadence gasped, working to catch her breath. "Thank you, Cam. I don't know what I would have done..."

He wrapped his arm around her—the three of them huddled on the grass together.

"I'd never let anything happen to you or Bodhi. He's okay, Cadence. We're all okay," he added gently.

She nodded against his chest. "I don't know what I would have done. And I couldn't get to him. I wasn't fast enough. If it wasn't for you..."

She trailed off again, but he didn't need her to finish the sentence. She couldn't lose Bodhi like she'd lost her husband. She couldn't say the words, but the fear written across her tear-stained face said everything.

He tightened his grip. "I've got you."

She smiled up at him through her tears. "I know you do, Cam."

The trust in her eyes hit him like a punch to the gut. He glanced over at Bodhi's upturned bike. Its handlebars twisted and front wheel spinning, and he knew one thing for sure. He hadn't lied to Cadence. The adrenaline coursing through his veins and that primal drive to protect Bodhi at whatever cost surged through him. He'd do anything to keep them out of harm's way.

From the moment he'd heard her scream on his first night back in Denver—even before he found out she was Daisy—he'd felt this need to keep her safe. This connection telling him to watch over her.

"Can Cam come with us to see Daddy," Bodhi asked as Cadence released a relieved breath.

"Bodhi, sweetheart, I'm not sure if Cam—" she began, but he stopped her.

"I'd like to join you, if that's all right."

She pulled back and he wiped a tear from her cheek.

"Are you sure?"

He'd never been more sure—certain that the only person

who could have cared for Bodhi and Cadence as much as he did was buried near his parents in that cemetery, and he wanted to pay his respects to the man whose wife and child had given him a summer to be more than just the runaway Bergen heir.

He nodded. "It would be an honor to pay my respects to the kind of man worthy of you and your son."

Camden flicked on the blinker of Cadence's truck then turned onto the road leading up to the cemetery. There were more cars in the parking lot today than when he last visited—which wasn't a big surprise since it was Father's Day—but something else was different.

He was different, and it wasn't just his appearance. He pulled into a parking spot and glanced in the rearview mirror at Bodhi, hugging his Teddy bear to his chest and leaning his head against the window.

For ten long years, he'd only cared for himself. Now, he couldn't sleep at night unless he'd made sure every door to the house he shared with Cadence and Bodhi was locked and secure —just like his father had done when he was growing up.

After Bodhi's near collision with the distracted driver, he'd carried the boy's bike back to the house. They'd set it on the porch, and he'd checked the frame and wheels for damage but only found a few scrapes to the handlebars.

They'd gotten damn lucky that was the only sign of what could have been a tragedy beyond measure.

Cadence had grown quiet, watching him as he went over all the parts of the bike with Bodhi, her hand going to her neck.

She hadn't put on the necklace with her husband's ring since she'd taken it off that first night they'd made love. He hadn't asked about it. It wasn't his place. She'd probably put it back on after he'd left. But after what had transpired on the street—that near miss, when they could have lost Bodhi—the thought of leaving them, of not watching her drift off to sleep in his arms, of not spending his evenings working on the cardboard boat with Bodhi seemed unthinkable.

He'd found his focus, but could he keep it? Could he trust himself to be that kind of man? And did Cadence even want him to stay?

They'd agreed on the summer, and she wasn't the kind of woman to push for more. She'd become a widow in her twenties. She was the sole provider for her son. She knew the hardships life could dole out. But when he held her close, when he was buried deep inside her, when words didn't matter, his heart knew what did.

It was her. It was her son. It was this perfect temporary life they'd created.

Could it be more? Could he come clean with her about Mountain Mac?

"Can I run down the hill, Mommy?" Bodhi asked, cutting into his spiraling thoughts, but Cadence didn't reply.

"Mom, can I take Mr. Cuddles and run over to see Daddy?" the boy tried again.

Cadence blinked as if she were waking from a trance. "Yes, but if you see people slow down. Remember, there are lots of moms and dads buried here, and we need to be respectful of all the people visiting their loved ones."

"Okay, Mom."

The boy took off his seatbelt, scooted off his booster seat, and opened the door. He skipped down the path leading from the parking lot and into the cemetery, dotted with trees and rows of flowers with the curved headstones and grave markers filling the emerald sea of rolling grass.

"Is Bodhi going to be all right on his own?" he asked.

She smiled. "He knows the way to his daddy. But you're right, we better catch up with him."

They got out of the truck and started down the path.

He rested his hand on the small of her back. "Are you all right?"

"I'm still just a little shaken."

He glanced down the path and caught Bodhi jumping over the cracks in the pavement.

"He's safe, Cadence. Just look at him. There's not even a scratch on him."

She stopped but kept her gaze trained on her son. "I keep wondering if that's what it looked like when Aaron was hit. I keep seeing that Jeep drifting, and Bodhi right in its path." She turned to him. "Thank you, Cam."

He tucked a lock of golden hair behind her ear. "Just a day in the life of a Flower Ninja."

She released a sweet chuckle. "I think you mean Flower Fairy and..."

"What?"

She gasped. "I forgot the flowers. They're still in the car."

"Want me to get them?"

She waved him off. "I could use a minute to get myself together. Would you mind catching up to Bodhi?"

He handed her the keys to the truck. "Sure, take your time."

She reached up and cupped his cheek—a sweet, gentle touch so familiar it was like he'd never lived without it. Like they lived in an alternate universe where days equaled years.

She set off back to the car, and he scanned the vast expanse of green and found Bodhi standing not far from where his parents were laid to rest. He'd set Mr. Cuddles on the headstone and gestured wildly with his hands.

Cam grinned, listening as the boy finished singing one of their camp songs then stilled at the mention of his name.

"Camden is my new friend," Bodhi began. "He's the biggest one out of all his brothers, and he taught me how to ride my bike, and he's helping me build my cardboard boat for the big regatta at Smith Lake. He makes Mommy smile, and I wish he didn't have to go back to Switzerland, but Mommy says you keep a little part of everyone you meet in your heart. So, I'll always have a little bit of Cam just like I'll always have a little bit of you, Daddy."

Cam took a step forward and cracked a twig and Bodhi looked over his shoulder then waved him over.

"Cam, this is my dad, Aaron Lowry," he said, taking his hand.

"It's nice to meet you," Camden replied, his voice thick with emotion.

"Where does your dad live?" Bodhi asked.

Cam pointed across the cemetery. "My dad lives here, too. Right over there. See those two big granite stones?"

Bodhi nodded.

"That's where my parents live."

Bodhi looked up at him. "Your mom is here, too?"

"Yeah, she is."

Bodhi scrunched up his face, thinking hard, then gasped. "I know! I could share my mommy with you."

"You'd do that, B?"

Bodhi nodded. "Yeah, you make her laugh a lot, and you're always smiling at her. She's an easy mom to love."

The breath caught in his throat. "She sure is."

Bodhi frowned. "She is going to make you eat vegetables and oatmeal with bananas."

He chuckled. "Do you think carrot cake counts as a vegetable?"

Bodhi leaned into him and sighed. "I already tried that. Mom says no."

He gazed down at the boy with emerald green eyes.

"I'm glad you're here, Cam," the boy said then squeezed his hand.

Three distinct little pumps.

I love you.

"Now, it's your turn," Bodhi said.

He glanced down at the boy's little hand curled around his and knew there wasn't a damn thing he wouldn't do for him. There wasn't a car he wouldn't jump in front of or a boat he wouldn't build.

Gently, he squeezed the boy's hand four times.

I love you, too.

And he did.

"Hey, you two," Cadence said with tears in her eyes.

"I'll do the flowers, Mom."

She handed Bodhi the bouquet of daisies, and the boy set to work arranging them in the vase at the base of the headstone.

He swallowed past the emotion in his throat. "Do you want me to give you a minute alone?"

She shook her head. "Remember, we agreed, this is our time when we don't have to be alone."

She turned to Aaron's headstone. "Hi, babe, I'm sure Bodhi let you in on all the excitement. He's riding his bike without training wheels, and he's still here with me thanks to the angel you sent into our lives." Cadence looked up at him and smiled. "I like to think that Aaron has a hand in all the good things that come our way. Last year, on the anniversary of his death, I went on that mountain biking forum, and that's when I met my friend, Mountain Mac who helped me find the courage to get back on a bike and gave me the strength to help Bodhi learn. And then, he sent us you."

Camden glanced at Bodhi, who'd retrieved Mr. Cuddles and was whooshing him around in the air like the bear could fly then met Cadence's sky-blue gaze.

"You think Aaron sent me?"

She nodded as something sparkled over her shoulder, and he looked on as the rays of golden Colorado sun shined on his parents' headstones. The light splintered off the onyx-colored granite just as it had off the water when he and his father had climbed into his cardboard boat and set off across Smith Lake with his mother cheering and waving to them.

Look at where you want to be. Find that spot and focus on it.

Cadence turned and looked over her shoulder. "Do you want to go visit your parents?"

"I think they know I'm here," he said as the weight of his shame and anguish melted away with each ray of sunlight glinting off the polished surface.

He took Cadence's hands into his. "Do you mind if we take a little detour on the way home?"

"Not at all. What were you thinking?" she asked then called Bodhi over as they started back to the car.

They made it to the parking lot, and he opened the car door for her then helped Bodhi into his booster seat in the back.

"I'd like to go by my house."

"Your house? But you live with us," Bodhi said, hugging Mr. Cuddles.

He ruffled the boy's hair. "I grew up not far from here. I haven't seen it in a long time."

"Does your family still own it," Cadence asked, securing her seatbelt.

He shook his head. "No, they sold it."

He started the truck and pulled out of the parking spot—the wheels in his head turning faster than the vehicle's. They drove in silence down the winding boulevard, past the streets and landmarks he'd never forget when he glanced into the rearview mirror and caught Bodhi, blinking his eyes, fighting to stay awake after the long, action-packed day. He reached over and rested his hand on Cadence's knee, and she set hers on top of his as he navigated the Denver streets.

"Your childhood home was near your grandparents' place?" Cadence asked as he turned onto the boulevard that led to Ray and Harriet's estate.

"Yeah, it wasn't as fancy as my grandparents' place. With three boys born so close together, my mom always said we should live in a barn."

Cadence chuckled. "Oh, I couldn't agree more—and I only have one."

He stopped at the intersection, turned, then slowed as the hazy light diffused by the grand beech trees lining the street led him home.

"That's it. The Tudor style home with the..."

"The one for sale with all the daisies growing next to the porch?" she asked.

"Yeah, that's it."

"It's a beautiful home, Cam."

It was just as he'd remembered. But the daisies. Those were new.

She sighed. "I always pictured Bodhi and I living in a house like this."

He wasn't expecting her to say that.

"What about Glenna and Gertrude's place—the paired homes? You've put so much work into them?"

She sat back and stared at the Tudor. "Those houses were Aaron's dream. Of course, I supported him, and I loved the idea of renovating them—but not alone. Not on my own."

"I can understand that," he answered, and he knew what he wanted to do.

It wouldn't be easy. He could lose her, or he could get everything he never dreamed possible. But he had to try.

"Are we still pretending that Camden is just your neighbor?" Elle asked with a smirk.

Cadence glanced around Ray and Harriet Bergen's backyard. It had been transformed into a summer evening wonderland with a live string quartet, twinkling lights, and tables dotted with votive candles. Wildflower bouquets scented the cool night air as people mingled and danced at Brennen and Abby's joint bachelor and bachelorette party.

"Are you sure that's just sparkling apple juice in your champagne flute?" she asked.

Elle downed the liquid. "Oh yes, because if this is Dom Perignon, then I'm Lady Godiva."

Cadence chuckled, and Elle set her empty juice flute on the table.

"We need to discuss your Man Find," she said, snagging another sparkling apple juice from a passing waiter.

Oh, not this again! She could almost kill Abby for making up those cheeky little monikers. Brennen was Abby's *Man Fast*. Jasper was Elle's *Man Feast*, and whoever Mountain Mac was— Abby had coined him into being her *Man Find*.

Cadence took a sip of champagne. "You mean my online mountain bike friend? The one you're sure is either in jail or living in his mother's basement?"

"Or a secret agent, unable to reveal his true identity," Elle added, her expression growing serious.

Cadence cocked her head to the side, and Elle gave a little frustrated shake of her head.

"Sorry, I shifted gears from travel books and started writing a thriller a few days ago. Blame it on all the pregnancy hormones. So, bear with the drama. And no, I'm not referring to your internet pen pal. I'm talking about my brother-in-law. You seem to have *found* yourself living next door to quite a *find*. He cleans up quite nicely," she added with that perfect Elle Reynolds-Bergen smirk back in place.

"What would make you think there's something going on?" Cadence asked, stealing a glance at Camden, who looked like a mountain of yummy wrapped in a suit.

But something was going on, and it wasn't the *something* Elle was referring to.

After Bodhi's close call with the distracted driver and their visit to Aaron's grave, Camden had started acting differently. It wasn't like he ignored them. Besides the few times he'd borrowed her truck to run to the store, the only time she wasn't with him was that first hour of the day when she'd wake with a daisy on her pillow.

Bodhi's Daisy Fairy.

Her literal live-in sex god.

But something was different. He'd checked in with Carrie everyday at camp, confirming she could still babysit for Bodhi so they could attend the party and had even gone as far as checking with Carrie's camp counterpart, Luke, to see if he could be their backup sitter in case Carrie couldn't watch Bodhi at the last minute. At first, it was sweet. But by Thursday, she'd asked if he had something up his sleeve.

And what had he done? He'd gone all Bergen bobblehead, shaking his head when she'd asked if he was up to something.

And then there was the texting and the furtive phone calls. Unlike ninety-nine percent of the civilized world, Camden Bergen had hardly glanced at his phone for the first two weeks she'd known him—until this week.

Elle gripped her forearm. "Scrub the Man Find intel," she said under her breath. "Bergen One and Bergen Three are at ten o'clock, and they're coming in hot."

Cadence glanced up to see Cam and Jasper headed their way and laughed. "Will you be talking like a secret agent all night, Elle?"

Elle pinched the bridge of her nose. "Damn! Am I doing it again? It's all the research seeping out into my real life. Last night, I found an old grocery list I'd written and set it on fire in the sink to destroy the evidence. Jasper thought I'd lost my mind."

"Speaking of losing your mind," Jasper said, then pressed a kiss to Elle's cheek. "I've checked the perimeter, per your request, and haven't identified any foreign operatives infiltrating the party."

Elle gestured with her chin, not so subtly, toward the cake table. "What about the French pastry chef? He was all sweaty and jittery when he arrived. What's he supposed to be doing?"

Jasper bit back a grin. "One, he brought the cake. And two, I think he's just afraid of Cam."

Camden blew out a tight breath. "I tried to apologize to the guy. I feel terrible about ruining his cake."

"Pierre gets a little edgy anytime he sees Cam walk by," Jasper added with a bemused smirk that matched Elle's.

"Edgy?" Camden echoed. "More like borderline homicidal.

The guy throws out his arms in front of the cake like I'm about to hurl myself at it every time I walk by. I hope he's not making the wedding cake, too."

Elle shook her head. "I don't think so. Abby and Bren are having the wedding cake flown in from some bakery in Kansas City."

Jasper nodded. "Yes, Brennen is friends with the chef who flew out to cook for us tonight. They met at the Aspen Food and Wine Festival a few years ago. His wife is quite an accomplished baker, and she'll be making the cake."

"Is it the same bakery that makes the strudel Harriet had for us when we were up at Bergen Mountain back in March?" Cadence asked.

"I believe it is. But I didn't come over to talk pastries," Jasper answered, pinning her with that Bergen steel-blue gaze.

"Oh! Is everything all right?"

Jasper had loosened up quite a bit since he and Elle had gotten together, but he was still the intense alpha CEO when he wanted to be.

"It's more than okay. I've had the Mountain Education Department share the changes and tweaks you've made along with the different teaching techniques Cam's introduced to the other Bergen Adventure Summer Camps in the metro area, and we're seeing great results. Increased time spent on the activities with less time spent corralling children and transitioning from activity to activity. Behavioral concerns have dipped, and parent surveys report a satisfaction bump up from seventy-five to ninety percent."

"Full stop!" Elle said, raising her hands. "Mr. Hollow Bunny, where are we?"

Jasper's CEO demeanor dissolved. "Is this a trick question?"

Elle exchanged a look with her husband. "No."

"We're at Bren and Abby's party," he answered slowly.

"Right! Party. Not boardroom. And you were just about to ask me to dance, right?" she said, grinning up at the oldest Bergen brother.

Jasper nodded with a sweet, barely-there blush to his cheeks. "Cadence, would it be all right if we talked next week?" He glanced at Elle. "During business hours. I've got something I'd like to discuss with you, but right now, I'm going to dance with my wife."

"That works for me," she answered as Jasper took Elle's hand and led her to the dance floor.

"My brothers are really happy," Cam said, standing just close enough that his arm grazed hers.

She glanced over at Abby, and found her friend smiling ear to ear on Brennen's lap, fork in hand and feeding him a bite of cake. Then out of the corner of her eye, she caught Jasper reach down and press his hand to Elle's pregnant belly.

"They've each found their person," she said and swayed to the music.

"You're right, they have," he replied, then took her hand. "Cadence?"

"Yes."

"I have a question for you."

"What is it?" she asked as her pulse kicked up.

"Do you think the most beautiful woman here would dance with me?"

She released a slow breath. What was she expecting? A proposal? A declaration of devotion?

She glanced around. "Where is she? I'll go ask her for you."

His expression grew serious. "You know I mean you. Of course, it's you. You're smart, gorgeous, and kind and—"

"And I didn't think you danced?" she said, needing to stop him—and more than that—needing to stop herself from thinking this was more than just a summer fling.

"What do you think I did for all those years by myself in a cabin tucked away in the Swiss Alps?"

She tried to keep a straight face but couldn't hold back a giggle.

Camden raised an eyebrow. "I see where your mind went, you naughty girl."

She laced her fingers with his. "Are you telling me instead of doing...that, you were ballroom dancing?"

"And basket weaving, crocheting, and ice sculpting," he answered with the sweetest smile, and the whole world just stopped.

What was she going to do when he left?

She was so sure of what her life was supposed to look like after Aaron's death—so sure of her priorities. But now, she couldn't imagine a night falling asleep alone in bed. She'd grown used to his arms wrapped around her and the rise and fall of his chest, slow and steady, pressed against her as he held her close as she murmured *sweetest dreams* to the man who occupied hers.

And then there was her son.

She'd heard Bodhi tell Cam he'd always keep a piece of him in his heart. She saw them do the secret *I love you* handshake.

What would they do when Cam's place turned back into Glenna's unit?

"Hey?" he said and ran his hand down her arm. "Where did you go?"

She blinked back tears. This was not the night for crying. That night would come soon enough.

She swallowed past the lump in her throat. "I'd love to dance."

"Good, because I wasn't going to take no for an answer," he said then led her to the dance floor and pulled her in close.

"Cadence, I..." he began but trailed off.

"What is it?"

"After the party, I'd like to take you somewhere. I have something important I need to tell you."

She stilled. "Are you not staying for the entire summer? Are you going back to Switzerland early?"

That had to be it.

"It's not that simple," he answered, then glanced at his watch.

His father's Patek Philippe watch.

She took in a sharp breath. Was it all too much for him? Had whatever that had driven him away after his parents' death become too much to bear?

Everything seemed perfect. No, more than perfect. Life felt right—as if by finding each other, they'd found a path to something real—even if it was only temporary.

"It's very simple, Cam. You're either staying, or you're leaving."

He'd gone pale and his throat constricted as he swallowed hard. "It's complicated. That's why I wanted some time alone with you."

She parted her lips to speak but got cut off as the crisp sound of a champagne flute being tapped with a knife cut through the night air, and the music stopped.

"Good evening, everyone," Brennen said, addressing the crowd from the elevated stage next to the quartet with Abby by his side. "Abby and I wanted to take a moment to thank all of you for coming to our joint bachelor and bachelorette party."

"And a special thanks to our hosts, Harriet and Ray Bergen. This night couldn't be more perfect," Abby added as Harriet and Ray raised their glasses to them.

"Welcome to the family, darling," Harriet added.

Abby wiped a tear from her cheek. "And a special thanks to my bridesmaids, Elle Reynolds-Bergen and Cadence Lowry.

The three of us made the lovely garland," Abby added with a teary chuckle. "But these women are much more to me than bridesmaids. Elle is family and so are you Cadence. You were my first friend in Denver, and I will never forget your kindness."

Cadence smiled up at her friend and did her best to rein in her emotions. Yes, she was over the moon for Abby and Brennen, but they had forever. She thought she had the summer, but Cam's expression seemed to say that might be over.

"And I wanted to say a few words about my groomsmen who also happen to be my brothers," Brennen continued. "Jas, you have always been the dependable one. The consummate older brother. You've always looked out for me—even when I was at my worst. I'm so grateful and so honored to have you as my best man."

Jasper wrapped his arm around Elle and nodded to his brother.

"And Cam," Brennen said, turning to face his younger brother. "I'm so glad you're here. It wouldn't be complete without you because you're the Bergen brother who found the beauty in everything—especially nature. You were always happier outside as a kid. Hiking, biking, climbing, skiing—if it was something that could keep you outdoors, you were there, taking it all in and helping everyone around you see the beauty in it. And do you remember what you called yourself?"

Camden raised his hands. "Wait, Bren. Don't..." but Brennen kept going.

"When Cam was little, he used to write the letters in his name backward. So, instead of Cam, *C, A, M,* he became Mac, *M, A, C.* And because he loved the mountains, my mom and dad used to call him Mountain Mac. You were only four or five. Do you remember, Cam?"

Mountain Mac was Camden?

Cadence glanced at Abby, whose jaw had dropped and then to Elle who looked just as shocked.

"Cadence..." Cam began, but she shook her head and waved him off, and like a key sliding into a lock, each groove working itself perfectly into place, all the tiny missteps made sense.

His reaction to her bike.

The times he called her Daisy.

The slips when he'd acted like they'd met before. Because they had. Because he'd been the person on the other side of the screen all those nights.

And he hadn't told her. He hadn't said one single word. And that had to be because...

Because he didn't want her to know.

She searched for the nearest exit then saw the gate leading from the backyard into the gardens.

"I need to go," she whispered, then turned and started running.

Her breaths came fast as she navigated the dirt path, pushing leaves out of the way until she made it to the main walkway. The place was empty—which was strange for a Friday night. There were summer concerts and weddings here all the time. It wasn't even nine o'clock—the time the gardens closed even without an evening event.

Maybe they'd closed early, and in that case, she was breaking in. Or was she, since she used the Bergen private entrance?

"Who cares!" she whispered through tears, walking down the path and deeper into the gardens as the pound of footsteps closed in behind her.

"Cadence, please, let me explain!" Camden called.

She shook her head, taking a page from his playbook.

"Cadence!" he bit out in a tight breath.

She stopped and turned to face him. "You mean Daisy? You mean Mountain Daisy?"

He scrubbed his hand down his face. "I didn't want you to find out like this. I didn't even remember how I'd come up with Mountain Mac until Bren started talking."

She steadied herself. "When did you know?"

"Know what?"

She lifted her chin. "That I was Mountain Daisy. And how did you know where to find me? I never gave Mac any personal information other than that I lived in Colorado."

He dropped his chin to his chest. "You sent a picture."

"But I wasn't in it. It was only..."

Only her handlebars with the Smith Lake trail in the background.

She gasped. "You've known I was Daisy from the first night, haven't you?"

He nodded.

She took a step back, remembering. "And I even messaged Mac that night. You said, Mac said, whoever you are said that you had some personal stuff going on."

"I didn't lie. That was true."

"You didn't lie?" she shot back. "Don't you see what this means? I haven't lost just you, Cam. I've lost Mac, too."

He moved toward her. "You haven't lost me. I came to Denver to find you. I'm not here for Bren and Abby's wedding. That was just...just a lucky coincidence. I came for you. I thought if I found you and you didn't know me as Camden Bergen, the damned runaway Bergen heir, then maybe we could have a life together."

She turned away, but he kept going.

"I know it sounds crazy, Cadence. But I knew from the picture you sent that you lived close to Baxter Park. So, I decided to come home and give myself the summer to find you. I planned on hanging around the park and looking for any bike with daisy stickers with the initials carved into your handlebars."

"*C* and *B*," she said softly.

He took another tentative step toward her. "I saw that in the photo, and the first thing I thought was that those were my initials. I thought it was a sign we were meant to be together. I hadn't strayed twenty miles from my cabin in Switzerland in ten years, but after I saw the *C* and *B*, I booked a flight home."

She brushed the tears away with the back of her hand. "So, your plan was to fly across the ocean to find Mountain Daisy and then try to make a life with her without disclosing who you were?"

He released a pained sigh. "I wanted to try to make a life with someone I cared for deeply without all the damn Bergen baggage."

"But once you found me—once you knew it was me—why didn't you say something? Did you decide I wasn't enough? I wasn't what you wanted?"

"You are everything I want," he said, anguish lacing each word.

She pinned him with her gaze. "Then, what? Why spend these weeks with me and say nothing?"

"Because my whole plan went to shit thirty minutes after I landed in Denver. I didn't even want my family to know I was back. But my cab driver figured out who I was and started snapping pictures of me and threatening to sell them. I couldn't do that to my grandparents. I couldn't let them find out I was back on some crap, quasi-celebrity website. And then, when I learned you were Mountain Daisy, it turns out one of your best friends is married to my oldest brother, and your other best friend is engaged to marry my other brother."

She threw up her hands. "So, you don't want me because I know your family?"

He ran his hands through his hair, pulling at the dark locks. "It's not just that."

She stared into his eyes and saw heartbreaking pain, and that's when it hit her.

"Bodhi," she said in a tight sob. "But I thought you..."

He closed the distance between them and cupped her face in his trembling hands. "I didn't think I could do it, Cadence. I didn't think I could trust myself to keep him safe," he whispered.

She shook her head and stepped back. "I never asked you to keep him safe. I never insinuated that I wanted you to act like a father to him."

"I know! I know! Just listen. I love Bodhi. I'd do anything for him. I was about to tell you I was Mountain Mac the morning after I got into town, but then Bodhi got dropped off, and I learned you had a son—"

Heat rose to her cheeks as anger edged out her shock. "And what? We seemed like too much of a responsibility? Too much of a burden?"

"Don't you see?" He bit out on a pained breath. "I thought I was the burden. I didn't trust myself. I could barely live with myself as it was. I don't know what the hell I'd do if my actions hurt a child—especially Daisy's child. Your child."

"Why would your actions hurt Bodhi?"

The sounds of the city at night wrapped them in a blanket of white noise as he crossed his arms and stared up at the starry sky.

"Because I killed my parents and then I ran."

Camden leaned over and braced his hands on his thighs. He'd never said it. He'd never spoken the words.

But there they were—nearly tangible. Once only the sound-track in his mind. Now spoken, the echo of his admission was everywhere.

The night air grew heavy, and Cadence shook her head as if that would change what he'd just said. But no amount of denial could alter the events of the night his parents died.

He hadn't planned on telling her this—on revealing the darkest part of himself. Especially tonight. Especially with what he'd hoped to accomplish.

Her heated expression transformed into one of confusion. "Your parents died in a car accident, Cam. Everyone knows that."

He shook his head. There was no sense in holding back now.

"Everyone thinks they know what happened to Griffin and Hannah Bergen, but that's only one part of the story. The cause of the accident—that's what the public doesn't know."

She took a step toward him. "It was dark, and the roads were icy. It was an accident. It was all over the news, Cam."

"It wasn't an accident, Cadence."

She reached out and squeezed his hand. "Then tell me what could be so bad that you left for a decade? What could make you think you were responsible for their deaths?"

He looked down at their hands and tightened his grip. "I was the one driving."

She gasped. "How did you not get hurt?"

He shook his head. "I wasn't driving the car my parents were in. I was driving the car that was in front of them."

"Another car?" she whispered.

This is what his family had kept from the public. This dark secret he'd carried all these years.

"It was after Brennen won big at the Winter X Games. Bren, Jas, and I were all in our Escalade. My mom and dad were following behind."

She frowned. "I still don't understand. How could you have had any control over your parents' car?"

The muscles in his chest tightened as the memories of that night came rushing back. The screeching tires. The acrid smell of burning rubber. The warped guardrail and the lights shining up from his parents' upturned sedan.

He shook his head, not sure where to start.

"You do not get to go bobblehead on me, Camden Bergen. Not now," she said, leading him to a bench.

He sat next to her, swallowed past the lump in his throat, then dropped his chin to his chest. He'd thought about that night at least a million times—maybe more. It was never far from his thoughts. But he'd never spoken the words. He'd never told his story.

Cadence cupped his cheek and gently tilted his head.

"One, two, three. Eyes on me," she whispered with a tender smile.

He held her gaze. She was the light that pulled him out of

the darkness when he'd met her as Mountain Daisy months ago. And now as Cadence Lowry, she wouldn't allow him to fall back into his self-imposed prison of emptiness and solitude.

He lifted her hand from his face and kissed her palm as a weight lifted. Whatever transpired after he spoke, whatever she thought or said—at least, she'd know everything. And until this moment, he hadn't realized how much he needed her to know.

Whatever the risk, he had to confess.

He released a slow breath. "On the drive back to Bergen Mountain, Jas, Bren, and I were messing around, laughing and talking. All of us amped up with Bren's win. The competition wasn't at Bergen Mountain that year. It was over at a resort in Vail, and we decided not to spend the night there because we all wanted to get back to the cottage to celebrate. It wasn't like I didn't know the roads. I know the mountains like the back of my hand, but I wasn't paying attention. One minute, the only thing cutting through the darkness were the car's headlights. I looked away for a second—just a second. I don't even remember what Bren said, but we were laughing. We were so damn happy, and then I glanced back at the road and saw it."

"What was it?"

A sad smile pulled at the corners of his mouth. "A deer. Just a deer. It was like she came out of nowhere. I slammed on the brakes, and she skittered off the road but not before..."

"Before your parents' car swerved and jumped the guardrail," Cadence offered, filling in the blank.

He nodded. "Yeah, my dad swerved so he wouldn't hit us."

She studied him, and all he wanted was for her to say something. Yell at him. Tell him he was a disgrace. He started to speak, to plead with her to tell him to go to hell, but she pressed her fingertips to his lips and silenced him.

"Listen to me, Camden. That's still an accident. I'm not saying it's not awful or heartbreaking, but I'm from Colorado, and you and I both know that accidents involving wildlife happen all the time. Even if Bren and Jas weren't with you in the car, that deer could have caught you off guard."

He knew that. He did. It was what happened next that sent a jagged jolt of shame through his heart. But there was no going back. He had to tell her everything.

He steadied himself. "But you see, I ran."

"From the accident?" she pressed.

He nodded. "It was like everything unfolded in slow motion. Jas jumped the guardrail and made his way down to my parents' car. It was stuck about fifty feet down on the side of the cliff. He was on ski patrol and had EMT training, and I'm sure he tried to save them. But when he climbed back up to the road, I knew they were dead by the look on his face, and then, I ran."

"Where did you go?"

A shiver passed through him as he remembered the cold night air and his brothers' frantic voices.

"At first, I thought if I didn't see them, if I wasn't absolutely sure my parents were gone, then maybe it would all disappear, like some kind of reset. I ran for hours and ended up at the cabin we have on a desolate patch of land. I'd gone there earlier in the week with my grandfather to see it after he'd purchased it. Somewhere in my mind, I must have known we weren't far from it. And then I stayed there. I thought, if I disappeared then it couldn't have happened. I couldn't have caused something so devastating."

Cadence laced her fingers with his. "How'd they find you? I remember seeing the pictures in the newspaper of you and your brothers at the funeral. I saw you on TV, too. Your parents' death made the local, national, and even the world news."

Those first days had blended together in one long, painful loop of numbness, shame, and utter disbelief. His parents had been larger than life. A power couple, attending galas, raising money for charities, and spearheading the Bergen Mountain Sports summer and winter education curriculums. It hadn't seemed possible anything could halt two lives that had shined so brightly.

He shrugged. "They knew where I was the whole time. I had GPS tracking on my phone. I used to do a lot of backcountry skiing with my brothers. My mom and my grandmother insisted we all have it on our phones. They used it to find me, and they brought me back in time for the memorial service. Then I went right from the funeral to the airport and flew to Switzerland."

She nodded, and he watched her, waiting for revulsion or hate or disappointment to color her expression. But all he saw in her eyes was compassion.

"I don't blame you for running, Cam."

"But it was weak. It was wrong."

She shook her head. "I didn't even know your parents, but I still cried when I heard the news of their deaths. Your family has always been like Colorado royalty, and everyone—even people like me who only read about them in the paper and saw them on TV—could tell they were kind people. They cared about the community. They championed more charities than I can count. But anyone could see that they cared the most for you and your brothers. A bond like that is rare. You loved your parents, and you couldn't imagine a world without them. I would have run, too."

A muscle twitched in his jaw. "But your husband died. He was killed, and you didn't run away from the world."

She blinked back tears. "I wanted to. I wanted what you wanted. I wanted it all to be some terrible dream."

"I should have stayed," he said in a tight breath.

"Even if you had stayed, it wouldn't have changed the fact that your parents were gone."

He stared into the darkness. "You don't think I'm a monster?"

There. He'd said it. The fear that had loomed in his mind for a decade.

Was he a monster? Was that the extent of his character?

"Camden, look at me."

He did as she asked.

She lifted her chin. "You are no monster. You're a man who would move heaven and earth to protect me—and my son. Cam, what happened was an accident. It's time you stopped blaming yourself and started living the kind of life you know your parents would want for you. You're not meant to be hidden away like a recluse. You're good with kids. You're a good teacher. Look what we've done with the summer program in only a few weeks. And you're just as much a Bergen as your brothers, and you have just as much to give."

"Do you really believe all that?"

"Do you think I'd lie to you?"

"No," he answered.

She held his gaze, unwavering. "Can I ask you something?"

"Anything."

"I always wondered why you chose to go to Switzerland?"

He glanced down at his watch. The Swiss-made Patek Philippe his dad had left him. "At the time, I just knew I had to leave. I didn't trust myself around anyone. And then I remembered my dad and I had found this cabin in the Alps on our last trip there when we'd picked up his watch—this watch—when we were scouting out locations for another Bergen resort. The place was pretty remote, and my dad said it looked like a cabin for somebody who wanted to forget. We didn't end up buying the property, and when I got there after the funeral and found I could rent it, I knew my dad was right. It was a place to forget. And all I wanted to do was forget who I was, where I came from, and what I'd done."

"But you came back, Cam. You came home to find me."

He tucked a lock of hair behind her ear. "Mountain Daisy made me feel like a person again—like someone out there needed me. I hadn't smiled in years until I saw your post warning D-canoes not to reply."

She chuckled then brushed a tear from her cheek. "I wrote that post on the anniversary of Aaron's death. Bodhi wanted to ride a bike like all the kids at school, and I knew I'd need to find the strength to not only teach him but to stop feeling so afraid. It wasn't like I couldn't figure it out for myself, but that day, I was going through a box and found a pair of Aaron's jeans mixed in with my things. I thought I'd donated all his old clothes, but there they were, nestled in with mine. I don't know why, but I checked the pockets. I'd found a piece of paper where he'd jotted down the mountain bike forum's website. It's almost like he was leading me to you. Like he knew you could be there for me when he couldn't."

He cupped her face and ran his thumb across her trembling lips. "The day I got back to Denver, I went to the cemetery and asked my parents to help me find you."

"And then you crashed into the cake party." Her eyes shining, she smiled up at him. "I think something bigger than us wanted us to meet."

"I believe that with my whole heart," he answered.

"And I believe in you, Cam. What happened with your parents—it was an accident, and I'm certain that if they were here today, they'd tell you the same thing. You're a good man. You've saved my son twice, and you saved me once."

"From the squirrels," he said with a little laugh.

"Even if it were a lion, you still would have charged through my door to protect me. You have a good heart. I hear you at night, locking the doors and looking in on Bodhi. You deserve to be happy. Whatever you think about yourself, I can tell you this for sure. You are worthy of your family and of the Bergen name.

You might have run away, but you came back, and you were here when I needed you."

He studied her beautiful face, bathed in moonlight. Cadence's face. Mountain Daisy's face. And all the things he'd thought that had prevented him from being with her—his past, her connection to his family, and her son—had turned out to be the gateway back to his life. She, with her glass daisy doorknobs, opened the door to his heart and allowed a tidal wave of love to wash away the shame and regret he'd carried all these years.

"Cadence, do you remember what you'd always write to me before you fell asleep?"

"Of course, I do," she whispered, her voice as soft as spring rain.

"Will you say it?"

She smiled at him through her tears. "Sweetest dreams, Mountain Mac."

He rested his forehead against hers. "Do you know how long I've dreamed to hear you say that?" He pulled back a fraction. "Cadence Daisy Lowry, I have loved you since the first night when you typed those four words."

"You have?"

"Yes. I found you, and from that moment on, everything changed."

"It looks like my *Man Find* finally found me," she said with a teary chuckle.

"Your *Man Find*?" he asked.

"Abby called Mountain Mac my *Man Find*. She'd say that I'd *found* someone who made me happy I just couldn't *find* him. She and Elle would tease me because I'd always grin like a schoolgirl when I read your messages. Elle said I'd go all googly-eyed when I looked at my phone like I was in love."

"Were you in love with Mountain Mac?" he asked.

His chest tightened. Even though she knew he was Mac,

she'd still lost the safety of confiding in her anonymous friend on the other side of the screen.

"I *am* in love with Mountain Mac," she answered, her tone resolute.

"And what about Camden Bergen?"

Her eyes sparkled with tears. "I love him, too."

There are moments in life so poignant they etch themselves into your soul. He'd kissed Cadence Lowry as Camden Bergen, but there was always that nagging voice, that slippery reminder that he'd been keeping a secret. As strange as it sounds, he'd held back kissing her as Mac. But there was nothing between them now. No fear of screwing up and giving away his identity. No worry she'd see him as only the runaway Bergen heir. And no judgment after he'd confessed his worst sin.

She leaned in, her lips a breath away from his. "I think we could use a little *redirection*."

Heat surged through his veins. "What were you thinking?"

"I think Mountain Mac should finally kiss Mountain Daisy."

And there she was, giving him exactly what he needed.

"How's this for redirection? I want to pull you onto my lap and kiss you. I want to kiss you for every time I couldn't kiss you as Mac. I want to kiss you for every night I imagined making love to you when you were two thousand miles away. I want to feel every inch of your perfect ass, and I sure as hell want to see whatever sexy panties you've got on." He paused and remembered what was in his pocket. "But there's something I need to show you first."

He stood and helped her up, then led her down a winding path, deeper into the gardens. They walked in silence until a rustling caught her attention, and she froze.

"What's that?"

He wrapped his arm around her. "It's probably security."

But it wasn't. And with a leafy crash, a pair of squirrels leaped from one dark tree branch to another.

"Squirrels," she said with a relieved sigh.

"Do they follow you everywhere you go?" he teased.

She leaned against him and shook her head. "I never thought of myself as a squirrel magnet. But they did bring a half-naked burly mountain man charging into my house."

"Don't kill the squirrels," he murmured.

"What was that?"

"It was my mantra that first night, when all I wanted to do was wrap my arms around you and never let go."

"I felt it, too—that connection. It was there from the moment I saw you. Do you think, even if there was no Mac or Daisy and if we had never met on that chat forum—do you think we would have found each other?"

He thought of the sun glinting off his parents' headstones. The bright light that echoed his father's words and showed him the way home.

Look at where you want to be. Find that spot and focus on it.

"I do," he answered.

She smiled up at him then glanced around the darkened path as another round of rustling came from the foliage a few yards down the walkway.

She frowned. "We should go. I think we're trespassing."

"We're not. I promise."

She stood in front of him, then glanced from side to side. "Cam, the gardens are closed. Your grandparents have their own private entrance, but I still don't think we should be here."

He couldn't hold back his smile. Even though his brother had outed him as Mac, he'd planned on telling her about his secret identity tonight. He hadn't planned on telling her about his parents—about his role in their death. But now that she knew, now that she'd listened to his story and still loved him, still gazed up at him with such trust in her eyes, what was about to happen, what he hoped would happen next, carried even more significance.

The woman he loved knew every dark part of him and still saw his light. Mountain Mac or Camden Bergen, it didn't matter. She loved them both.

He took her hand and pressed a kiss to her knuckles. "We're the only people who should be here."

She cocked her head to the side. "What does that mean?"

"Remember when I told you that there was somewhere I wanted to take you after the party?"

"Yes."

"We're here. I rented out the gardens for the evening."

"You rented it?" she asked with a hint of skepticism.

"Yeah."

"All the gardens?"

"Yeah."

"The entire place?"

"Every square inch."

She frowned. "Doesn't that cost a fortune?"

He bit back another grin. "I'm sort of worth a fortune."

Her eyes went wide. "But I didn't think you wanted any part of that. You barely accepted the watch your father left you."

He took her into his arms. "Cadence, you've helped me see who I am. You've helped me realize where I need to be in this world."

"And where is that?" she whispered.

"It's here, with you and Bodhi." He leaned in to kiss her when a sharp, quick whistle pulled them apart.

"Psst! Mr. Bergen, is that the sign?"

Cadence gasped. "Who's that?" she asked, staring down the dark path.

"It's just me...Calvin," came a whisper-shout from the bushes.

Cadence's jaw dropped. "Who the heck is Calvin?"

Camden shook his head. Jesus! He'd forgotten all about Calvin!

"When I rented the gardens, I asked if they had someone who could turn on the lights when we got to the spot."

"Yeah, I volunteered," came the voice from the bushes.

"Calvin is one of the security guards here. The same one who chased me through the gardens when I crashed the cake tasting party."

"Has he been here all night?" she asked.

"Only for like ninety minutes," Calvin answered.

"Ninety minutes!" Cadence exclaimed.

"It's not a big deal, miss. I've been listening to the game on my phone. Lucky for you, I just saw you pass by."

Sweet baby Jesus! This was not the way he'd expected this part of the evening to go.

"Calvin, if you don't mind," he said.

"Oh sorry," the man replied as the click of a switch cut through the air and all the trees in the outdoor courtyard lit up with twinkling white lights.

Cadence gasped. "It's—"

"Should I stick around, Mr. Bergen? The Rockies are up by two, and I'd really like to watch the end of the baseball game in the security office if you don't need anything."

Cam turned toward the bushes. "We're fine, Calvin. Enjoy the game. We'll take it from here."

He listened as the sound of footsteps disappeared into the night then turned toward the lights and froze. Cadence stood in a small courtyard, bathed in the twinkling light and surrounded by white and yellow daisies.

"Cam," she breathed. "You did all this?"

He joined her in the center of the space. When he'd come to the garden's events manager earlier in the week and told them he wanted to fill one of the garden's intimate courtyards with daisies, he had no idea they'd create such a magical place.

"This is where I wanted to tell you I was Mac. After we visited the cemetery on Father's Day, it all became clear to me. I belong here. I belong with you and Bodhi. I can honor the memory of my parents and the memory of your husband by spending the rest of my life loving and protecting you and your son. That is, if you'll have me."

She touched the delicate petals of one of the daisies. "This was only supposed to be for the summer."

"I know," he answered, his heart in his throat.

She looked up. "But it's turned out to be much more."

Relief washed over him. "I want forever with you and Bodhi. I want to put down my own roots here. Our roots. I don't want to sleep on the other side of the wall anymore. I want you in my arms every night all night." Surrounded by daisies, he took a knee in front of her, pulled a small box from his pocket, and opened the lid. "Mountain Daisy, will you marry me?"

"Oh, Cam, I never imagined I could be this happy. I didn't expect to ever love again. I thought life had already given me that gift, but I believe with all my heart that Aaron wants this for me and for Bodhi. I believe he chose you—and I choose you, too." She reached for his hand and squeezed it three times.

I love you.

He replied with four gentle pumps.

I love you, too.

"Is that a yes?" he asked.

"Yes," she whispered with tears in her eyes.

He removed the ring from the box and slid it on her finger.

She stared at the large center diamond surrounded by six smaller stones. "It's a flower."

"It's a daisy," he answered. "You'll always be my Daisy."

"Always," she answered.

In the space of a breath, he stood and gathered her into his embrace. She wrapped her arms around his neck and tilted her head up. He leaned in, his lips millimeters from hers.

"Kiss me, Mac," she whispered.

He closed his eyes as she said the words he'd longed to hear and pressed his lips to hers. She hummed a sigh, a sound so sweet yet so sexy, it sent a hot bolt of lust tearing through him. She parted her lips, and he deepened the kiss. Mac or Cam, it didn't matter. He was both men to her, and he kissed her with a heated ferocity as she weaved her fingers in the hair at the nape of his neck.

He slid his hands down her back, palmed the globes of her ass, then stilled.

She smiled against his lips. "Remember how you said you wanted to find out which pair of panties I was wearing tonight?"

"Yes."

"I hate to disappoint you, but with this sheer dress, I'm not wearing any."

"I don't think there's a man on the planet who could be disappointed with that statement."

She giggled then gasped when he lifted her into his arms. She wrapped her legs around his waist, and the hem of her dress rode up her smooth thighs. Their mouths locked in a feverish kiss as he carried her past the rows of daisies and into a hidden alcove.

Lit only by the twinkling lights diffused by a curtain of aspen leaves, he lowered himself to a bench tucked away beneath the trees.

"You've felt like mine from the minute I saw you. It had to be you, Cadence. My heart knew it had to be you."

She cupped his face in her hands and the rush of having the

woman he loved in his arms intertwined with the dizzying prospect of a real life not clouded by a veil of guilt but the warm embrace of infinite possibilities. To be a husband. To be a father. To be a part of the business his parents and grandparents had built.

With Cadence by his side, he could do anything. Be anything. Be the man Aaron and his parents needed him to be.

Earlier in the week, he'd visited an antique shop, hoping to find one of her daisy doorknobs only to find a different daisy. A vintage diamond ring in the shape of the flower that had brought them together. And he knew. He just knew that was the ring Cadence would wear every day for the rest of her life.

He gripped her bare ass as she arched against him, her skirt riding up her thighs another few inches as carnal desire took over. She reached between them and undid his belt. His hard length strained against his pants as she unbuttoned his trousers then unzipped them.

He slid his hand between her thighs and found her hot and wet—her body responding to his touch, his kiss.

"I'm going to worship your body every day," he bit out, his breaths growing heated.

"Show me," she answered.

He shifted beneath her, lowering his pants just enough to allow his cock to come free of the confines of his clothing. She lifted her hips and positioned him at her entrance.

"I found you, Cadence, and I will never let you go."

"My *Man Find* is all mine," she whispered and lowered herself onto his hard length.

"All yours," he repeated, weaving his hand into her hair before sucking in a tight breath.

Then, the time for talking was over.

He thrust his hips and guided her up and down in delicious, fluid strokes. She met his body, matching his rhythm as she rode his cock, grinding against him. With a breathy gasp, she leaned forward and held onto the back of the bench, changing the angle of penetration as she rolled her hips, taking every hard inch of his cock.

He wanted all of her. Everything. He wanted to ravage her body and own her pleasure. He growled into her ear then kissed a trail down her jawline, tightening his grip on her ass and dialing up their frenzied pace. The friction between them intensified. Joined together, they became one in a sea of passion, writhing, pumping, and grinding.

She tightened around him, and he held her close, maintaining their rhythm and reveling in her release, until he couldn't hold back any longer. He followed her over the edge. Wave after wave of pleasure crashed over them. Mac and Daisy. Cadence and Camden. Every part of them now exposed and raw —their lovemaking a symbol of the two separate worlds coming together.

"Cam," she moaned as he worked her body, lengthening their release.

She was his everything, and life began anew with her. Right there. Right now.

He held her close as she caught her breath and rested her head on his shoulder.

"I'm glad you're Mac. In my heart, I wanted you to be him. I wanted to have you both, and now I do."

He took her hand and kissed the daisy diamonds. "You always will. You're all I've ever wanted."

She stared down at the ring. "Do you know how excited Bodhi's going to be? He's crazy about you."

"I'm a lucky man. I get the girl of my dreams and the greatest kid I've ever met." He cupped her face in his hand, and she leaned in to kiss him when a woman's voice carried through the night air.

"We've waited long enough. I'm ready to kick that Bergen bobblehead right in the balls!"

Cadence gasped. "That's Elle."

"She's…"

"Intense, but she's got a heart of gold and would do anything for the people she loves," Cadence added with a sweet twist to her lips.

He cringed, remembering their walk around the lake. "I'm not sure she loves me yet."

"She will. She finally came around and warmed up to Brennen. He's changed his ways but, he used to be quite a player. That has to say something."

Cam chuckled then stilled.

"Holy flip! Look at this place!"

"Speak of the devil," he whispered, still not used to his brother's PG vernacular.

"They came looking for us," Cadence whispered.

He hadn't told a soul what he was up to—which, in retrospect—was probably a shit idea.

She raised up, and he helped her off his lap. They adjusted their clothes, buttoning and smoothing, as a surprised chorus of oohs and aahs filled the air.

"I think they found the daisy courtyard," he said, smoothing a lock of her hair.

"How do I look?" she asked.

With her mussed hair and wrinkled dress, she'd never looked more beautiful to him.

"You look perfect."

She glanced down at her now very wrinkled dress. "You may be a little biased," she answered with a chuckle.

"Cadence! Camden! Are you guys here?"

"That's Abby," Cadence whispered. "I think everyone is out there."

"We'll be fine as long as my—"

"Camden, darling! Cadence, dear!"

Oh, for Christ's sake! His grandmother—and most likely his grandad—were there, too.

Cadence's jaw dropped. "I can't see your grandparents like this. We just..." She gestured to the bench. "And I'm all..." She waved her hands around her body.

"We'll just walk out like we were chatting back here. No one will think anything of it," he offered.

"Chatting?" she said and raised her left hand.

Yep, that might get their attention.

He squeezed her hand. "Chatting and deciding to get married. People do it every day."

She glanced down at his pants. "Okay, but you should probably zip your fly first," she said with a wry grin.

Jesus! In the space of an hour, he'd thought he'd lost her, poured his heart out to her, asked her to marry him, and then had crazy-amazing newly engaged sex on a public bench. It had already been one hell of a night, and now they were cornered by his family—and his fly was open.

He fixed his pants then tilted her chin up. "I'll do my best to get us out of here unscathed."

She nodded, and he pushed back the curtain of leaves to find Bren, Jas, Abby, Elle, and his grandparents standing in the center of the courtyard with their backs to them.

"Here we are," Cadence said with a slight shake to her voice.

"Are you all right, dear? You left in quite a rush," his grandmother asked as the group turned to face them.

"I'm fine, Mrs. Bergen. I was just a little shocked—"

"That Camden is Mountain Mac? We're shocked, too!" Elle glanced around at all the flowers. "Now, what's with Daisyville, USA?" she asked, eyeing him.

He shared a look with Cadence. "I'm not sure where to start. How much do you already know?"

"Abby and Elle filled us in on the whole Mountain Mac internet pen pal thing," Jas said, clearly biting back a smirk.

"Is Cadence what brought you back to Denver, Cam?" his grandfather asked.

"Yes," he answered. There was no turning back now.

"And how did you know Cadence was Mountain Daisy? Did you have her under surveillance? Did you tap her phone?" Elle pressed.

Jas rubbed his wife's back. "Elle, honey, I think your book research may have you jumping to conclusions."

She threw her hands up. "Well, he had to have figured it out. When Bren said Mountain Mac, Camden looked like he'd been caught red-handed."

Camden wrapped his arm around Cadence. "I was going to tell Cadence that I was Mountain Mac tonight, but Bren let the cat out of the bag before I could bring her here."

"Sorry, bro," Bren said.

"It's all right." He glanced at Cadence. "We're good."

Abby pressed her hand to her chest. "All the daisies are for Mountain Daisy. That's so sweet."

Elle shook her head. "But Cam's been living a double life. When did you find out she was Daisy? You can tell us now, or we can take you down to the station?"

"Honey?" Jasper said.

"I'm doing it again, aren't I?" Elle asked.

Cam took a step forward. "It's all right. I can answer that. Cadence sent me a picture."

"Bro..." Brennen said, eyeing him with a warning glare.

Cam waved him off. "Not that kind of picture."

"What kind of picture did you think Cadence sent?" his grandmother asked, confusion marring her features.

He wasn't about to go there. Tonight was not the night to school Harriet Bergen on sexting.

"It was just a picture of Cadence's bike at Baxter Park. I recognized the location immediately and gave myself the summer to try to find her." He turned to his grandparents. "I went to visit Mom and Dad at the cemetery and asked them to help me find her. That's when the whole cab driver paparazzi dude figured out who I was. I wasn't planning on letting anyone know I was here but..."

"But your parents found a way to lead you to Cadence and back to your family," his gram answered, her gaze growing glassy.

"Yes."

"And is that what I think it is on your hand, Cadence?" his gram asked.

Like a tennis match, everyone's gaze shifted from him to Cadence's left hand.

Elle snapped her fingers. "I was right! I knew something was going on!"

"It must be your supersleuth mind, Nancy Drew," Jasper replied with a straight face.

"Holy flip, Cam! Are you guys engaged?" Bren asked.

"We are," he answered.

"This is wonderful news!" his grandfather said, shaking his hand. "We should celebrate. The staff's cleaning up from the party, but there's plenty of champagne left."

Cam glanced at his watch. "We better get going."

Cadence nodded, following his lead. "Right, we told the babysitter we'd be back by ten."

"And then there's all the laundry we have to do," he added.

Cadence pressed her lips together, holding back a grin. "So much laundry."

"You just got engaged, and you're heading home to do laundry?" Abby asked.

He exchanged a look with Cadence. "Yep, all the laundry."

She nodded. "We may be doing laundry all night."

"Then we'll do brunch at the house tomorrow. You must bring Bodhi!" Harriet said, giving Cadence a hug.

"I'm so excited for you! I want a closer look at your ring before you go," Abby said, hugging Cadence next.

The women circled Cadence as his brothers and grandfather gravitated toward him.

"Does this mean you're staying in Denver?" Bren asked.

He looked from his brothers to his grandfather, taking in their Bergen steel-blue eyes. The same eyes as his father. The trait that bound them together. Christ, he'd missed them. Missed belonging. Missed being part of a family. Bren was getting married. Jas had twins on the way. And now, he'd be here, starting his own family with Cadence and Bodhi. He searched their eyes for contempt or derision. They knew how his parents had died, but the blame he'd showered on himself was nowhere to be seen in their warm expressions.

"Yeah, I'm staying."

"It's good to have you home, Cam," his grandad said and patted him on the shoulder.

"It's good to be home."

Jas gave him a curt nod then pulled out his phone. "Thank Christ! We can put you to work cleaning up the Bergen Mountain Ed Department," he said, back to business, but there was a slight curve to his stoic brother's lips that spoke more than any words could.

He looked over Brennen's shoulder and caught Cadence's eye.

She smiled at him. "Are you ready to head home?"

Home.

He held Mountain Daisy's gaze. "Yes, let's go home."

"Come on, Mountain Daisy. I've got a secret spot I want to show you."

Cadence smiled up at her fiancé as he took her hand and led her out of the ballroom, teeming with wedding guests dancing and celebrating, at the grand lodge at Bergen Mountain.

And life was a fairy tale.

It had been a little over a month since Brennen had outed Cam as Mountain Mac. A little over a month since she'd said yes and agreed to marry the man that the universe had bent over backward to help her find.

Her Man Find.

Her Bergen bobblehead.

Her Mountain Mac.

Her fiancé.

She glanced over her shoulder and scanned the bustling room.

"Bodhi's with my grandparents," he said, reading her mind.

"Are you sure they don't mind keeping an eye on him? Carrie and Luke are here, we could ask them to watch him for a little bit?"

He turned and pointed into the room, decorated with flowers and twinkling lights, and she found Bodhi doing the "Chicken Dance" with Harriet.

"Let's see," Cam said and pressed a kiss to her temple. "My granddad has taken him fishing every weekend, and my gram can't stop having his favorite strudel flown in from that little bakery in Kansas City. They adore him, Cadence, and they're going to be his great grandparents."

She leaned into him and nodded. It still didn't seem real.

She'd gone from being Bodhi's sole provider and his only living relative to a woman, marrying into Colorado royalty and —more than that—into a family that welcomed her with open arms.

Now, she'd be related to her best friends. It seemed like a dream and absolutely uncanny that she'd asked Abby in jest at the beginning of the summer if there were any extra Bergen brothers lying around.

Granted, there was no lying around when it came to Camden Bergen. No, he burst into her life like a Mack truck. But here they were, at the end of July. Summer camp winding down. The regatta a week away and her life had become something she'd never imagined possible.

She'd never expected to find love again—not like this.

She'd feared that if she even tried to love again, that would somehow diminish the affection she'd had for Aaron. But the funny thing she'd realized about love is that it's infinite. Her love for Camden didn't erase her feelings for Aaron. If anything, it bolstered them. Anytime she saw Bodhi with his head rested on Cam's shoulder as they worked on his regatta boat or caught a glimpse of Cam ruffling her son's hair, she knew Aaron—with his wide grin and open heart—would be grateful, grateful for the love and kindness shown to their son.

Fate, coincidence, destiny. Whatever you wanted to call it,

she and Cam had found each other. Had needed each other. They'd boxed themselves in. They'd told themselves solitude was the only choice for people like them.

But they were wrong. So very wrong.

Cam pressed his hand to the small of her back. "See, Cadence. They're fine. Plus, I told my grandad we were going to go look for Mr. Cuddles."

"He's still missing?"

That bear!

Cam nodded. "I checked the car. I checked our room. He had him when we got here, right?"

She nodded. "Yes, I remember because he fell asleep on the drive up today and used Mr. Cuddles as a pillow."

"He has to be somewhere. We'll find him. But I have a little detour we can check before we call a search party together."

She chuckled. "I should have bought two."

Cam frowned. "Two of Mr. Cuddles?"

"Yep, maybe three."

"We'll have to remember that trick," he replied.

"For what?"

"For our next one," he replied.

She cocked her head to the side. "You mean a child?"

He grinned. "Yeah, wouldn't it be great for Bodhi to have a brother or a sister? I loved growing up with brothers. Being the youngest meant always trying to keep up, but I wouldn't have had it any other way."

She stared at this stunning man—so handsome in his wedding attire—completely transformed from the burly, barely verbal Bergen bobblehead she'd met back in June.

She'd stood next to Elle during the wedding ceremony. It was a beautiful sunset service on the lodge's outdoor terrace. And while she'd done her best to focus on her dear friend at the altar, her gaze had wandered from the beautiful couple reciting their vows to the man—her fiancé—standing on the other side of the happy couple next to Jasper.

He'd caught her watching him and had winked. A quick, silent admission that he was thinking the same thing she was.

The happy couple at the altar would soon be them.

She looked up at him. "I think Bodhi would love to have a sibling."

He took her hand, and they continued down a long corridor. "Or two or maybe three?"

She shook her head and chuckled. "You never saw me pregnant, Cam."

"I'm sure you were beautiful."

"If beautiful is swelled feet and power eating saltines twenty-four seven, then yes, I was the epitome of beauty."

"As long as you don't start writing crime novels then stake out the local bakery after they're out of your favorite chocolate chip muffin because you assume there's a mafia connection to their lack of your preferred pastry, I'm all good."

Cadence giggled. "And that was just last week. God, I love Elle."

They passed through the kitchen and then down a dim forgotten hall.

She glanced around the desolate place. "Okay, now this is getting a little crazy. Where are you taking me?"

"Here," he said and pointed to the wall.

"How much have you had to drink?" she asked.

He frowned. "Not a drop."

"Did you hit your head?"

"No."

She crossed her arms. "You led me through the lodge down the creepiest hallway ever to show me a wall?"

He grinned like a kid in a candy store. "This part of the lodge is the original cabin. My grandparents purchased Bergen Mountain in the late sixties, and this smaller structure was the only thing here at the time. They built the Bergen Lodge around it."

"That's fascinating, Cam, but why did you need to show me this now?"

"This cabin was a pretty hopping spot during Prohibition back in the twenties," he added as if that gave her anymore to go on.

She stared at the wood paneling. "Do you think Mr. Cuddles is off somewhere drinking moonshine?"

"He could be. He's one elusive bear."

He wasn't wrong.

"It's honestly a miracle we haven't lost him yet. Bodhi's left him all over Denver."

"Then it wouldn't hurt to look for him in here." Cam lifted a strip of wood, and with a click, the panel opened.

She tried to look past him. "What's in there?"

"Nothing, now. But it used to be where the bootleggers would hide their jugs of moonshine."

"How do you know about it?"

"My gram and grandad showed it to me years ago. They told me that we were the only ones who knew about it."

"Wow!" she said, gazing into the dark space. "What are we supposed to do in there?"

His gaze grew carnal. "Do you know what it's like to look at something so beautiful all day and not be able to have it?"

She mirrored his naughty disposition. "I have a little idea."

"This entire day has been about me on one side with my brothers and you on the other with Elle and Abby."

She trailed her fingertips down the plunging V-neck collar of her dress. "I guess it's just the price we have to pay for being part of the wedding party."

He licked his lips. "Do you know how hard it was, watching you during the wedding ceremony and not being able to touch you, to tell you all the vows and promises I want to make to you?"

Butterflies erupted in her belly as her pulse kicked up.

This man.

She cupped his cheek in her hand and brushed her thumb across his sexy stubble. "You have officially de-bobble-headed yourself, Camden Bergen."

He kissed her palm. "Want to go inside?"

"In there?" she asked, imagining they were about to disrupt about six thousand spiders from whatever spiders do in the dark —something she had no desire to discover.

"Yeah, I always thought it was the greatest space, and it's kind of been a fantasy of mine to bring a girl here."

She chewed her lip. "Just to make this all crystal clear, you want to make out with me in a dusty old hidden room that used to store bathtub gin and bootlegged hooch and is most likely now the home to many, many creepy crawly things?"

"Yes," he answered without a hint of hesitation.

"Hmm," she answered, trying to figure out a new plan. They were in a giant lodge that his family owned with hundreds of beds. A scary hidden booze room couldn't be their best option.

But when he leaned in and captured her lips in a heated kiss, spiders vanished from her thoughts. She sighed as he deepened the kiss, and she melted into his touch. His hands slid past her shoulders, down the length of her back and settled on her ass. In the space of a breath, he lifted her into his arms and had her back pressed to the wall.

She wrapped her arms around his neck and swiveled her hips. His hard length pressed between her thighs, and she really needed to thank Abby for choosing a loose, flowing bridesmaid dress. This would not have been an easy maneuver in a mermaid-style gown.

She ached to feel him inside her, her body growing greedy,

desperate for sweet release, as his thick cock stroked her most sensitive place and she gasped as the heat between them blazed.

"I'm okay with the spider room," she breathed, tilting her head back as he dropped a trail of kisses down her neck.

"You didn't mention anything about spiders, Jas!"

Cadence stilled, and Cam stopped mid-kiss at the sound of Elle's voice. They looked down the hall, turning their heads in unison, to find Jasper and Elle coming toward them.

"Do you guys bring all the girls here?"

But Cam looked just as surprised as she was.

His brows knit together as Jasper and Elle got closer.

He stared at his brother. "I thought I was the only one who knew about this place. Gram and Grandad showed it to me years ago."

Jasper frowned. "They told me about it years ago and said *we* were the only three who knew about it."

A bubbly giggle rang out, and Brennen and Abby came into view. They stopped at the end of the hall, her white dress billowing around her.

"What are you all doing back here?" Brennen asked.

Jasper pinched the bridge of his nose. "Let me guess. Gram and Grandad showed you this secret spot."

"Yeah, I'm the only brother who knows about it," he answered.

"Wait! Is this some weird Bergen brother thing?" Elle asked, eyeing her husband.

"No, I've never brought anyone back here."

"Me neither," Brennen echoed.

Cadence leaned in. "You should probably put me down," she whispered into Cam's ear.

He blinked as if he couldn't believe anyone had found them. "Yeah, right."

"What's so special about this place?" she asked, smoothing out her dress.

"Seriously! What's up with the Scooby-Doo scary hallway? I feel like I need to make sure my tetanus shot is up to date," Elle added, batting at a spider web.

Abby lifted her dress so it wouldn't brush against the gritty floor. "Bren, we just snuck out of our wedding reception. You said we were going to a secret spot."

"I thought this was a secret spot," he answered.

Cam shook his head. "Gram and Grandad showed me this place on my tenth birthday. They shared the history of the lodge and then opened the secret door."

"Yep, that's how it went for me too," Jas answered.

"Ah flip! That's exactly what they said to me," Brennen echoed.

"Well, I call dibs. Cadence and I got here first," Cam said with a resolute nod.

Jasper shook his head. "I learned about the secret room when I was ten, so I knew about this place before either of you. So, I call dibs."

"No flipping way! It's my wedding day. I call dibs," Brennen shot back.

Elle glanced between the brothers. "Your family owns nineteen resorts worldwide. Why are we fighting over a musty old hidden room?"

"Because it's cool," Jasper answered with a twinkle in his eye.

"It's a secret room! It doesn't get any better than that," Brennen said as Abby pulled her dress in closer to her body.

Cadence chuckled.

"What is it?" Cam asked.

"The entire wedding party snuck out of the reception to come here," she answered.

"It did seem a little more impressive when I was a kid," he answered as his brothers nodded.

"Yeah, when Gram and Grandad showed it to me, it was like finding a hidden treasure," Brennen said.

"Just for the record. Nobody's going in there, right?" Elle asked and rubbed her pregnant belly when quick footsteps coming down the hall caught their attention.

"Wow! This is awesome!" Bodhi said, skipping down the corridor with Ray and Harriet Bergen following close behind.

The little boy stopped and stared at the couples. "Did you guys find the secret door to the secret room?"

The Bergens took in the scene as Harriet turned to her husband.

"I think we've been found out."

"Grandad, Gram, this was supposed to be our secret place," Brennen said.

"Yeah, I spent the last twenty years thinking I was the only brother who knew about it," Jasper added.

Ray sighed. "You boys shared everything. We thought it would be fun for you each to think you were the only one who knew about the old moonshine room—like a secret hideout."

"Now I get to see it!" Bodhi said with an excited whoop, but Cadence noticed his eyes were red and dried tears trailed down his cheeks.

She knelt down. "Are you okay, B?"

"Bodhi was missing Mr. Cuddles. We thought that showing him the secret door might cheer him up and get his mind off his missing Teddy bear," Harriet replied.

Bodhi gasped. "Mommy! Cam! I just remembered where I left Mr. Cuddles!"

"Where, sweetheart?"

"Remember when I woke up on our drive to Bergen Mountain and I had to go pee?"

"Yes."

"I left him at that coffee shop."

"Are you sure?"

Cam nodded. "That's right! Now I remember. We set Mr. Cuddles on the counter."

"Can we go get him, Mom?"

"I could call and have one of the Bergen Mountain staff go?" Jasper offered.

"No, don't trouble anyone. We can go get him," Cam said, patting Bodhi's shoulder.

"Bodhi, do you want to stay here at the lodge? We could go back to the party and hit the dance floor again," Harriet offered.

But Bodhi shook his head. "No, thank you. Mr. Cuddles needs me."

Cam lifted Bodhi into his arms. "Let's go track down a bear."

"Be careful with those bears," Elle said, sharing a glance with Jasper.

"And we should get back to our wedding reception," Abby added. "I hope nobody's missed us!"

"Very true, darling," Harriet said with a chuckle.

"Hey, why *are* you guys all down here?" Bodhi asked.

Nobody said a word—not even the spiders made a sound.

"I'll let you know in about twenty years," Cam answered, patting the boy's back.

Cadence walked next to Cam as the wedding party proceeded down the hallway and back toward the ballroom with the three of them parting ways with the group and heading out to their car.

"Sorry, Mommy," Bodhi said with a yawn, his head resting on Camden's shoulder.

"It's all right, B. Everyone knows how important Mr. Cuddles is to you."

"Can I do the 'Chicken Dance' again when we get back?" Bodhi asked, followed by another yawn.

Cam chuckled as Bodhi's little body went limp in his arms. "I think our little guy is chicken danced out."

Our little guy.

It almost seemed too good to be true. A chill passed through her, remembering when she'd felt this way before—those few years ago when she'd thought she'd be starting a new life in Denver. When she'd kissed Aaron goodbye then watched his image disappear behind them in the rearview mirror.

Cam shifted Bodhi to one arm and wrapped the other around her. "Are you cold?"

She swallowed past the lump in her throat and nodded, pushing the painful memory away. "I forgot how chilly it could get up in the mountains at night, even in the summertime."

"Hold on," he said, opening the door to the Range Rover then settling a sleeping Bodhi into his booster seat.

Cam had made little tweaks in his life this past month. Baby steps toward life as a billionaire Bergen brother. A car. Some new clothes. He'd tried to get her to accept rent money, but she'd waved him off. It seemed silly now that they were engaged.

He hadn't leapt into the life of extreme wealth he'd left a decade ago, and she was grateful he was taking it slow. She'd lived paycheck to paycheck for years, cutting coupons and budgeting her salary to the last penny. It was hard to believe that wasn't going to be her life anymore. She couldn't lie—there was a sense of relief in not having to worry about paying the mortgage or wondering what they'd do if the truck broke down—but she'd never be the type to throw money around. She'd been raised to work hard and help others. Rich or poor, that's the example she'd set for her son.

"Here," Cam said, shrugging out of his suit jacket and wrapping it around her shoulders.

She inhaled his scent, that clean, outdoor fragrance she'd breathed in every night before drifting off to sleep in his arms. He opened her car door and helped her in. Out of habit, she glanced back at Bodhi in the rearview mirror, sleeping peacefully, his head resting against the edge of the seat as Cam got in and started the car.

The dash lit his features, and she watched him as he put the car in reverse.

"Do you want to tell me what's on your mind?" he asked, easing the car out of the lodge's parking lot and onto the road that led to the highway.

She touched his cheek. "I'm just remembering what you looked like the first day we met."

"I think you went all *Harry Potter* and called me a Hagrid."

"And don't forget, a D-canoe."

He chuckled and shook his head. "I could never forget that."

She sighed as the oncoming traffic cast shadows on his face. "I'm really happy, Cam."

He glanced over and rested his hand on her knee. "Me too. Happier than I ever imagined possible."

They drove in silence as if they needed to let whatever new life was to come, sink in. Brennen and Abby's wedding served as a preview and with Jasper and Elle expecting, that too could be on their horizon.

Cam slowed the car as flashing lights loomed in the distance.

He leaned forward. "Looks like they've got the westbound lanes closed for road work. We should be fine going east."

"What about getting back to Bergen Mountain?" she asked.

He squeezed her knee. "Did you forget who you're engaged to? I could hike from here and find my way back."

"That's right. I may have shaved off the mountain man beard, but you can take the man off the mountain, but you can't take the mountain out of the man."

"I like that," he said then flicked on the blinker as the coffee shop came into view.

He pulled up in front and shifted the car into park. "I'll run in," he said, leaning over and pressing a kiss to her cheek.

Cam got out of the car, and she sat back and pulled his jacket around her. The gentle hum of the engine purred, and she watched him speak to the man at the counter who nodded and pulled Mr. Cuddles out from beneath the register.

She glanced back at her sleeping son. "We found Mr. Cuddles, baby."

Bodhi mumbled softly, and she envied his ability to fall into a deep sleep at the drop of a hat—or in their case—loss of a bear.

"We've got our cuddle bandit back," Cam whispered, handing her the Teddy bear then settling himself in the driver's seat.

She turned and tucked the bear under Bodhi's arm.

"He'll be glad to wake up with Mr. Cuddles," she said, patting the little boy's leg.

"You know what I'll be glad to wake up next to?" Cam asked with a naughty bend to his words.

"I sure hope the answer's not Mr. Cuddles."

"I can promise you, it's not," he replied, taking them out of the parking lot and passing the westbound ramp to get back on the highway.

He turned onto a narrow road that snaked into the mountains, and they drove in the inky darkness as the drone of the engine and the whirl of the breeze created a cocoon of serene sound.

She glanced at the clock on the dash. It had only taken them fifteen minutes to get to the coffee shop. But the drive back was proving to be much longer.

"Are you sure you know the way?" she asked.

He turned to her. "Cadence, I told you, I—"

Movement flickered in the corner of her eye, and she gasped.

"Cam! Stop!" she yelled and pressed her hands to the dashboard reflexively as the eyes of a mature bull elk flashed in the headlights.

Cam hit the brakes, and her body heaved forward, the car screeching to a stop in front of the majestic animal. The elk didn't move. Its canopy of antlers and massive body stood stock still. She'd never been this close to one before, and the sheer size of its body, with smooth fur, pulled taut over thick, muscled limbs, left her in a state of shock.

The elk stared at them, unblinking, his dark eyes glinting midnight blue in the beams of light.

Cadence took one breath and then another before the animal tossed its head, like a warning, then sauntered off the road into the darkness. And with the animal's exit, she regained her senses. She flipped around in her seat and breathed a sigh of relief.

"Bodhi's still asleep. It's okay. We're okay," she said, catching her breath.

But Camden said nothing as the dim light of the dashboard illuminated his trembling hands and clenched jaw.

"We're all right, Cam. Let's just get back to the lodge. We don't want to miss out on saying goodbye to Abby and Brennen before they leave the reception and head out on their honeymoon," she said, working to keep her voice calm and even.

He didn't answer, his gaze trained ahead of them. The road was empty, but she knew what he saw. She could almost see it herself. Three brothers, panicked and shouting. The commotion. The fear.

And then she saw the police officers that had knocked on her door. She'd known before they even uttered one word that Aaron was gone.

"I'll make sure you and Bodhi are taken care of," he said in a low, hollow whisper.

She swallowed hard. "I hope you're not talking about money, Camden Bergen."

"What else would I be talking about? It's the only thing of value I can offer you."

She glanced back at Bodhi then got out of the car. She crossed her arms and stared up at the starry sky. Everything about nighttime in the mountains was comforting. The sound of the wind rustling through the aspen leaves. The dark, magnificent peaks, a humbling reminder that no matter what happened, the sun would rise and set and day in and day out, they would be there. She tried to absorb it, but her hammering pulse and racing thoughts edged out any hope of calm.

The car door closed behind her, and she turned to find Cam standing a few paces away.

She glanced into the car at Bodhi, hugging his bear and sleeping peacefully, then turned to Camden. "Don't you dare for a second make this about money. I don't want your money. I want you."

He shook his head. "No, you don't."

"Cam, we're safe. We're fine. Bodhi's asleep in the car."

"Christ! Bodhi!" he said in a pained whisper then met her gaze, his eyes blazing. "Do you know what would have happened to us if I'd hit that elk? That was a mature bull, Cadence. He probably weighed upwards of eight hundred pounds. It would have been like crashing head-on into a brick wall."

She gestured to the car. "But you didn't, and we're all fine. Don't do this. I'm begging you."

It was like watching a wrecking ball in slow motion.

"I'm an idiot. I'm a damn idiot," he murmured.

She took a step toward him. "You're not. You're just a little shaken."

"A little shaken? Would you like to know the only thing that could possibly be worse than me killing my parents?"

She shook her head. "Stop it!"

He scrubbed his hands down his face. "Hurting you. Hurting Bodhi. Jesus! I won't do it. I can't risk it."

The wrecking ball inched closer, but she wasn't ready to admit defeat.

"You think you're the only person who lives with regret?" she asked.

He shrugged, sliding back into bobblehead mode, but she pressed on.

"What would have happened if I told Aaron he needed to come with us? What if I told him to forget his work? Forget the packing. Just come with us. Drive back to Grand Junction the next day. Do you think he'd be here? Do you think Bodhi would have his father?"

Another shrug.

She steadied herself. "I don't know. None of us know. You can't live like that, Cam. You can't carry the blame for everything. And you can't predict the future."

"I can if I'm not a part of it. You'll be better off. I'll tell Jas and Bren. They'll make sure—"

She blinked back angry tears. "I don't need your brothers looking after me. And I won't allow it. I won't have it. I'm not some charity case, Camden, and I'm not scared to face this world on my own. I just thought I wouldn't have to. I thought we'd do it together."

He stared past her. "Keep heading west. This road turns into the service road that runs parallel to the highway. You can get back on the interstate there. You'll have passed the road work, and then you'll see the exit for Bergen Mountain."

"Why are you giving me directions? Where are you going?"

He glanced at the car, and the wrecking ball hit.

"Somewhere where I can't hurt anyone," he answered, his tone robotic. And just like the giant elk, he turned and disappeared into the night.

Cadence opened a tattered box and fanned away a cloud of dust.

"Please don't tell me it's another box of doilies," Abby said, sitting across from her at the kitchen table, sorting through Glenna and Gertrude's animal figurines.

Cadence wrinkled her nose and peered inside. "Doily box *numero tres*," she said and tried to muster a smile.

It had been eight days since Cam left her on that darkened road.

Eight days since the fairy tale life she'd feared was too good to be true vanished into the night.

And no one had heard from him. Not a call. Not one text.

She'd even messaged Mountain Mac, thinking maybe they could go back to how things used to be. But that message went unanswered because there was no going back. There was no undoing what had been done. No pretending promises weren't made and no forgetting the man who'd told her she was his forever, then disappeared without a trace.

"It's really nice of you to do this with me—especially the day after coming home from your honeymoon," she added.

Abby set a miniature squirrel next to a gathering of other

glass woodland creatures. "You should have said something the night of the wedding, Cadence. We would have..."

"What? Canceled your honeymoon to Fiji? I wouldn't hear of it."

Abby sighed. "You should have told Elle or Jasper or Ray or Harriet. I hate that you had to spend all this time alone with no one to talk to."

"Camden's a grown man, Abby. If he wants to leave, he should be able to leave. And I didn't want to trouble anyone on such a happy day. You're here now, and I'm grateful for that," Cadence answered, again trying to find her smile.

After Camden's departure, she'd arrived back at the lodge amid the newlyweds being carted off to meet their private plane set to whisk them away to an island paradise. It was the perfect amount of chaos and well-wishing that allowed her to bring Bodhi back to their room. No one had thought anything of a mother carrying her tuckered out little boy away from the excitement. No one had asked about Cam, surely assuming he was nearby. On such a joyful occasion, nobody contemplated that the runaway heir had disappeared again.

"I'm glad you're still wearing your engagement ring," Abby said with a hopeful glint in her eye. "I'm sure this is going to work itself out."

Cadence glanced out the window at Bodhi, paintbrush in hand, putting the finishing touches on his cardboard regatta boat before the race that afternoon.

"I'm wearing the ring for Bodhi."

"And maybe a little bit for yourself, too?" Abby offered, her gaze trained on the figurines.

Cadence shook her head. Cam had left. What chance was there that he'd come back? But the thought that Abby could be right stoked the embers of hope that still burned in her heart.

"No, I'm just not sure what to say to Bodhi or how to say it yet."

"What does he think?"

"I told him the story Elle came up with that we used for all the articles about his return to Denver."

"That he's out in the wilderness testing Bergen gear?" Abby asked, moving on to wipe the dust off a porcelain rabbit.

"Yeah, Elle came up with a great story."

"Knock, knock! I heard my name, and I hope you don't mind that I let myself in," Elle said and entered the kitchen. "By the way, some guy just dropped off a realtor sign. Are you selling one of the houses?"

Abby gasped. "You're not moving, are you?"

Cadence tried to put on a brave face. "Not exactly. It's a coming soon sign. I spoke to a real estate agent a few days ago, and she suggested putting it up to build buzz."

"Buzz for eventually selling one of the houses?" Elle pressed.

"Actually, I'm going to sell both."

"Why both?" Abby asked.

Cadence glanced outside at Bodhi, humming the "Chicken Dance" tune and painting away.

She lowered her voice. "Renovating two historic homes was never my dream. Aaron was the one who loved building and tinkering but caring for two houses is a lot of work and not easy on the pocketbook. Even if I were able to rent out the other unit, I'd still have to maintain it. That's just more than I can handle on my own. It would be best for Bodhi and me to live somewhere easier to manage."

And somewhere that didn't pull so strenuously on her heart-strings.

Her friends stared at her, wide-eyed.

"But you'll stay in Denver?" Abby asked.

Cadence nodded. "Yeah, that's the plan, for now."

She'd spent the night Camden left alone in her room at the lodge watching Bodhi sleep and doing the one thing that got her through Aaron's death.

Making to-do lists.

Finish painting.

Go through Glenna and Gertrude's things.

Get Elle's help assessing the value of the antiques.

Find the last set of daisy doorknobs for the laundry room door.

Start fresh. Start over. Refocus. And possibly...relocate.

Elle sat down next to her and pushed an old, dusty box out of the way. "Why would you want to leave the city?"

Cadence swallowed hard. "When Aaron died, Bodhi was just a toddler. He'd asked for his daddy, but as time passed, he stopped asking. He was so young when we lost Aaron, and *dad* became just a man in a photograph. But now, Bodhi's six, and six-year-olds remember. He's going to remember Cam. Cam taught him how to ride a bike. They've been working on his regatta boat every night this summer. He's become a part of our lives. And after Cam proposed, Bodhi asked me if he could call Camden his dad after we were married."

Elle reached across the table and squeezed her hand and Cadence blinked back tears.

"There's only one door that's missing the daisy doorknobs. I told myself that as soon as I found the last set, that would be the sign that it was time to move on. Time to officially put the houses up for sale and see what new path the universe has in store for me and Bodhi."

"Oh, Cadence," Abby whispered and pressed her hand to her heart.

Cadence steadied herself. "But there's one thing I know for sure. After Bodhi learns Cam's gone—really gone—it's going to hurt him. I think a fresh start somewhere new could help ease the pain of that loss."

Elle crossed her arms and rested them on her pregnant belly. "Jesus! I should have kicked Camden in the balls when I had the chance."

"Are you guys going to play kickball?"

Cadence glanced over to see Bodhi, standing just outside the propped-open back door, holding a paintbrush dripping blue dots on the daisies.

"No, B, we were just talking."

Bodhi peeked into the kitchen.

"Hi, Mrs. Bergens!" he said to her friends with a bright grin. "Is Cam with you guys?"

Elle glanced at her cousin, who'd grown quiet.

"No, honey, he's not," Elle answered.

"How long until the regatta, Mom?" Bodhi asked.

"Five hours, B. You have plenty of time to keep working on your boat."

Her sweet boy wiped his cheek and left a smear of blue paint under his eye. "I painted my name and Cam's name on the inside of the boat since he's going to be my co-captain," he added, a smile stretched across his face.

She exhaled a slow breath. "Remember, honey, Cam's busy working."

"He'll be back. Don't worry, Mom," Bodhi said over his shoulder as he returned to his cardboard boat and her heart splintered into a million pieces.

She hated that she wanted her son to be right. Hated that she longed to see Cam. And hated that in five hours, she'd not only be trying to hold together the pieces of her broken heart but those of her son's, too.

With Bodhi back attending to his boat, no one said a word.

Even the vivacious and always loquacious Elle Reynolds-Bergen remained silent.

Cadence pressed her fingertips to her eyelids, needing a moment to pack away the tears she'd cry if she were alone when Abby's phone buzzed and cut through the heavy silence.

"Excuse me," she said, glancing at her cell. "It's Bren. I better take this."

Abby left the kitchen, and Elle opened one of the old boxes.

"I'm going to say one thing about the Bergen brothers, and then we don't have to speak of them anymore today," Elle said, brushing at a seam of dust on the box.

Cadence nodded. If she tried to speak, if she tried to do anything other than sit there, she'd fall apart.

And just like with Aaron's death, she couldn't fall apart. With a young son and two mortgages to pay, she didn't have that luxury.

Elle picked at the corner of the box. "I can tell you from experience, those men can really screw things up spectacularly. But as much as I still want to kick Camden in the balls, he may still surprise you."

"It's been over a week, Elle. The regatta's today. The countdown's almost hit zero," she answered.

"All right, then," her friend said with a resolute nod. "Why don't we start going through these and see if we can find Amelia Earhart's hair comb or one of Moby Dick's teeth."

Cadence released a teary chuckle, grateful her friend understood how badly she needed this distraction. "I'm not so sure Glenna and Gertrude were friendly with Amelia, and we're pretty landlocked here in Colorado. I'd be surprised to find anything related to a sperm whale, fictional or not, in these houses."

"Oh my!" Elle said, peering inside the box. "It looks like Glenna and Gertrude skipped the sperm altogether."

Cadence knocked over a stack of doilies. "What in the world would make you say that?"

"Because they've got a Dr. Macaura's Pulsocon Blood Circulator," Elle answered as she removed a tattered rectangular box a little smaller than a carton of eggs.

Cadence leaned in and tried to make out the faded image on the lid. "Blood circulator? Is it some old-fashioned medical device?"

A wry grin pulled at the corners of her friend's lips. "That's what upstanding young ladies of a certain era would hope you thought it was," she answered, opening the box and removing a small metal device.

Whatever the heck a *pulsocon* was, it fit neatly in Elle's hand. It looked like a cross between a pencil sharpener and an eggbeater with a delicate, polished wood handle connected to a small metal body which was equipped with a little hand crank and a peculiar flat disk, barely larger than a quarter, fixed to the bottom.

"How does it work?"

Elle pinned her with her gaze. "Put out your hand."

Cadence raised an eyebrow.

"It won't hurt. I promise."

"All right." Cadence held out her hand as Elle pressed the disc to her palm and rotated the crank.

A sharp buzz pulsed through her hand, and she gasped. "It's..."

"Vibrating!" Elle answered with a naughty grin.

Cadence's jaw dropped. "It's a vibrator?"

"Oh yes! It's an old school hand crank vibrator. They were around in the twenties and thirties. A blood circulator is what they used to call them."

Cadence stared at the device. "How in the world do you know that?"

Talking antique vibrators was the last thing she'd imagined doing this morning, but it was just what she needed.

Elle held up the pulsocon. "There's a vibrator museum in San Francisco. I wrote about it in my California Coast travel guide."

"What did you write? 'When in San Francisco, in between visiting the Golden Gate Bridge and riding the cable cars, go check out a dildo museum?'"

"Something like that," Elle answered, glancing into the large box then stilled.

"What?"

"There's another one."

"I guess that makes sense. Glenna and Gertrude were twins, and from what I've heard from the neighbors, they did like to have all the same things."

Elle handed her the second box then turned the crank on her pulsocon like a mad scientist. "Even in the realm of masturbation, the sisters were identical."

Cadence sighed through a chuckle. It felt good to laugh.

"Well, help me out, world travel expert. Are these hand-crank dildos worth a lot?"

Elle shook her head, apologetically. "I don't think so. These vibrators are collectors' items, but I doubt they'll be paying off your mortgage."

Abby entered the kitchen, eyeing them warily. "What's going on in here?"

"While you were gabbing with your husband, we found matching antique vibrators," Elle answered.

They turned the crank on their pulsocon at the same time, and Abby reared back.

"Have you guys been touching those things?" she asked, raising an eyebrow.

"Yeah, the vibration is pretty amazing. Want to try it?" Elle asked, holding out the device.

Abby waved her off. "If those are what you say they are, I'm hoping you wiped them down first. It's probably been years, but just imagine where they've been."

Cadence exchanged a glance with Elle, and the women dropped the antique vibrators back into their respective boxes.

Elle's eyes went wide. "Ew! I didn't even think..."

"I didn't either," Cadence replied, holding her hands away from her body.

Elle pulled a travel size bottle of hand sanitizer from her purse, squirted some into her hand then handed her the bottle.

"So, how's Brennen?" Elle asked, adding another dollop of sanitizer to her palm.

Abby looked away and blushed. "Oh, he's fine."

"Can't go a day without you?" Elle pressed.

Abby smiled, but there was something odd in her expression. "Here," she said, setting a small box on the table. "I saw this in that secretary desk you've got in your living room. It looks about the same size as your antique vibrator box."

"Ooh! Maybe they had a spare? I'm really starting to like Glenna and Gertrude," Elle said, reaching for the box.

Abby gave a furtive glance to her phone then plastered on a smile that didn't quite reach her eyes.

Cadence watched her friend, who pocketed her phone then handed the old box to her cousin.

Elle picked off the dried tape and opened the lid. "Oh my God!"

"Is it another one?" Cadence asked, but her friend's voice had lost its teasing tone.

"No, it most certainly isn't."

Abby craned her head to see. "What is it, Elle?"

Elle looked around the kitchen. "Grab that dishtowel, Abs. Cadence, let's clean off the table."

Cadence narrowed her eyes. "Elle, you're freaking me out!"

"Well, Miss Lowry, if I'm right, that'll make two of us."

"Please tell me there's not a vile labeled Bubonic plague or a mummified body part in there," she said, moving the figurines and boxes off the table while Abby wiped the dust away and laid down the crisp white dishtowel.

"How much do you know about watches?" Elle asked, completely changing gears.

"I can teach second graders how to read one," she answered, growing impatient. "Come on, Elle. What's in the box?"

Whatever was in there, it had Elle transfixed.

"And Gertrude and Glenna...they came from money, right?"

"Yeah, their father had made quite a fortune here in silver, but he lost everything in the end."

Elle carefully removed a small item wrapped in a cloth bag with the words Patek Philippe embroidered on the soft cloth.

Cadence froze as the breath caught in her throat and Cam's watch came to mind.

Cam's very, very expensive Patek Philippe watch.

"Hey! That's the brand of watch Bren and I brought to Camden," Abby said as they watched Elle remove the outer bag to reveal a polished cherrywood box.

"Hold on," Elle said, pulling out her phone. "I want to send some pictures to my antiques friend before we go any further. Where did you find this, Abby?"

"On the desk."

Cadence sat back. "It hasn't always been there. The first night Cam was here. Two squirrels must have gotten into the house when I was painting earlier in the day. They started running around the living room. I screamed, and Cam burst in to save me."

"From squirrels?" Elle asked, cocking her head to the side. "I'm not sure how that has anything to do with this watch box."

A tear trailed down Cadence's cheek, and she brushed it away. "It does. Just listen. The squirrels squeezed in and hid behind the secretary desk. Cam pulled it out so I could catch the squirrels in a box and put them back outside. He found the box you've got there when he went to put the desk back in place."

"That makes sense," Elle said, nodding her head.

"What makes sense?"

"I'm pretty sure the bank had people poke around Glenna and Gertrude's stuff before they sold you the houses and all their contents. And I bet that's how they missed this."

Cadence stared at the gleaming box that looked brand new. "Elle, for all we know, it's empty."

Elle pulled out the drawer built into the bottom of the box, revealing a slim leather sleeve. "Looks like we've got papers," she said, handing it to Abby.

Abby slid a yellowed certificate from the sleeve. "It says this watch was made in 1914 in Geneva, Switzerland."

Elle released an audible breath. "Cadence, if what I think is in this box is what's actually in here, this may be a one of a kind piece."

"Well, open it, already," Abby exclaimed.

Elle's phone chimed. "It's my friend. She wants us to do a video call for the unboxing. Abs, hold my phone."

Unboxing?

Cadence sat back as the women maneuvered around the polished cherrywood box, listening as Elle spoke with the antique appraiser. She lifted the lid, and the midmorning light glinted off the gold rim of a pristine pocket watch. With its elegant numbers spanning the circumference and three smart little dials dotting the face, the watch was breathtaking in its craftsmanship.

Elle carefully held the watch, revealing the backside with four more intricate dials representing the day of the week, date, month, and even the phases of the moon.

And then the expert started spouting out dollar amounts.

Dollar amounts that included the word million.

"Cadence," Abby whispered as Elle continued her animated conversation with the appraiser. "This could change everything for you."

It could. Her friend wasn't wrong. It just wasn't the everything she'd dreamed of since the moment Mountain Mac had come into her life. She glanced out at Bodhi, still painting away. Their lives were going to change—but not because of this watch, but because the regatta was now only four hours and thirty minutes away.

18

Cam zipped his pack and surveyed the inside of the cabin. There was a sad kind of symmetry in that he'd chosen to go back to the same place he'd fled to after his parents' death.

But that was who he was.

The runaway heir.

The person who hurt the ones he loved the most.

The man who couldn't be trusted to keep Cadence or her son safe.

The night of Bren and Abby's wedding blurred through his mind. Everything seemed perfect. And then, like one of those funhouse mirrors, the image skewed and warped, and all he could see were the midnight-blue eyes of the bull elk staring at him as if the animal could see straight into his soul and had found him lacking.

He'd run into the night all the way back to his family's place in Bergen Mountain, known to all as Bergen Cottage. The massive mountain mansion sat empty with everyone on the other side of the resort at the lodge. And like a thief in the night, he entered their mountain home and had gone from room to room, grabbing gear and clothing. He'd been operating on autopilot since he left Cadence on that dark road, systematically going through a checklist of all the things he'd need for a long hike back to the cabin he'd run to a decade ago.

His family had made improvements to the tidy structure. The space was still rustic and could only be reached by foot, and it still was without electricity, but they'd added running water and a little wood-burning stove.

When he was last there, it had been frigid; the temperatures dipping well below freezing. He'd stayed two nights before his family tracked him down, wrapped him in blankets, and carted his ass back to Denver for his parents' funeral.

Summer was different. There was no frostbite to fight off. He'd hike all day, traversing the punishing mountain. Climb until his fingers bled and then, exhausted, he'd return to the cabin where he'd dream of Cadence and Bodhi. He'd wake the next day then do it all over again.

A cycle of physical exertion he'd hoped would quiet his mind.

It hadn't.

Days rolled into nights, and he'd lost track of time—his father's watch and his phone, forgotten and tucked away in the bottom of his pack.

But it was time to stop the charade. Time to stop dreaming he'd ever be worthy of Cadence and Bodhi and return to his Swiss exile. But there was one thing he needed to do first. One loose end that needed to be tied up.

He strapped on his pack, opened the front door, and found himself eye to eye with his oldest brother.

"Jesus Christ, Cam! Why'd you have to come all the way out here again?" Jasper asked.

Brennen shook his head. "Bro, what's going on?"

Cam looked back and forth between his brothers.

What the hell were they doing here?

Then it clicked. "Gram?" he said, walking past them and starting down the mountain.

"Yes, Gram," Brennen answered, following behind him. "We didn't even know you were gone until Abby talked to Cadence last night after we got back from our honeymoon."

"Then we called Gram, and she checked your phone's location," Jasper answered.

Of course, the phone she'd insisted he keep had GPS just like his mother had insisted when he was younger. But it didn't matter. He was going to call his family today.

"I'm glad you're here. I need your help setting up a trust for Bodhi and Cadence."

"Why the hell would we need to do that?" Jas asked.

"Because I'm leaving. Because I'm a liability to them. I can't keep them safe, and they're better off without me."

His brothers stared at him, mouths hanging open as he strode past them. But soon, he heard their footsteps behind him, crunching against the dried grasses and pine needles. They walked in silence for almost half an hour until Bren's words stopped him in his tracks.

"Bodhi thinks you're coming back."

Fuck!

"The regatta," he replied in a tight whisper.

His thoughts mired in the past, and his days spent numbing the pain through hours of hiking and climbing, he'd lost touch with his commitments.

"Yes, the regatta," Brennen echoed. "And you might want to know that Cadence is going to sell the houses, and there's a good chance she'll leave Denver."

Cam faced his brothers. "She's leaving?"

Bren nodded. "I spoke with Abby before we lost cell service coming up here. She and Elle are with Cadence, going through all the antiques, trying to see if there's anything of value. And you know those glass daisy doorknobs she's always looking for?"

"Yeah, of course, I do."

"Abby says Cadence has one more door left that she needs to find knobs for and once she finds them, she's decided that's the universe's way of telling her that it's time to move on and make a life with Bodhi somewhere else."

A sick sensation washed over him. At least in Denver, Cadence had her friends and his brothers to look after her. But if she moved, if she left the city, she'd be on her own.

And whose damned fault was that?

His.

"How could you leave them, Cam?" Jas asked.

"You don't think it kills me not to be with them? Did Abby tell you what happened? Did Cadence tell her why I had to leave?"

Bren shook his head. "Cadence hasn't said much about that night. Abby says it's because of Bodhi. Cadence isn't sure what to tell him, so she used the story Elle came up with for the press."

"Testing Bergen gear."

"Yeah."

Cam scrubbed his hands down his face. "You know how we left your wedding reception to go get Bodhi's Teddy bear? On the way back, they were doing road work on the westbound side of the highway. So, I decided to take the back roads. A bull elk came out of nowhere, and I nearly hit him."

"Don't go there, Cam," Bren said, but he waved off his brother's words.

"Had I hit that animal, they could have died. I could have killed them just like I killed Mom and Dad."

He looked from Bren to Jas—shame rushing through him. They'd never talked about that night. They'd barely spoken at the funeral, and then he'd left. But now he'd ripped the bandage off and exposed the raw, gaping hole in his heart.

"You can't blame yourself for what happened to Mom and Dad," Bren said gently.

Cam barked out a tight incredulous laugh. "You know, I almost believed that. I almost let myself think I could do right by Cadence and Bodhi and keep them safe. But that night proved I was wrong."

Jas stared up at the sky. "Holy hell, we Bergen brothers really know how to fuck things up in this family."

"Mom and Dad's deaths weren't your fault, Jas. You weren't the one driving."

Jas held his gaze. "Maybe not, but I had EMT training, and I couldn't save them."

"And Mom and Dad wouldn't have even been in Colorado if I hadn't told them I wanted them to be there for my competition," Bren added.

Jasper blew out a pained breath. "Bren and I each felt responsible for Mom and Dad's death. We let it consume us, and it took a decade of our lives. A decade where Bren numbed the pain with partying, and I worked myself to the bone. We were the worst versions of ourselves all because we felt responsible."

"Well, you can let yourself off the hook. I was responsible. And I almost got Bodhi and Cadence killed, too."

"You know who almost got you killed, Cam?" Jas asked, his expression stone cold.

"What the hell are you talking about?"

"Dad," his brother answered, his steel-blue eyes darkening. "You were three, and you couldn't get enough of the cardboard boats Bren and I were building for the regatta, so Dad made one for you."

Brennen took a step back. "Holy flip, that's right. I was only five, but I remember Mom calling out and running into Smith Lake."

Cam closed his eyes as a carousel of blurred images and fuzzy sensations came together. The chill of his mother's wet arms wrapped around him. The sound of her tight breaths. And his father's face, dripping with water, pale and petrified.

"Dad threw the boat together quickly and forgot to use waterproof tape on the seams," Jas continued.

Bren nodded. "And he put my life jacket on you, Cam, and it was too big."

"Halfway across Smith Lake, the boat sank. Dad expected you to float in the vest, but you slipped out," Jasper added.

Cam rubbed his nose, his body remembering the sharp sensation of his nostrils filling with lake water and the darkness all around him.

"It had to have only been seconds, but it felt like an eternity, watching Dad go under, trying to find you," Jas said.

Bren nodded. "And Mom in her dress, running into the water. I think she lost her hat."

Jasper nodded. "Yeah, she did."

Cam ran his hands through his hair. "Why are you telling me this, Jas?"

"Do you think Dad meant for that to happen?" his brother pressed.

Cam turned away from his brothers, but Jasper kept going.

"What if Dad decided to leave us in order to keep us *safe*? Do you see how that makes no sense?"

"It's not the same, Jas," he bit out.

"What did Cadence say to you that night? Did she tell you she didn't want you in her life?"

"No."

Bren put a hand on his shoulder. "Jas and I almost lost Elle and Abby because we couldn't let go of the guilt we felt about the past. Don't make the mistake of letting Cadence and Bodhi go."

Cam shook his head. "I need you to make sure they're taken care of."

Jas released an audible sigh. "You know she won't take it."

"Then hire her to run the Bergen Mountain Education Department. She's more than qualified."

"I was hoping you'd both agree to lead the department together," Jasper offered.

"Like Mom and Dad did?" he asked.

His brother's sharp gaze softened. "Yes."

Cam shook his head. "I can't."

A muscle ticked in Jasper's jaw. "What's it going to take to make you see that you're making the biggest mistake of your life? Do you need a sign from above? Maybe a lightning bolt to knock some sense into you?"

"Jas, let's just hike to the bottom," he said and continued down the mountain.

Bren caught up to him. "Where were you going when we came up to the cabin, Cam?"

"Back home."

"To Denver?" Bren asked with a hopeful bend to the words.

"No, Switzerland."

"Were you going to tell us?" Jas interjected, catching up to hike alongside them.

"Yes, to ask you to look out for Cadence and Bodhi."

Jasper shook his head. "I don't know if you've noticed, but Cadence doesn't need to be taken care of. She works hard. She's got her shit together. She's raised a pretty amazing kid all on her own. She needs a partner, not a protector," his brother added then walked ahead.

Cam glanced over at Brennen. "I know what Jas is trying to say, but Cadence needs someone she can count on."

"That's you, Cam. She loves you, man. Bodhi loves you," Bren said, emotion lacing each word.

"I love them, too," he answered.

"Then stay," Bren said when Jasper's voice cut into their conversation.

"Yes, stay put. Right now. Right where you are," Jasper called, standing in front of a fallen tree.

Cam shook his head. "Jas, I told you—"

"Skunks!" Jasper whisper-shouted, staying stock still.

What the hell was wrong with his brother?

After a few more steps, he saw what the hell was wrong.

Cam stared at the ground near Jasper's feet as four black and white balls of fur frolicked on his brother's hiking boots.

"Jas, those are western spotted skunk kits."

"Kits?" Jas echoed.

"That's what the young are called," Cam bit out.

"Flip, Jas!" Bren said, taking a careful step back. "You stepped on a bunch of baby skunks?"

"Not on purpose! Should I run? Are they going to spray me?"

Cam glanced around. Jas had walked right into a skunk den. "Only if they feel threatened."

"Are they threatened?" Jas asked on a low whisper.

Cam shook his head. "No, I think they like you."

Jas looked at him and gave him the international expression for *what the fuck, dude*!

"Move slowly. I don't see the mother. She's the one we'll have to worry about."

"Would she be about triple the size of the kits with that swirly black-and-white pattern on her fur?" Bren asked.

"Yeah, why?"

"Because one of those things just brushed past my ankle, moving pretty flipping fast."

Cam looked over his shoulder as the mama skunk stamped her feet.

"That can't be good," Jas said. "Maybe she'll just bite me instead of spraying."

Cam shook his head. "You don't want that. It's practically guaranteed you'll get rabies."

Jas cringed. "Bears and skunks! Jesus, I cannot catch a break!"

Cam watched the mother skunk. "We're okay unless she raises her hind legs. Step away from the kits slowly and get on the other side of the tree trunk."

"This is why I don't like to leave the boardroom," Jas muttered under his breath.

Jas moved slowly, lifting his foot when the mama skunk let out a high-pitched screech and shot toward her kits.

"Run!" Cam called.

The brothers took off, crashing down the mountain, batting their way past prickly evergreens and leafy aspens.

"Do you smell anything?" Bren called.

"No!" Cam answered.

"Is she chasing us?" Jas asked.

Bren pulled ahead. "I don't want to look!"

Jasper kicked up his pace. "Somebody needs to look!"

"Can she chase us and spray us at the same time?" Bren asked.

Cam shook his head and caught up to his brothers. "I don't think so?"

Jas glanced over at him. "You're the brother who knows all the outdoorsy summer shit!"

"How does that include knowing what happens after somebody steps on a skunk nest?" he shot back.

Christ! After this, he'd never complain about squirrels again.

"You think I wanted to do that?" Jas threw back.

"Shut the *flip* up and keep running!" Brennen called, taking on the role of the middle child, otherwise known as the sibling peace negotiator.

They kept sprinting until they made it down to a winding gravel road, and Cam caught Jasper's eye, and the two started laughing.

"What?" Bren asked with a heaving breath.

"Bren, you're with us. You don't have to talk like you're making balloon animals at a toddler's birthday party!" Cam said, grateful to be laughing with his brothers.

Brennen threw up his hands. "I can't help it, man! I used to have a vocabulary that would make a sailor blush. But after meeting Abby, I changed. Love makes you do crazy things."

Jasper nodded. "I can second that."

They walked down the road, catching their breaths, as a small gas station and a few old shops came into view.

"Where'd you park?" Cam asked, checking the gas station's small cracked asphalt lot.

"There," Jas said and pointed out to a clearing where a helicopter sat.

Cam's jaw dropped. "You took a helicopter here?"

Jasper frowned. "What did you think we'd take? A hot-air balloon?"

"A car! I figured you drove here."

"Cam, we're Bergens. We have things. Expensive things that fly," Jas answered.

"Hold on," Bren said and pointed toward the shops. "I need to go check and see if they have any of those doorknobs Cadence has been looking for."

"In that rundown antiques place?" Jas asked, pointing to the small building with a sun-bleached sign reading *antiques and other novelties*.

Bren nodded. "I was here at the beginning of the summer

and stopped in. They didn't have any at the time, but the shop-keeper said he might be getting some in."

The breath caught in Camden's throat. "So, there might be a daisy doorknob in that store?"

"Yeah."

Cam swallowed hard. "If there's one in there, then I know I'm meant to stay."

Jasper looked at him as if he had ten heads. "I tell you all about how you almost drowned and how I almost lost Elle to try to make you see that you need to forgive yourself and let the past go. But it's a damn doorknob that may keep you here and bring you back to Cadence and Bodhi?"

He nodded. "Abby told Bren that she needed one more set of knobs for the house, and that would be fate's way of telling her where she needed to be, right?"

Brennen nodded.

"If I have the doorknobs, that'll be the sign that she and Bodhi are meant to be with me," Cam said as fear and excitement surged through his veins.

Bren let out a low whistle. "That's a whole flipping lot riding on a doorknob, bro."

No shit.

Cam turned to Jas. "If that doorknob is there, I'm going to need to make a pretty big purchase. We have lawyers to do that kind of thing, right?"

Jas grinned. "In spades, little brother, in spades. Whatever you need, they can make it happen."

"What time is it?" Cam asked as the rush wore off and a calm set in.

He was doing this.

Brennen glanced at his watch. "It's two."

Cam blew out a slow breath. "And the regatta's at three?"

"Yeah," Bren answered.

He stared at the antiques shop and thought of his father's words.

Look at where you want to be. Find that spot and focus on it.

"If I find that glass daisy doorknob in there, can we make it to Smith Lake in time for the regatta?"

Jas crossed his arms. "It'll be damn close, but I think so."

Mountain Daisy had given him hope. Daisies had brought him home. If he were meant to stay, the daisies would let him know.

He closed his eyes and thought of his parents and Cadence's husband, Aaron.

The ball's in your court. If there's a daisy doorknob in that shop, I'll know what it means—and I'll never forget.

He opened his eyes then nodded to his brothers. "All right, here goes everything."

"Bodhi stay where I can see you and don't put your boat in the lake yet!"

"Okay, Mom! Tell Camden I'll be down by the water when he gets here."

Cadence glanced around Smith Lake as families congregated near the water's edge, laughing and carrying cardboard regatta boats.

"Are you okay?" Abby asked.

Cadence scanned the boathouse and then the playground.

Why was she looking for Camden? That was a stupid question. She still loved him. She loved this man who carried the weight of the world on his shoulders. But she also wanted to kill him when she caught a glimpse of Bodhi searching the crowd as well.

"I don't know what I am, Abby," she answered.

"Well, probably rich," her friend offered with a little smile.

Elle's antique expert friend had gone nuts over the watch—the two of them talking quickly and going back and forth over video chat. If what they thought was true, this pocket watch could easily garner over a million dollars at auction.

A million dollars.

She'd spent the last three years pinching pennies, convincing Bodhi that mac and cheese three nights in a row was a fun game instead of a cost-saving measure when her bank account had dwindled down to almost nothing in the days before her paycheck got deposited.

Would she have known the watch was there had those squirrels not caused her to scream and brought Cam crashing into her life?

"Okay, Cadence," Elle said, dropping her phone into her bag. "My friend's flying out first thing tomorrow."

"She's coming here? To Colorado?"

Elle nodded and fanned herself. "This is huge. It could change everything for you, and Christ on a cracker, it is hot out!"

A few families glanced over at Elle, and she smiled brightly. "It's okay! I'm six months pregnant with twins and allowed to say anything I want at this point. Doctor's orders."

"Oh, Elle!" Abby said, shaking her head.

"You try walking around in this heat with two watermelons wreaking havoc on your uterus, and then I'll let you sing all the cookie jar and head's up seven up chants you want."

"Your friend really thinks it's the real deal?" Cadence asked, still finding it all so hard to believe.

Elle stopped fanning herself. "You've got the papers. The watch is in pristine condition. This is the kind of find antiques lovers dream about. Yeah, she needs to see it herself, and she knows a watch expert who also wants to take a look, but she just told me she's ninety-nine percent sure you're in possession of an extremely valuable timepiece."

"Holy pickles and relish," she said with a dazed whisper.

"That's a shit ton of pickles and relish," Elle added then pointed to her belly when a woman walking by gasped.

Cadence pressed her hand to her mouth and chuckled. "I'm

glad you and Abby are here. Thank you. I'd never have known the value of that watch without you."

Tears welled in Elle's eyes. "God, help me! I hate hormones. If I'm not cursing out my flat iron, I'm crying when the guy at the bakery hands me a bagel and tells me to have a nice day. *A nice day*! So sweet, right?"

Cadence rubbed her friend's back. "I was the same way when I was pregnant with Bodhi. For me, it was fabric softener commercials. I'd burst out in tears because I'd never used fabric softener before, and I couldn't help thinking of all the cuddle fresh softness I'd missed."

"Okay, that's really messed up, Cadence!" Elle replied through tears when Harriet Bergen's voice rang out.

"Hello, darlings!" Harriet said and pressed a kiss to their cheeks. "How are you feeling, Elle?"

Elle grinned warmly. "Like I want to punch Jasper in the throat."

Harriet nodded. "That sounds just about right. When I was pregnant with Griffin, I would dream about what it would be like if Ray had to give birth."

Elle patted her belly. "It's good to know that homicidal tendencies run in the family."

"And Cadence, dear, I don't know what to say. When Brennen called and told me what had happened, I made sure he and Jasper sprang into action."

Cadence shared a look with Abby. "What did you say to Brennen?"

"Just that Camden may need a...reminder."

"A reminder?" she echoed.

She should have guessed Abby would say something. And she'd looked off when she returned to the kitchen after her phone call with Brennen.

Harriet sighed. "Bergen men have hearts like no other,

Cadence. But it's a double-edged sword, darling. To love that deeply means that when they make a mistake, that pain eats at them. It weighs them down, and they can lose perspective." She turned to the group. "You three smart, driven women brought my grandsons back from a very bleak existence. I'm grateful to each of you."

Cadence blinked back tears. "But Cam's gone, Mrs. Bergen."

Harriet waved her off. "None of that, Mrs. Bergen. I'm Harriett. And you can never say never with my grandsons. Camden loves you, and he loves Bodhi, too."

Cadence swallowed past the lump in her throat. "But he left me."

Harriet nodded then squeezed her hand. "He did, darling—and he shouldn't have. But it's not because he doesn't care," she added then glanced over her shoulder as Ray Bergen approached. "I can tell you that after more than fifty years of marriage to a Bergen man, I know for a fact it's because he does."

Ray pointed at his watch, and Harriet nodded.

"Well, then," she said, composing herself. "I always blow the foghorn to start the regatta. Looks like it's time for me to stand on my perch at the boathouse."

"We'll find you after the race," Abby said as they waved goodbye to Ray and Harriet.

"How many minutes do we have until the regatta starts?" Cadence asked.

Abby bit her lip. "Thirteen."

"Thirteen," Cadence echoed as a low mechanical hum filled the air, and a helicopter made a pass over Smith Lake, rippling the smooth surface.

Cadence stared open-mouthed as the chopper landed in the middle of Baxter Park's empty sports field. "Is that..."

"Yep, it is," Elle said, shaking her head.

"Those brothers do know how to make an entrance," Abby

added as the helicopter blades slowed, and all the children cheered.

"Mom!" Bodhi cried and ran to her side. "It's Cam and Brennen and Jasper! They're here! I told you Cam would come."

She was standing, so she knew she was still breathing, but the sight of him, her Mountain Mac striding toward her, left her breathless.

Abby leaned in. "What do you want us to do?"

"Yeah, I'm pretty sure he's going to want to talk to you," Elle whispered.

"It's okay. I'm okay," she answered.

Liar. She was the furthest thing from okay.

The brothers made their way to them, their matching strides and steel-blue eyes were a riveting sight, but she couldn't take her eyes off Cam. What was she supposed to say to him? What's up? How was your impromptu vacation?

Luckily, Bodhi was the first to speak.

"That was awesome! Will you guys take me up in a helicopter someday?"

Jasper and Brennen greeted their wives, then high fived Bodhi.

"We sure will," Brennen answered as Cam held her gaze.

"Are you ready for the regatta, Bodhi?" Jasper asked.

"The SS Daisy is ready for action!" her son replied then reached for Cam's hand. "I knew you'd be here. I painted our names on the boat this morning."

Cam took a knee to be eye to eye with the boy. "That's awesome, Bodhi. Do you mind if I talk to your mom for a minute before the race?"

Bodhi threw his little body at Cam and wrapped his arms around the man's neck. "I'm glad you're back. Mommy smiles a lot more when you're here."

"I'm glad I'm back, too, B," Cam said, emotion lacing his words.

"Will you show us your boat, Bodhi?" Brennen asked.

Bodhi pulled away from Camden and smiled up at Brennen and Jasper. "You guys won't believe how cool it looks! Come on!" he said over his shoulder, skipping away toward the lake.

"Hey," Cam said and set his backpack on the ground.

"Hey," she echoed, completely at a loss for what to say.

"I've missed you so much, Cadence."

"We'll give you guys a minute," Abby said, but Elle stayed put and eyed the man.

"Not before I warn you, Camden Bergen. I may be six months pregnant and as big as a house, but I could still take you down if I wanted."

"Duly noted," he answered.

Elle turned to her. "Are you going to be all right if we leave, Cadence?"

"Yes, I'll be fine."

There she was, again, lying.

Her friends made their way to the lake toward the guys and a waving Bodhi, and she steadied herself.

"How are you?" Cam asked.

"About as good as someone who got left on a darkened road by the man that she thought had loved her."

He took her hand. "I do love you. I love you and Bodhi so much. I'm sorry I left you like that. But I ran down a mountain to get to you today. I dodged angry skunks to be here."

She frowned. "That would explain the smell."

Cam gave her the hint of a smile. "They didn't spray us. This is just what a guy smells like after a week in a cabin."

She released a sad little chuckle. "Do you know how angry I am with you?"

His shoulders crumpled. "I can imagine."

"Do you know how hard it was keeping it together for Bodhi when all I wanted to do was scream and cry and curse your name?"

"I'm sure it was torture."

"Why are you back?" she asked, unable to rein in her frustration.

He lifted his chin. "Because I love you. Because I know we're meant to be together. You, me and Bodhi are meant to be a family."

She released a shaky breath. "You've told me this before. What's going to happen the next time Bodhi gets hurt, or something happens to me? How will I know you won't leave us again? Because Cam, I don't think I could stand it and can't even imagine what it would do to my son."

He tightened his grip on her hand. "I thought I had to bear it all. I thought, if I couldn't keep you and Bodhi safe, I didn't deserve you."

She shook her head, hating that they were back to this. "Nobody has that power, Cam."

He held her gaze. "I know that. And I know that there are going to be hard days. But instead of me trying to control everything that happens, trying to save you from heartache or pain, I understand now that we need to meet those days together. You and me."

She dropped her chin to her chest as tears slid down her cheeks.

He tilted her head up gently. "One, two, three. Eyes on me," he said softly.

"That's my line," she replied with a teary smile.

He cupped her face in his hand. "You've given me so much, Cadence. You were the spark of hope that gave me the strength to come home. I thought I had to be your protector. I thought it was my job to never let anything hurt you or Bodhi—but I didn't take into account your strength and your resilience. As much as I don't want anything to hurt you—that's just not how life works. My brothers helped me see that I need to be your partner, not your protector. We'll meet whatever life dishes out to us head-on, and we'll do it together."

How she wanted to believe him! How she wanted to rest her head against his chest and melt into his warm embrace. But she couldn't because it wasn't just her heart that was on the line.

"How can I trust you? It's one thing for you to break my heart. I'm a grown woman. I've buried a husband. I can take the pain. But Bodhi..." she trailed off.

Cam blinked back tears. "I have something I need to give you. Something I have to show you that will prove I'm not going anywhere."

He unzipped his pack and pulled out a worn brown paper bag.

"What is it?"

He reached inside it and removed two glass daisy doorknobs. "It's the universe telling us Mountain Daisy and Mountain Mac were always meant to be together."

He handed her the final set, the last items she needed for the houses to be completed and the renovation to be over.

"Brennen told you what I said," she whispered, staring at the intricate daisy encased in glass.

He nodded. "When I got to the bottom of the mountain, Bren pointed out a rundown antiques shop. He said he'd spoken with the owner back at the beginning of the summer and that there was a chance he'd have your daisy doorknobs."

She nodded. "I remember him mentioning it."

He ran his index finger across the glass surface. "I stood outside the shop and silently called on my parents and your husband to show me the way. I just knew if the knobs were there, it was a sign—just like the daisies and the initials on your handlebars—that we were meant to be together."

Her heart hammered in her chest. She'd told herself finding this last set of daisy doorknobs would be the key to starting over —the key to the next phase of her life with her son.

She parted her lips to speak but paused when a young man in a suit came running toward them, waving a folder above his head.

"Sorry, Mr. Bergen. I've got the papers right here. The house is all yours," the man said on a winded breath, handing Cam a folder.

Cadence stared at him. "Who are you?"

"I'm an attorney from Bergen Enterprises legal department, ma'am," he replied, then mopped his brow with a handkerchief.

"And why are you here?"

The lawyer looked to Cam.

"Thanks for your help. I'll take it from here," Cam replied to the man who gave her a polite nod before walking back to a car parked on the street.

"Cam, what's this about a house?" she asked.

"After I found the knobs, I knew there was one more thing I wanted to do for you and Bodhi. So, I bought my house for us."

"Your house?"

He smiled. "The house I grew up in. The house I showed you with the daisies growing in the front yard. The house filled with so many happy memories. Remember, it was for sale."

She shook her head. "I don't need you to buy me a house."

"Cadence, I want to give you and Bodhi a good life. I want a place for us—a place for our family. I know you're thinking of selling the paired homes. Bren told me that, too."

"Yes, I am, but there's a good possibility that I'll be coming into quite a bit of money thanks to those squirrels and you crashing into my life."

He cocked his head to the side. "What do you mean?"

"Do you remember when you found that box behind the secretary desk on your first night back in Denver? After we trapped the squirrels?"

"Of course, I remember that night."

"Abby, Elle, and I opened it today. It contained a pocket watch. A Patek Philippe watch from 1914 that was owned by Gertrude and Glenna's father. Elle has an antiques expert friend who thinks it's worth over a million dollars."

"A Patek Philippe, like my dad's watch," he repeated.

She nodded.

"That's crazy," he said with a stunned expression as two sharp foghorn honks got their attention.

"Is it time?" she asked, then glanced at the shoreline and the families preparing to launch their cardboard vessels.

"That's the two-minute warning," he answered.

Two minutes.

She had two minutes to decide her future. She glanced at the doorknobs and then to her son.

"If you get in that cardboard boat with Bodhi, that's a promise more powerful than any words. That's you showing him —and me—that you'll never leave us again."

Cam didn't say a word as he took her hand, kissed the diamond daisy ring on her finger, and led her to the lake.

"Are you ready, Cam?" Bodhi asked as Brennen adjusted her son's life vest.

"I've never been more ready for anything in my entire life," he answered, his gaze locked with hers.

Bodhi stretched out his hand. "For luck, Mommy," he said, giving her hand three quick pumps.

She held back tears and returned the secret *I love you, too* handshake reply.

"Cam," he said, reaching for his hand.

They exchanged the squeezes as Cam brushed a tear from his cheek.

He turned to her. "Do you know how much I love you?"

She smiled up at him through tears. "I do."

"I found you, Mountain Daisy, and I swear, I will never let you go." He glanced down at Bodhi. "I'm going to kiss your mom, and then we're going to go win this regatta. Is that all right with you?"

Bodhi smiled up at Camden. "Mom said I could call you dad. Can we start that today?"

"Do you think Aaron would mind?" Cam asked, emotion lacing his words.

She pictured the boy she'd grown up with and the kind man she'd married. He never had a jealous or vindictive bone in his body. And then she remembered the scrap of paper that led her to the mountain bike forum and to Mountain Mac.

"I don't think he'd mind at all. He chose you, Cam. He picked you to help raise his son."

Camden nodded then blew out a slow breath. "Yeah, B, I'd love it if you called me dad."

Bodhi grinned then pulled a taped piece of cardboard with Cam painted in sloppy six-year-old letters off the boat to reveal the word *Dad* hidden beneath.

A loud honk—but not a foghorn—pulled their attention to Elle, sobbing a few feet away.

"Can you just kiss her? This is like ten times more touching than the bagel guy telling me to have a nice day," she wept then blew her nose again.

Bodhi pressed his hands to his eyes. "Okay, I'm not looking."

Cam ruffled her son's—no, their son's hair. "Thank you, Cadence Daisy for giving me the kind of life I never dreamed possible."

"It looks like my Man Find is all mine," she replied when Elle blew her nose again.

"Camden Bergen, help a pregnant woman out and kiss your fiancée!" Elle said, dabbing at her eyes with a tissue.

"Seriously, Cam, can you speed things up a bit. My wife's having a moment here," Jas added, but he was holding back a grin.

"Oh, I can do that," Camden answered then cupped her cheek in his hand, tilted her head, and pressed his lips to hers.

She'd never believed in fairy tales, but that kiss was the closest thing to magic she'd ever felt. This kiss sealed the promises Cam had made to her and to Bodhi with the approval of everyone who'd ever loved her. This beautiful, caring man was her future. She sighed, relief and love and joy washing over her in sweet, rippling waves when a real wave, albeit small, splashed her heels and a foghorn blasted through the air.

"Come on, Dad! It's time!" Bodhi cried.

Cam smiled against her lips at Bodhi's words. "I better go. My son and I have a regatta to win."

"Good luck! I'll find you after the race," she said, taking a step back, but he reached for her hand and gave it three gentle squeezes. She responded back with four.

He smiled, and the whole world disappeared. "Don't worry, Mountain Daisy, no matter what, we'll always find each other."

EPILOGUE

CAMDEN

"Good morning, Mrs. Bergen."

Cadence nuzzled into him, her body warm and loose from a night spent sleeping in his arms.

"Good morning, Mr. Bergen," she said with a sexy sigh.

He smoothed back her hair and stared out the window as a gently falling snow blanketed Bergen Mountain, but his thoughts were diverted from the weather the moment his wife's hand trailed down his chest. Her warm fingertips drew a lazy line past the plane of his abdominal muscles and teased his now rock-hard cock.

That was the thing about being married to a goddess. Each day, he woke up to the woman of his dreams—and that meant a lot of morning wood.

A hell of a lot.

Thank Christ, it wasn't for nothing.

He slid his hands down the length of her naked torso, every curve and every sweet stretch of soft skin, turning his thoughts more carnal by the second.

Cadence stretched like a cat, arching into him and doing absolutely nothing to calm his raging hard-on.

"Do you think everyone is still asleep?" she asked, tightening her grip on his hard length.

"I'm not thinking of anyone but you at the moment," he whispered into her ear.

His entire family had gathered up at the Bergen Cottage to celebrate Thanksgiving. His grandparents, Bren and Abby, and Jas and Elle were all here, not only to celebrate the holiday, but to have some time to relax before Elle's scheduled C-section next week.

Change was on the horizon for the Bergen brothers.

Once splintered and scattered, the bond between them now couldn't be stronger. Jasper had talked Cadence into leaving the classroom to head up the Bergen Mountain Education Department—along with him.

They were a team working together, just like his parents.

It hadn't been an easy decision for his wife to leave the traditional classroom, but once she learned Carrie Mackendorfer, one of their lead counselors, was the top contender to be hired on and take over her class, she knew the students at Whitmore would be in good hands.

And speaking of good hands…he knew exactly what his wife wanted him to do with his. Because as much as he would love to come by her touch, he had other plans this morning.

"Turn onto your stomach," he growled.

She released his cock, and for a split second, he questioned his plan until the curve of her sweet ass and her breasts pressed to the mattress reminded him it was damn good to plan ahead. All Cadence's to-do lists had rubbed off on him in the best possible way.

He'd also become a pretty amazing Laundry Ninja—to go along with his title of Flower Ninja.

When it came to Cadence Daisy Lowry Bergen, he had all the ninja skills to make her body writhe with pleasure.

She reached up and held on to the iron rods attached to the headboard then looked over her shoulder and bit her lip.

"Like this?" she asked with a sultry bend to her words, knowing damn well it was.

He prowled the length of her body and dropped kisses and gentle nips to her supple ass.

Holy hell! Monuments should be made to commemorate its perfection.

He brushed her golden hair to one side and kissed her neck as he straddled her body, pinning her beneath him. He lowered himself, careful not to crush her with his imposing six-foot-five frame and slid his hands along her arms to where she gripped the iron rods attached to the headboard.

His cock pressed between her thighs, and she released a breathy moan, muffled by the pillow. A great trick they'd picked up in the world of *parents trying to get it on without their kid being any the wiser.*

They'd moved into his childhood home which had given them quite a bit more space and a butler's pantry to add to their naughty time location line-up in addition to the laundry room.

Options were good—and in a six-bedroom five thousand square foot house, they had plenty.

But they'd decided not to sell Glenna and Gertrude's paired home. At Cadence's suggestion—and after they'd refurnished the units and de-doilyed the place—they'd created a Bergen residency. Anyone having just graduated from college in Colorado and starting a career in a field that served the community was welcome to apply. And they couldn't have been happier to choose Carrie and Luke Parker, the other lead counselor who had chosen to begin his law career in legal aid, as recipients of the two awards which included free housing.

Not a bad gig.

And all this husband and wife business? Well, they'd

followed Bodhi's lead, and he'd officially became Bodhi's step-dad, sopping wet, right after he and his son had kicked ass and won the regatta.

It had been an impromptu ceremony just inside the boathouse overlooking Smith Lake. With rings made out of twists of wet cardboard from the SS Daisy, Harriet and Ray had procured the services of their dear friend, a former Colorado State supreme court judge, who'd been attending the regatta with his family to marry them in a lightning-quick ceremony and make their union official.

And he had to admit, despite years of trying to forget who he was, it wasn't half bad being Colorado royalty—especially when you want to marry the girl of your dreams and become a father to a child you loved more than your very life right on the spot.

"Cam," Cadence breathed, and he grinned against the shell of her ear. Cadence was one of the most kind, giving people he'd ever met, but in bed...he liked his wife greedy.

"Do you need something, Daisy?" he purred in her ear.

She lifted her hips and rubbed her sweet ass against his thick cock.

It was time to take care of his wife. This stunning, driven woman who'd taught him what love, commitment, and forgive-ness looked like each day he was blessed to call her his own.

And now, he was ready to own her pleasure.

With one hand gripping her wrist, he slid the other beneath her hip and found her wet and so damn ready for him. He thrust inside her from behind, working her throbbing bundle of nerves with his hand as heat built between them. Christ! He'd never tire of the delicious slide of their bodies coming together and the feverish pace they'd reach, climbing higher and higher.

And just when he thought he couldn't last a second longer, she laced her fingers with his, squeezed hard, and met her release, flying over the edge. Her body belonged to him and him alone, to love and worship and ravage. And all it took was hearing her sexy heated breaths, and he was there, too. Flying, falling, riding the wave of their intense connection so deep it pierced his soul.

He gently rolled off of her and gathered her into his arms. "I like making love to my sugar mama," he said with a low, teasing tone.

She chuckled. "I'm no sugar mama."

"How much was the last offer for the pocket watch?"

"Oh, something a little north of one point five million," she answered, stroking the scruff of his beard.

"And all because of a pair of damn squirrels."

The watch had caused quite a kerfuffle—a word he did not use lightly or really ever—in the world of antique timepieces. Glenna and Gertrude had left Cadence quite a prize, but they'd decided not to sell the mint-condition pocket watch. It was an heirloom bought with the riches from the days of the Colorado gold and silver rush which they'd agreed to loan to the Colorado History Museum. But the offers to purchase the pocket watch continued to roll in, giving him ammunition to tease his generous wife.

"What do you want to do today?" she asked.

He glanced out at the mountain. "It looks like there was quite a storm last night. There's probably six inches of fresh powder, and the snow's still falling. We could hit the slopes."

"Bodhi's a little speed demon out there," she said, still stroking his scruff.

"He's caught the Bergen bug. And with a name like Bodhi Lowry Bergen, the kid's destined to be a ski legend. Bren, Jas, and I will have him skiing triple black diamond runs backward any day now."

Cadence pushed up onto her elbow and grabbed a pillow. But just before she could smack him with it, a knock came at the door. Like professional parent ninjas, Cadence grabbed her robe, and he pulled on his pajama bottoms in two-seconds flat.

She twisted her hair into a bun. "Is that you, B?"

"No, it's me," came Jasper's voice. "I think we're having the babies."

"Are you just now realizing this, Jas?" he asked, but his brother's worried expression had him up and at the door in an instant.

Cadence tied the belt on her robe. "Where's Elle? Have you called the doctor?"

"She's in our closet, and yes, I made the call."

"Why is she in the closet?"

"That's where she was when the contractions started, and she told me she wasn't moving."

"Okay, let's go," Cadence said as they rushed down the long hallway to Jasper and Elle's room.

"What's all the commotion?" Abby asked, opening the door to the room she shared with Bren.

"Elle's having contractions," Cadence answered as Abby and Brennen followed them down the hall.

"But she's scheduled to have a C-section in a few days," Abby said.

Jasper shook his head. "Yeah, don't tell her that. I tried and let's just say she had some colorful language as to where I could stick my comments."

"What time is it?" Harriet asked, opening the door.

"Early, Gram. But Elle's started having contractions. She's in Jasper's closet," he answered.

"The closet?" Ray said, joining his wife.

"It's a walk-in closet," Jas replied as if that made her location any less weird.

"Let's just get to her," Harriet said with a nod.

"How about I make sure Bodhi is all right while you all tend to Elle," Ray offered.

"Good idea, darling. There's strudel in the kitchen."

"Yes, thanks, Ray," Cadence said as the party of six made their way to Jasper and Elle's walk-in closet.

"Cam, is this really happening?" Bren whispered.

"Sounds like it," he answered.

"How are you doing, Elle?" Cadence asked, rushing alongside Abby and Jasper to her side.

"I've been better. I'll be much better when we get to a hospit —" she cut off as a contraction hit and his sister-in-law tensed.

"I'm just going to check you," Jasper said calmly.

"I know you were an EMT, Jas. But that was a decade ago," Elle said through clenched teeth.

"Well, it doesn't take an EMT to see that the first baby is crowning."

Holy hell! This was happening.

He shared a glance with Cadence as Elle endured another contraction, and his wife took his sister-in-law's hand.

"You've got this, Elle. Just breathe."

Quick footsteps padded down the hall, and a woman dressed ready to hit the slopes entered.

"Dr. Anderson? What are you doing here?" Elle huffed on a shocked breath.

"Didn't Jasper tell you?" the doctor asked, shedding her ski coat and opening her medical bag.

"You can never be too prepared," Jas said.

Another woman clad in ski gear walked into the room.

"Hi, I'm Joyce. I'm one of the labor and delivery nurses."

Elle turned to her husband. "Jasper, you've got the entire labor and delivery team here at Bergen Mountain?"

Jas shrugged. "Just everyone that's not on call at the hospital in Denver."

"It's been amazing!" the nurse said, donning gloves. "It's like the whole department's gotten a ski getaway the last three weekends."

"You've been doing this for three weeks?" Elle growled between pants.

Jasper paled. "Well, four. A month ago, I invited the neonatologist association to have their annual conference here at Bergen Mountain free of charge."

"Am I really going to have these babies in a closet," Elle asked between contractions.

"Kind of like a pioneer woman," Jasper offered.

The women stared at his brother.

Jasper blushed. "I'm just going to stop talking."

The doctor patted Elle's knee. "Elle, you've powered through this pregnancy, and we know the babies are both head down. You're an excellent candidate for a vaginal delivery."

"In a closet?" she bit out.

The doctor looked under Elle's robe. "It looks like it. Don't worry. We've got an ambulance on the way, but these babies are coming now."

Cam stepped back and watched as Cadence took Elle's hand, and the miracle of life unfolded before his eyes. Had someone told him a year ago that he'd be a father, married to Mountain Daisy, and participating in the birth of his brother's children, he would have thought they were nuts. But as he looked at his wife, holding the first twin wrapped in a Bergen Resort towel, he knew he was right where he needed to be—a Bergen brother, building the company his parents had devoted their lives to and building a life with the woman he couldn't live without.

Lila and Hannah, named after Elle's mother and their mother, came into the world in a walk-in closet ten thousand feet above sea level.

A baby in her arms, Cadence glanced up and smiled, and he saw a life filled with love and more Bergen babies to come.

"Aren't they beautiful?" Harriet said with tears in her eyes.

He wrapped his arm around his grandmother as Bodhi and his grandfather joined them, and they gazed at the babies.

Cam squeezed Bodhi's shoulder then smiled at Jasper. His oldest brother glanced at him, tears streaming down his cheeks as he held his daughter in his arms.

"What do you think, Gram?" Cam began, surrounded by all the people he loved. "Do you think this world is ready for the next generation of Bergens?"

"Oh, darling, all I can say is, watch out. Here they come."

SHARE THE BERGEN BROTHER LOVE

Thank you for reading *Man Find*, the last book in the Bergen Brothers Series. Would you like to be a part of sharing Camden and Cadence's story with others?

Reader reviews are a vital part of ensuring the success of a book. If you enjoyed spending time with the Bergen Brothers, I would be very grateful if you would post a review on Goodreads, Amazon, Apple Books, Google Play, Barnes & Noble, or Book-Bub. There's a bunch! Take your pick!

I read every review and also respond personally when readers reach out. If you have a moment, email me with your thoughts at KSandor@KristaSandor.com.

Your kind words make my day and help others find and fall in love with the Bergen Brothers Series.

ACKNOWLEDGMENTS

I'm never sad when I write the last book in a series. In my Langley Park Series and the Bergen Brothers Series, I've loved having the opportunity to bring the characters together and send them all off on their happily ever afters. And, if you've read all my books, you may have caught some Langley Park/Bergen Brothers crossover moments. If you really paid attention, you'll see two characters in Man Find who may just pop up again.

That's the great thing about romance...it never stops.

I have many people to thank. Let's start with this beautiful cover. Juliana Cabrera crafted a perfect Cam. She's done all the Bergen covers and knocked each one out of the park.

I'm grateful to Tera, Kendra, and Shayne. These eagle-eyed mavens are the superstars of editing. I love you guys to pieces! Thank you for your edits and thoughtful suggestions. A very special thank you to Marla for pulling the manuscript together with her meticulous attention to detail. And thank you to Courtney for beta reading all my Bergen books—and always keeping me supplied with inspirational photos.

And to my author tribe. I don't know where I'd be without authors Michelle Dare, S.E. Rose, Ashley Hastings, Lynne Leslie, and Emma Renshaw. These are the writers I turn to when I need a second opinion or a pep talk or just a good laugh. Honestly, I could list a hundred more friends in the romance author, reviewer, and blogger communities. So many talented women—and men (yep, they're there) who band together and support each other.

I hold you all in my heart.

This acknowledgments page would not be complete without thanking my husband, David.

I moved to Denver in my early twenties. I was single and pretty sure, after only a few months here, that I'd dated every jerk in the city. One night, out on a walk with my dogs in the Wash Park neighborhood in Denver (the inspiration for Baxter Park), I said a little prayer to the Universe. I asked to have one of the good ones cross my path—someone with a kind heart, unwavering integrity, and a protective nature. Not a week later, I was set up on a blind date with a handsome architect. Six months later, we were engaged.

And to you, dear reader, your kind words, reviews, and recommendations mean the world to me. It's an honor to share my stories with you. Thank you for your love and support!

ABOUT THE AUTHOR

KRISTA SANDOR

If there's one thing Krista Sandor knows for sure, it's that romance saved her. After she was diagnosed with Multiple Sclerosis in 2015, her world turned upside down. During those difficult first days, her dear friend sent her a romance novel. That kind gesture provided the escape she needed and ignited her love of the genre. Inspired by the strong heroines and happily ever afters, Krista decided to write her own romance novels. Today, she is an MS Warrior and living life to the fullest. When she's not writing, you can find her running 5Ks with her handsome husband and chasing after her growing boys in Denver, Colorado.

Never miss a release, contest, or author event! Visit Krista's website and sign up to receive her exclusive newsletter.

ALSO BY KRISTA SANDOR

The Bergen Brothers Series

A sassy and sexy series about three brothers who are heirs to a billion-dollar mountain sports empire.

Book One: Man Fast

Book Two: Man Feast

Book Three: Man Find

The Langley Park Series

A steamy, suspenseful second-chance at love series set in the quaint town of Langley Park.

Book One: The Road Home

Book Two: The Sound of Home

Book Three: The Beginning of Home

Book Four: The Measure of Home

Book Five: The Story of Home

Sign up for my newsletter to stay in the loop.

https://kristasandor.com/newsletter-sign-up/